JÓN KALMAN STEFÁNSSON

THE SORROW OF ANGELS

Translated from the Icelandic by
Philip Roughton

MACLEHOSE PRESS
QUERCUS·LONDON

First published in the Icelandic language as *Harmur englanna*
by Bjartur, Reykjavík, in 2009
First published in Great Britain in 2013 by MacLehose Press
This paperback edition published in 2015 by

MacLehose Press
an imprint of Quercus
55 Baker Street
7th Floor, South Block
London W1U 8EW

This book has been published with the financial support of

 MIÐSTÖÐ ÍSLENSKRA BÓKMENNTA
ICELANDIC LITERATURE CENTER

ISBN (MMP) 978 0 85738 912 1
ISBN (Ebook) 978 1 84866 293 3

10 9 8 7 6 5 4 3 2 1

Designed and typeset in Albertina by Libanus Press, Marlborough
Printed and bound in Great Britain by Clays Ltd, St Ives plc

THE SORROW OF ANGELS

A guide to the pronunciation of Icelandic consonants, vowels and vowel combinations can be found on p.331

Our Eyes Are Like Raindrops

Now it would be good to sleep until our dreams change to sky, a quiet, calm sky, an angel feather or two floating down, otherwise nothing but the bliss of the oblivious. Sleep, however, eludes the dead. When we close our staring eyes memories overtake us, not sleep. At first they come singly and even as beautiful as silver, but quickly turn into a dark, suffocating snowfall, and that's the way it's been for more than seventy years. Time passes, people die, the body sinks into the ground and we know no more. Otherwise there's little of sky here, the mountains take it from us, as do the storms that these same mountains intensify, dark as the end, but sometimes when we catch a glimpse of the sky following a blizzard we believe we can see a white streak left by the angels, high above the clouds and mountains, above the mistakes and kisses of man, a white streak like a promise of great bliss. That promise fills us all with childish happiness and a long forgotten optimism stirs within us, but it also deepens despair and hopelessness. That's the way it is, a great light creates deep shadows, great fortune contains great misfortune and human happiness seems condemned to stand at the point of a knife. Life is quite simple but a person is not; what we call the puzzles of life are our own complications and murky depths. Death has the answers, it says somewhere, and it frees ancient wisdom from its fetters; of course this is damned nonsense. What we know, what we have learned has not sprung from death but rather from a poem, despair and finally memories of happiness, as well as great betrayal. We do not possess wisdom, but what trembles within us takes its place, and is perhaps better. We've travelled far, further than anyone before us, our eyes are like raindrops, full of sky, pure air and nothing. So it's safe for you to listen to us. But if you forget to live you end up like us, this hounded herd between life and death. So dead, so cold, so dead. Somewhere deep within the lands of the mind, of this consciousness that makes a person sublime and devilish, there still dwells a light that flickers and refuses to go out, refuses to give in to the heavy darkness and suffocating death. This light nourishes us and torments us, it persuades us to keep going instead of lying down like dumb beasts and waiting for what might never come. The light flickers, and thus we go on. Our movements may be uncertain, hesitant, but our goal is clear – to save the world. Save you and ourselves with these stories, these snippets from poems and dreams that sank long ago into oblivion. We're in a leaky rowing boat with a rotten net, and we're going to catch stars.

Some Words Are Shells in Time,
And Within Them Are Perhaps Memories of You

I

Somewhere within the murky snowfall and frost, evening is falling, and the April darkness squeezes between snowflakes that pile up on the man and the two horses. Everything is white with snow and ice, yet spring is on its way. They toil against the north wind, which is stronger than everything else in this country, the man leans forward on the horse, holds tightly to the other's reins, they're completely white and icy and are likely about to change into snow, the north wind intends to gather them before the arrival of spring. The horses trudge through the deep snow, the trailing one with an indistinct hump on its back, a trunk, stock-fish or two corpses and the darkness deepens, yet without turning pitch black, it's April, despite everything, and they press on from the admirable or torpid obstinacy that characterises those who live on the border of the habitable world. It's certainly always tempting to give up, and in fact many do so, let everyday life snow them over until they're stuck, no further adventures, simply stop and let themselves be snowed over in the hope that sometime it will stop snowing and clear skies will return. But the horses and the rider continue to resist, press on despite the seeming existence of nothing in this world except for this weather, everything else is gone, such snowfall wipes out directions, the landscape, yet high mountains are hidden within the snow, the same ones that take a considerable portion of the sky from us, even on the best days when everything is blue and transparent, when there are birds, flowers, and possibly sunshine. They don't even lift their heads when a house gable suddenly appears in front of them from out of the relentless snowstorm. Soon another gable appears. Then a third. And a fourth. But they fumble along as if no life, no warmth has anything to do with them any longer and nothing matters except for their mechanical movement, faint lights can even be glimpsed between the snowflakes, and lights are a message from life. The trio has come up to a large house, the mounted horse moves all the way up to the steps, lifts its right foreleg and scrapes vigorously at the lowest one, the man grunts something and the horse stops, then they wait. The lead horse is upright, tense, its ears perked, while the other hangs its head, as if thinking deeply, horses think many things and are the closest of all animals to philosophers.

Finally the door opens and someone steps out onto the landing, his eyes squinting into the obtrusive snowfall, his face drawn against the ice-cold wind, the weather controls everything here, it models our lives like clay. Who's there? he asks loudly and looks down, the blowing snow sunders his line of sight, but neither the rider nor the horses reply, they just stare back and wait, including the horse standing behind with the hump on its back. The person on the landing shuts the door, feels his way down the steps, stops just over halfway down, thrusts out his chin to see better before the rider finally makes a hoarse and rattling sound, as if clearing ice and muck from his language, opens his mouth and asks: Who the Hell are you?

The boy steps back, up one step, I really don't know, he replies with the sincerity that he hasn't yet lost, and which makes him a fool or a sage: No-one special, I suppose.

Who's out there? asks Kolbeinn, the old skipper, who sits hunched over his empty coffee cup and directs the broken mirrors of his soul towards the boy, who has re-entered and wants more than anything to say nothing, but still blurts out, Postman Jens on an ice horse, he wants to talk to Helga, before hurrying past the skipper, who sits in his eternal darkness.

The boy quickly ascends the interior staircase, rushes into the corridor and clears the steps to the garret in three leaps. Gives himself entirely to the race, shoots like a phantom up through the opening and then stands panting in the garret, completely motionless, while his eyes become accustomed to the change of light. It's nearly dark there; a little oil lamp stands on the floor and a bathtub appears against a window full of snow and evening, shadows flicker about the ceiling and it's as if he's in a dream. He discerns Geirþrúður's coal-black hair, white shoulder, high cheekbones, half a breast and drops of water on her skin. He spies Helga next to the bathtub, with one hand on her hip, a lock of hair has come loose and falls across her forehead, he's never seen her so carefree before. The boy jerks his head as if to wake himself, turns around abruptly and looks the other way, even though there's nothing special to see besides darkness and emptiness, which is where a living eye should never look. Postman Jens, he says, and tries not to let his heartbeat disturb his voice, which is of course entirely hopeless: Postman Jens has come, and he's asking for Helga. It's perfectly safe for you to turn around, or am I so ugly? says Geirþrúður. Stop tormenting the boy, says Helga. What can it hurt him to see an old woman naked? says Geirþrúður, and the boy hears her stand up from the bath. People get in the bathtub, think something, bathe themselves and then stand up from the bathwater, all of this is rather ordinary, but even the most ordinary thing in this world can conceal considerable danger.

Helga: It's safe for you to turn around now.

Geirþrúður has wrapped a large towel around herself but her shoulders are still bare and her December-dark hair is wet and wild and possibly blacker than it's ever been. The sky is old, not you, says the boy, and then Geirþrúður laughs quietly, deep laughter, and says, you'll be dangerous, boy, if you lose your innocence.

Kolbeinn grunts when he hears Helga and the boy approaching, contorts his face, which is covered with lines and deep grooves from the lashes of life and his right hand moves slowly across the table, feels its way forward like a weak-sighted dog, pushes aside the empty coffee cup and glides over the cover of a book before his expression slackens suddenly, fiction doesn't make us modest, but sincere, that's its nature and that's why it can be an important power. Kolbeinn's expression hardens when the boy and Helga enter the Café, but he continues to rest his hand on the book, *Othello*, in the translation of Matthías Jochumsson. "Be still, hands! Both you, my men and the rest; were it my task to fight, I could perform it without prompting."[1] Helga had thrown on a thick, blue shawl; she and the boy walk past Kolbeinn, who pretends not to be interested in anything, and then they're outside. Helga looks down at Jens and the horses, all three nearly unrecognisable, white and icy. Why don't you come in, man? she asks, somewhat sharply. Jens looks up at her and says apologetically: To tell the truth, I'm frozen to the horse.

Jens generally chooses his words carefully, and is, what's more, particularly reticent just after finishing a long and difficult winter delivery trip; what's a person supposed to do with words in a blizzard anyway, up on a stormy heath and all directions lost? And when he says that he's frozen to the horse, he means it; then the words are completely transparent and hide no meanings, no shadows, as words are wont to do. I'm frozen fast to the horse: which means that the last large stream that he crossed, around three hours ago, concealed its depth in the darkness of the storm; Jens was soaked from his knees down yet the horse is tall, the April frost clamped around them in a second, horse and man froze together so tightly that Jens couldn't move a muscle,

1. Matthías Jochumsson (1835–1920) is an Icelandic poet, dramatist, and translator. Among his works are the popular play *Skugga-Sveinn* and the lyrics to what became the Icelandic national anthem. Here, the original text in *William Shakespeare, The Tragedy of Othello, Moor of Venice*, Act I, Scene 2, reads: "Hold your hands,/ Both you of my inclining, and the rest:/ Were it my cue to fight, I should have known it/ Without a prompter."

couldn't dismount and had to let the horse scrape at the lowest step in order to announce their arrival.

Helga and the boy have to work hard to pull Jens off the horse and then assist him up the steps, which is no easy task, the man is big, around a hundred kilos, no doubt; Helga's thick shawl has turned white with snow by the time they manage to get Jens off the horse, and there are still the steps. Jens snorts angrily; the frost has deprived him of his virility and transformed him into a helpless old man. They plod up the steps. Helga once wrestled down a drunk fisherman in the Café, a man of above-average size, and then threw him out like a piece of rubbish; Jens thus transfers most of his weight automatically to her; who is this kid, by the way? There doesn't seem to be much to him, he could break beneath snowflakes, let alone a heavy arm. The horses, Jens mutters on the fifth step; yes yes, replies Helga simply. I was frozen fast to the horse and can't walk unsupported, says Jens to Kolbeinn as Helga and the boy half carry, half drag him in. Take the trunks off the horse, says Helga to the boy, I'll handle Jens myself from here on; then take the horses to Jóhann, you should know the way, and then let Skúli know that Jens is here. Can this one manage the trunks and the horses? asks Jens doubtfully, glancing sidelong at the boy; he's more useful than he looks, is Helga's only reply, and the boy carries the trunk into the house with difficulty, dresses warmly and heads out into the darkening night and gloomy weather with two exhausted horses.

world during the long winter months, when our only company is the stars, the darkness between them and the white moon. Three to four times a year Jens goes all the way to Reykjavík to fetch the mail, when he replaces the postman for the South, but otherwise he travels from the Dalir district, where he lives on a small farm, surrounded by gentle mountains and the summer-green countryside, along with his father and sister, who was born with such clear skies in her head that there was little space left for thoughts, although no sins took root there either. Jens' postal route is likely the most rugged in the country, costing two postmen their lives in the last forty years, Valdimar and Páll, storms claimed them both on a heath in the month of January fifteen years apart. Valdimar was found soon after, frozen solid, not far from a newly built mountain refuge, but Páll not until spring, after most of the snow had melted. The post itself, the letters, newspapers, was fortunately undamaged in the trusty canvas-lined trunks and in the bags that hung over the men's dead shoulders. Valdimar's horses were both found alive, but were in such bad condition from the cold that they were put down on the spot. Valdimar's body was intact, for the most part, whereas ravens and foxes had gotten to Páll and his horses. The postman for the South transmits to Jens the news that he hears in Reykjavík, Jens delivers it to us, besides everything else that he learns of on his route; this person died, that one had a bastard child, Gröndal was drunk down on the beach, fickle, changeable weather in the South, a thirty-ell long whale beached in Eastern Hornafjörður, the Fljótsdalur Valley Cooperative Society is drawing up plans for a steamboat service on the Lagarfljót River and has ordered a steamboat from Newcastle, which is in England, adds Jens. As if I didn't know that, replies Skúli brusquely, without looking up; he questions Jens and writes so rapidly that the paper nearly ignites. The boy observes how the editor proceeds, how he formulates his questions, even tries to look over his shoulder, to see whether there's much difference between what the postman says and what's put down on paper. Skúli is engrossed, so focused that he hardly notices the boy, yet twice looks up, half annoyed, when he comes unnecessarily near. Time is pressing, Jens has finished eating, filling his big body with curds, smoked lamb, English cake, coffee, warm as Heaven, black as Hell; the time has come for his first beer and first shot of liquor, which Helga brings him. Liquor has the tendency to change our ideas about significance, birdsong becomes more important than the world's newspapers, a boy with fragile eyes more precious than gold and a girl with dimples more influential than the entire British navy. Of course Jens says nothing about birdsong or dimples; that he would never do, yet after three beers, one shot, he's a poor informant for Skúli. He becomes rather complacent, loses interest in momentous events, major news, troop movements, whether the governor of the country sits or stands or appoints his young and inexperienced son-in-law as pastor at Þingvellir. Did he do that? asks Skúli, hotly, my poor fellow, what does such a thing matter now, it all turns out the same anyway, they're all the same on the loo, says Jens, on his third beer, before telling Kolbeinn new stories about Páll, who roams the heaths in search of the eyes stolen by ravens

21

III

The night is dark and very silent in the winter. We hear fishes sigh at the bottom of the sea, and those who climb mountains or traverse high heaths can listen to the music of the stars. The old folks, who possessed the wisdom of experience, said that there was nothing up there but exposed terrain and mortal danger. We perish if we don't heed experience, but rot if we pay it too much attention. In one place it says that this music wakens in you either despair or divinity. Setting out for the mountains on still nights, sombre as Hell, in search of madness or bliss, is perhaps the same as living for something. But there aren't many who undertake such journeys; you wear out valuable shoes and the nocturnal vigil makes you incapable of taking on the day's tasks, and who is to do your work if you are unable to? The struggle for life and dreams don't go together, poetry and salt fish are irreconcilable, and no-one eats his own dreams.

That's how we live.

Man dies if you take his bread from him, but he withers without dreams. What matters is rarely complicated, yet we still need to die to come to an equally obvious conclusion.

The nights are never as quiet down in the low-lying areas, the music of the stars is lost somewhere along the way. But they can still be quite silent here in the Village, no-one out and about except perhaps the night watchman, doing his rounds between unreliable streetlamps, making sure they don't smoke and are lit only when necessary. And now night lies over the Village, dispensing dreams, nightmares, solitude. The boy sleeps soundly in his room, has curled up beneath his quilt. Never before has he had his own space to sleep until Bárður's death brought him to this house three weeks ago, and at first he had difficulty falling asleep in the silence; no breathing close by, half-stifled coughs, snoring, the sound of some-one tossing and turning in bed, farting, sighing in the depths of sleep. Here it's he who decides when to extinguish the light and can therefore read as long as he likes; it's a dizzying freedom. I'm extinguishing the lamp now, said the farmer, when he felt they'd stayed up long enough in the family room, and then the darkness clutched them. He who stays up too late is poorly fit for the next day's work, but he who doesn't follow his dreams loses his heart.

And day breaks slowly.

Stars and moon vanish and soon day comes flooding in, this blue water of the sky. The delightful light that helps us navigate the world. Yet the light is not expansive, extending from the surface of the Earth only several dozen kilometres into the sky, where the night of the universe takes over. It's most likely the same way with life, this blue lake, behind which waits the ocean of death.

IV

I miss you lads and somehow I find it harder to live now, writes Andrea from the fishing huts. She'd sat down on their bunk in the garret, used her knees and the English-language textbook for a desk. They were at sea: Pétur, Árni, Gvendur, Einar, and two itinerant fishermen brought in to replace the boy who lived and the man who died. The sea breathed heavily somewhere out in the snowfall that filled the world, and swallowed everything. Andrea couldn't even see the other fishing hut, nor did she give a damn. Yet the breath of the sea could be heard clearly through the storm, the heavy aspiration of a senseless creature, this treasure chest and grave of thousands. They rowed away early in the morning and were perhaps waiting over their lines as she wrote her letter, Pétur with fear in his veins, because everything seemed to be leaving life, *I miss you lads,* she writes. *Sometimes, though, I wish that I'd never met you, yet little better has ever happened to me. I don't know what to do. But I feel as if I should and need to make a decision about my life. I've never done so before. I've just lived, and I don't know of anyone whom I can ask for advice. Pétur and I barely ever speak, which could hardly be comfortable for the others, except maybe Einar. He's a vermin. Sometimes he stares at me as if he were a bull and I a cow. Oh, why am I writing you such things,*

25

you're far too young, and have enough of your own to deal with. And my scrawls are hardly legible. I think I'll tear up this letter, and then burn it.

I miss; days have passed.

The distance between Bárður and life grows relentlessly every day, every night, because time can be a rotten bastard, bringing us everything only to take it away again.

The boy is awake, sits up in bed, stares out into the semi-darkness, the dreams of the night evaporate from him slowly, vanish, turn to nothing. It's approaching six o'clock; perhaps Helga had knocked lightly on the door, awakening him instantly. Nearly three weeks since he arrived here with deadly poetry on his back. Of what other use is poetry unless it has the power to change fate? There are books that entertain you but don't stir your deepest thoughts. Then there are others that cause you to question, that give you hope, broaden the world and possibly introduce you to precipices. Some books are essential, others diversions.

Three weeks.

Or thereabouts.

A room as large as the family room in the countryside, where eight to ten people worked and slept together; here he's alone with all this space. It's like having an entire valley for oneself, a solar system next to life, he probably doesn't deserve it. But fate deals out fortune or misfortune, fairness has nothing to do with it, and then it's a person's job to try to change what needs to be changed.

You'll have the bedroom, Geirþrúður had said, and here he

is, sitting confused between sleep and waking, half waiting for everything to disappear: the room, the house, the books on the bedside table, the letter from Andrea, no, she didn't burn it, the fishing-station postman stopped by the huts shortly after she finished writing it, constantly in doubt as to whether she should burn the letter or not, sort of let the postman have it inadvertently, changed her mind immediately and ran out to demand it back but he was gone, swallowed up by snowflakes, gulped down by the whiteness.

Afternoon and evening can be quite tranquil in this house, except when the Café is occupied; the stream of patrons had been rather heavy half a month ago, when the clouds lifted for two days and sailors from the ships poured into the Village. Then the boy served beer, toddies, shots, received taunting remarks in return; in general it's easy to use words and some believe that a harsh or uncivil demeanour makes them bigger. Yet most evenings are calm. Helga closes the Café, the four of them sit together in an inner room of the house, the pendulum in the big clock hangs motionless, as if trapped in bottomless melancholy, the boy is reading for Kolbeinn from the English poet Shakespeare and most often the two women listen as well. He's finished with *Hamlet*, is halfway through *Othello*, but it certainly didn't start off well; Kolbeinn was so angry after the first reading that he swung his cane in the direction of the boy. Soon started snoring softly during the reading, which wasn't exactly encouraging, the boy's mouth went dry and for a time it felt as if his throat were going to close; he chirped rather than read. You shouldn't read as if you're out of breath, said Helga when Kolbeinn was gone, having left the room like an angry ram; just read as naturally as you breathe, it's very simple when you get the hang of it.

When you get the hang of it.

The boy could barely fall asleep that evening. He tossed and turned, drenched in sweat, in this glorious bed, lit the lamp numerous times, scrutinised *Hamlet*, plunged into the dizzying stream of words and tried to make some sense of it. I'll be thrown out, he muttered; how the hell does one breathe words?

The next reading was disastrous as well.

So unsuccessful that this English poetry, which has the flavour of deep sky and great despair, was turned into lifeless, arid wasteland.

After five minutes Kolbeinn stood up, the boy shrunk instinctively but no blow came, the cane lay lifeless against the chair and Kolbeinn reached out a hand that resembled the paw of a shaggy old dog, held it out most impatiently. You're supposed to hand him the book, said Helga finally, extremely calmly, and then the old ogre stalked out of the room, swinging his cane, which had acquired a cranky spirit of its own in his hands. Well, thought the boy, sitting there, a failure, so it's over, I'll just try to get work salting fish this summer; this was also too good to be true, it was a dream and now it's time to wake. He stood up but for some reason sat right back down. Geirþrúður sat in her chair holding a cigarette; that was likely the worst reading I've ever heard, she said, slightly hoarse, having, as she did, a raven's heart. But don't fear, you haven't hit the bottom, you could get even worse if it continues like this. I hardly think so, he muttered. Yes yes, never underestimate humankind, there's extraordinarily little that it can't ruin. She took a drag on her cigarette, held in the sweet poison for several seconds before blowing the smoke out through her nose; but as Helga said last night, you shouldn't think, just read. Read the text up in your room later; then you'll have time off around midday tomorrow to prepare, read until you stop distinguishing between the text and yourself – then you can read without thinking. But Kolbeinn took the book.

You'll get it back later, we'll go and fetch it, he can hardly read much of it himself.

The boy is still sitting in bed.

Listens to the dreams of the night trickle from his blood and disappear into oblivion, then gets out of bed and pulls back the heavy curtains. The light is almost grainy, hiding nothing, yet it's as if everything is slightly distorted, or blurred, as if the world is slowly sorting itself out after the night and the snowstorms of the last few days. No tracks in the snow below, but now of course it's six o'clock and soon someone will set out and spoil the purity. A housemaid on her way to a shop, Reverend Þorvaldur on his way up to the church to be alone with God, seeking the strength not to bend beneath the back-breaking struggle of life, kneels at the altar, closes his eyes, tries unsuccessfully to ignore the ravens that shuffle on the edge of the roof, stepping heavily, as if sin itself were plodding there, making its presence felt. Maybe it wasn't God who created sin, but vice versa.

The boy sits in the soft chair, runs his hand over the letter as if to say, I haven't forgotten you, and how could I forget, then grabs a book from the bedside table, poems by Ólöf Sigurðardóttir.[2] Is going to read one or two poems, needs to go downstairs, Helga is no doubt waiting with some work for him to do, shovel snow from around the house, clean, scrub the floor, read to Kolbeinn from newspapers or magazines, go down to Tryggvi's Shop. He reads, and she speaks, such words:

> She speaks; such words. She laughs, oh, ringing heart.
> She hates, such spite. She commands; what a sentence.
> She labours; such vim. She loves; oh, sweet fire.
> She threatens; such power. She implores; what a prayer.[3]

He stops reading and stares into space. She loves, she threatens, what a sentence.

2. Ólöf Sigurðardóttir from Hlaðir (most often referred to as Ólöf frá Hlöðum) (1857–1933), a midwife and poet.

3. Originally from Ólöf's first volume of poetry, Several Ditties (Nokkur smákvæði; Reykjavík, 1888).

V

It's been nearly a week since Helga sent him down to Tryggvi's Shop. He was supposed to buy a few trifles, chocolate and boiled sweets for the evening coffee and bitter almonds that Helga was going to daub with poison and scatter throughout the cellar for the mice that have made themselves far too much at home. Gunnar had been standing behind the counter, with his moustache and sardonic sneer, clearly planning to say something to amuse himself and the bystanders and making the boy sigh; there never seems to be a scarcity of those who take trouble to put down others with their words. The Devil drives his claws into them and they open their mouths. And there stood Gunnar with his mouth open, two shop clerks watching, but didn't manage to say much more than "Well", because Ragnheiður came out and pointedly asked the three of them whether they had anything to do. The two clerks disappeared so swiftly that it was as if they'd gone up in flames, but Gunnar didn't go far, simply stepped to the side and started fumbling with some tins, his expression sombre.

Ragnheiður regarded the boy from beneath her brown hair, meditative, distant; he cleared his throat and asked in a low voice, hesitantly, for delicacies for humans, death for mice. She didn't move, her eyes didn't leave his face, her lips were slightly parted, he caught a glimpse of her white teeth, rising like icebergs behind her red lips. He cleared his throat again, about to repeat his question about chocolate and almonds, but she started to move and all he could think was: Don't look at her.

She prepared his order.

And he watched.

But why watch a girl; what use is that, what does it do for the heart, uncertainty; does life become better in some way, more beautiful?

And what's so remarkable about shoulders? he thought, trying unsuccessfully to take his eyes off them, everyone has shoulders and always has had, throughout the entire world. People had shoulders in the days of the ancient Egyptians and will probably still have them after ten thousand years. A shoulder is the area where the arm connects to the shoulder-blade and collarbone; it's surely a waste of time to look at such things, no matter how rounded they are, don't look, he ordered himself, and managed to look away as she turned her white and cold profile towards him. Gunnar watched them, and so closely that he didn't pay attention to what he was doing, bumped into a stack of cans, which toppled loudly to the floor. When the boy looked away from Gunnar, who stood swearing among twenty or thirty cans, Ragnheiður was standing before him, with only the counter between them, and had a boiled sweet in her mouth. Now, there's nothing remarkable about having a boiled sweet in one's mouth, not a whit, but she sucked it slowly and they looked each other in the eye. And a thousand years passed. Iceland was discovered and settled. Or just under two thousand; Jesus was crucified, Napoleon invaded Russia. And then she finally took the wet and shiny sweet from her mouth, leaned over the table and stuck it in the boy's mouth. His hand trembled slightly as he counted out the money. Ragnheiður took it and suddenly it was as if he no longer mattered.

Maybe she's just tormenting me, he thought as he tramped off from Tryggvi's Shop, through the snow, astonished at how good it could feel to be tormented. The sweet was also incredibly good, the boy sucked it enthusiastically and his heart pumped agitation through his blood. That agitation had its ridiculous outlet the next night when he woke suddenly from a dream about Ragnheiður; she lay naked next to him, with one leg over him, though he had no idea how she looked naked, but she was delightfully warm and she was incomprehensibly soft and he woke with a start, all wet. Had to sneak into the basement to rinse out his underwear, among mice that died slowly from the bitter poison.

VI

The boy has finished dressing; he reads two poems by Ólöf before going down.

Jens' snoring meets him on the stairs. The postman is sleeping in the guest room on the lower storey the few days that he's here in the Village, never stops longer than two days, just long enough to let the horses rest, though longer if there's a storm, if foul weather ascends from the bottom of the sea, bearing ancient malice. The aroma of coffee blends in with the snores after the boy has come down, breakfast awaits him, bread and porridge. Kolbeinn chews his bread, spread with a thick layer of pâté. You've come to save me from Kolbeinn's ceaseless merriment, says Helga, and the boy feels so much at home that he smiles and doesn't let the skipper's sombre expression trouble him. How can Jens sleep through his own snoring? he says. Bliss for some to sleep, says Helga, listening to the coffee brew, the previous brewing intended only for Kolbeinn, who's so grouchy before his morning coffee that most living people, and even life itself, shrink back from him.

The coffee brews.

Oh, the aroma of this black drink!

34

warms her veins, makes her heart feel better; she sighs. If there's a Heaven, coffee beans must grow there. Shouldn't I put ointment on those scratches, they could become infected, says Helga. How did you get them? asks the boy, without waiting for Kolbeinn's reply, too young to be tactful. Kolbeinn snorts, wriggles to his feet, walks out of the kitchen like a grumpy ram, swinging his cane all around him, knocks it against the wall, twice hard close to Jens' room, Jens wakes up with a start, his snoring ceases abruptly and he has a piercing headache. They listen as Kolbeinn goes up the stairs, lashing out with his cane, hoping perhaps to wake Geirþrúður as well. Damn, he's fun sometimes, says the boy. Yes, but you shouldn't have asked like that; those scratches assuredly didn't come from anything good. They hear a door slam upstairs, Kolbeinn has entered his cave, has slammed the door hard enough to be certain they hear it down in the kitchen. He can't tolerate anyone but himself now, mutters the boy into his porridge, are you so certain he even does that? says Helga softly, looking up, as if to try to see into Kolbeinn's room, through the floor and walls.

The old skipper lies dressed in bed, stroking his cane as if it were a faithful dog, his room as big as the boy's, a heavy bookcase next to the bed, around four hundred books, some thick and many in Danish, all from the time when Kolbeinn could see, when his eyes had purpose. Now he lies in bed and his eyes are useless, they can be tossed into the sea, they can rest on the seabed, full of darkness. The skipper sighs. It's sometimes good to talk when you feel awful, Helga had said as the coffee brewed and it was just the two of them, I have excellent ears; but Kolbeinn had just muttered something that he himself hardly understood. Many choose to keep silent when life stings them hardest, since words are often just lifeless stones or torn and tattered garments. And they can also be weeds, harmful disease vectors, rotten pieces of wood that can't even hold an ant, let alone a man's life. Yet they're one of the few things that we actually have handy when everything appears to have betrayed us. Keep that in mind. As well as that which no-one understands – that the least important, most unlikely words can, entirely unexpectedly, carry a great load and bring life undamaged over dizzying ravines.

Kolbeinn's eyes shut, slowly but surely; he sleeps. Sleep is merciful, and treacherous.

VII

It has started snowing again when Ólafía bustles in to join them. The sky holds an endless amount of snow. Here come the angels' tears, say the Indians in northern Canada when the snow falls. It snows a great deal here and the sorrow of the heavens is beautiful, it's a cover protecting the earth from the frost and bringing light to a heavy winter, but it can also be cold and devoid of mercy. Ólafía is dripping with sweat as she knocks on the door of the Café, so lightly that she needs to wait many minutes, perhaps twenty; her sweat has become chill against her flesh and she's started shivering, a bit like a big puppy, by the time the boy finally opens the door. You should have knocked harder, he says, without realising how absurd it is to demand such a thing. Ólafía would never have been able to indicate so determinedly, even impertinently, that she existed. Well, I've still managed to come inside, is all she says, and starts changing her shoes; she'd diligently brushed herself off outside and there's hardly a snowflake left on her as she steps in. The boy sticks his head all the way out and his black hair whitens, the ground lies everywhere beneath a thick layer of the sorrow of angels, no grazing either in pasture or on beach, all the livestock kept inside and the farmers counting every hay-blade going into them, in some places little remaining but leavings and the animals bleat and low for a better life, but the clouds are thick and no sound is carried to Heaven. Ólafía's track cuts desolately down the road and is starting to be erased, drifting snow has long since covered the track of Þorvaldur, who trudged his way up to the church early in the morning to thank God for life and grace; what grace? we ask. Þorvaldur cursed the ravens when he came out, threw several snowballs in their direction but seemed perfectly unable to hit them; they didn't move from their places there on the roof ridge, simply looked down at the priest and croaked derisively. The boy closes the door on the world, opens the inner door and calls out loudly, yes, Ólafía's here! She's startled to hear her name called out so loudly and unhesitantly, because what name has deserved to be called out loudly enough for many others to hear, what life has earned it?

Fate can actually create unexpected connections, let us be thankful for that, otherwise much would be predictable, with little movement in the air surrounding us, so little that it would stagnate and life would be sleepy and dull. Surprise, the unexpected, are the catalytic forces that stir the air into motion and give life an electric charge: you remember Brynjólfur, hopefully? The skipper of Snorri's ship, who slumped onto the table in the Café, overwhelmed by twelve beers and chronic insomnia. The boy had sat down opposite Brynjólfur but stared at his dead friend behind the skipper until he dissolved into cold air. Dead was the beauty of the world.

Helga had simply laid the skipper on the floor; he doesn't deserve better, she said, when Geirþrúður wanted to have Brynjólfur brought into the guest room where Jens snored until Kolbeinn hammered the wall with his cane out of innate sulkiness, or the despair of one who's lost his sight and is incapable of speaking. Yet Brynjólfur's deeply etched head was given a pillow to lie on. It's like a chunk of rock, muttered the boy as he struggled to position the pillow. Helga spread a blanket over the skipper, a thick Scottish woollen blanket, and then went to Ólafía.

She had an idea of where Brynjólfur and Ólafía lived, but not much more than that, had never spoken to Ólafía, never stood close enough to her to scent the heavy, semi-sweet smell of her big, awkward body, much less look in her eyes, which are oval and often appear to be full of rain and wet horses. Those eyes follow me everywhere and force me to drink, said Brynjólfur, leading many here to blame Ólafía for his excesses; just a glimpse of the woman filled one with hopelessness. The truth is, few things can have more influence on a person than eyes, we sometimes behold all of life in them and it can be unbearable. But perhaps Brynjólfur drinks because he's given in, despite his enormous physical strength; a man's misfortune comes from within more often than we suspect. Helga was just going to let Ólafía know where her husband was, that was her only errand, she found the house after a little searching, Ólafía opened the door, guardedly, and Helga looked into the oval eyes full of rain and wet horses.

Since then, Ólafía has come several times to help with one trifle or another.

Has come in the morning, left in the evening, before supper, before they close the Café, sit down in the parlour and the boy begins his reading, which improves continuously, one can even detect a satisfied look on Kolbeinn's face at times, although it could be an illusion. Ólafía blushed when Helga asked her once to sit with them, muttered a goodbye and hurried away without any further reply.

You're so kind-hearted that life would kill you if I weren't with you, Geirþrúður had told Helga after meeting Ólafía for the first time. Would you be opposed to her coming here now and then? No, no, it's good to have fragile people around; it helps us to understand this world better, though I don't always know what I'm supposed to do with that understanding.

Ólafía doesn't work quickly, she moves a bit labouredly, as if there's sand in her blood, but she's constantly busy and does her job well. Her hands are thickly calloused and hard as wooden boards, her fingers slender and quite dextrous, as it turned out.

Helga had woken Brynjólfur from a twelve-hour sleep, or a twelve-hour coma, and rather harshly.

Ólafía deserves a much better man than you, said Helga, as Brynjólfur sat stooping over his coffee and hearty plate, with a horrendous headache; someone was trying to tear his skull apart. He was going to say something about the repressive eyes of his wife, her ponderous presence and even sheepish manner, everything that made it difficult for him to stay at home, but he had the sense to keep quiet, besides his having to work hard to keep the copious meal down; his imposing shoulders slumped; he looked like an old man. My ship has rejected me, he finally said, softly, as if to himself, or to the tabletop that didn't reply, since inanimate objects don't know many words. Helga looked at the boy; go up to your room for a moment, she said.

Half an hour later she asked the boy to take Brynjólfur down to the ship, accompany this old seadog to his own ship, renowned for his daring but now old and weak, according to him, and convinced that the ship had rejected him. Helga told the boy to take him down to the spit, where the ship was waiting; I told him that you had special abilities, sometimes it's vital to lie in order to help people.

Snorri's ship is the only one still waiting on the shore, held upright by large posts, the others long gone. Brynjólfur stopped when they still had several hundred metres to go, looked at the ship, which most resembled a dead whale, then grabbed the boy's shoulder tightly, deriving strength from it. The boy simply stood there motionless, pretending to have some special abilities, as Helga had told him to do, but bit his lip because for a time it felt as if Brynjólfur were going to crush his shoulder. Then they boarded the ship; it welcomed its own skipper. Brynjólfur lay down flat on the deck and kissed it.

It took Brynjólfur some time to open the fo'c'sle, the hatch was frozen shut. You'd think I wasn't meant to go down, he muttered, sighing, yet in the end it opened, they went down into the fo'c'sle, which was so dark and cold that it was as if Brynjólfur had cut a hole in existence and they were about to descend into hopelessness itself, were it not for the morning light that streamed down through the opening and stuck like a spear into a dark, giant beast. Brynjólfur fumbled his way forward in search of light, because living men see nothing in such darkness, finally found a kerosene lamp; the light kindled and with it hope. Shortly afterwards, the crew members, whom Helga had got to their feet, started coming on board, one by one.

First to arrive was Jonni, the cook, a short and burly, shaven-headed man with a swollen face and curious but friendly eyes. He threw his arms around Brynjólfur, as if the latter had been recovered from Hell, which wasn't entirely ludicrous, and was almost completely swallowed up in the skipper's expansive embrace; the boy saw only the bald crown of the cook's head, making it look as if Brynjólfur were embracing the moon itself. Jonni went and grabbed a bucket, clambered back down to the spit, filled it with snow, returned and started brewing coffee. Struggled to light the stove, needing to blow on the embers for a long time in order to wake a flame; one must blow on the embers constantly to keep the fire alive, no matter what name we give it: life, love, ideals; it's only the embers of lust that one never needs to blow on, the air is their fuel and air envelops the earth. The aroma transformed the icy fo'c'sle into human living quarters; it ascended through the open hatch like a cry of joy, and the men streamed aboard. Most were the same age as their skipper, men with rough skin, nearly cured, their movements stiff, they don't loosen up until the ship is at sea. A stranded whale here on the foreshore, a lifeless whale, yet which shines like silver as soon as it hits the waves.

They sat for a long time down in the fo'c'sle and Jonni went to

43

fetch more snow, which he transformed into black coffee, a bit like a comical god; they shook themselves in the cold, chewed tobacco, swore happily, gulped down coffee, it'll be lively here tomorrow, said one of the men to the boy, who sat squashed between two broad-shouldered men and was warmed by them. Their rough, weather-beaten faces all gazed at Brynjólfur with such warmth and joy that they were as beautiful as a summer day. One of the bunks was boarded up, two slender planks in a cross; there's Ola the Norwegian's bunk, you didn't know Ola, they say to the boy, now there was a champion, and then they sighed over the memory, but also at how time passed, they sighed, had another cup of coffee, more tobacco and shared stories about Ola. Blew into the embers of memory, imitated his unique language, moved nearly to tears. He'd lost most of his Norwegian and never learned Icelandic to any useful degree, invented a new language that was right in between, sort of both and neither, and it was only his shipmates who understood him without difficulty. Then he died, simply drowned up near the Lower Pier in a dead calm, saw the moon reflected in the tranquil sea and tried to dive in after it. Drowned in the pursuit of beauty. Oh, indeed. And settled himself in the best bunk for when we sailed next, here's where he wanted to be and nowhere else. How tedious it's been for the poor man these long winter months! But this is why the bunk is boarded up, you see, they tell the boy in conclusion, Ola needed a place to stay and he chose the best bunk, we had to accept it, and he in return protects us from many evils. Such as what? asked the boy. The men looked at him in surprise, one really shouldn't ask such a thing. They shifted in their seats, had more tobacco, chewed it silently, perplexed, well, he's got to sleep somewhere, the dear man, said Jonni finally and the men nodded; this was a good answer, Jonni's clever. And then, of course, the boy blurted out: But do the dead sleep?

VIII

The boy's first task this day, which began so slowly, almost brightly, or bright enough for us to remember the spring and the green grass of summer, but was soon obscured by falling snow, is to translate a short English text into Icelandic, armed with a poor dictionary and his wits. He sits in the Café, Kolbeinn is still up in his room, perhaps asleep, perhaps dreaming of sunflowers and laughter; yes, hopefully he's sleeping, hopefully the old skipper has managed to open the hatch that leads to the underworld of sleep, where the grass has many colours and it's possible sometimes to find a peculiar peace. Where does that world come from, and what happens to it when you die?

The boy stares at the English text and barely understands a word, *It was the best of times, it was the worst of times.*

You're to translate this, Helga had said, handing him the page with the English text, a dictionary, a pen and paper. A person who holds a pen and paper has the possibility to change the world. Translate, repeats the boy. You're to be educated, Helga said, this is the start, and many have begun with less. He wanted to ask questions, be given some explanation; whence, for example, came this text, and why in English, and why was he to be educated; so does he make a difference and may he stay here, even much longer, protected from the world, be educated, what does that involve, is he to learn English to be able to converse with Geirþrúður's skipper? Does one understand the world better if one knows many languages, and is it important to understand? But a heavy, determined knocking on the main door of the house prevented any questions. Helga looked at the boy, who went to the door. The knocking came again before the boy reached the door, impatient pounding; damn it, the blows said, isn't anyone going to come?! The boy hurried to open the door but immediately retreated before the gloved fist that rose threateningly over him, as if its owner, a tall, sturdy-looking man, were considering driving his fist into the boy's face to punish him for his tardiness; but then the fist opened, changed into a palm that dusted snow off the thick capote with its lined collar.

Good day here, I need to find Geirþrúður, said this man, speaking somewhat like a rifle, because some words are like bullets and some people are like rifles.

The man stopped brushing himself off, perhaps yielding to the snow and the sky, which is larger than everyone; even this tall, strong-looking person seemed to realise it, came in, looked down at the boy; the man was almost a head taller, gave him a quick, crooked smile and asked, who ate your tongue? Took off his fur hat, his hair was grey but his beard black and well-groomed, his eyebrows unkempt and beneath them grey eyes set deep, seemingly endowed with great power. It isn't always good to talk, replied the boy, feeling as if he were suffocating. The man removed his coat, gave another quick smile and said, you're absolutely right, and the boy felt as if he'd won a great prize. But go fetch Geirþrúður anyway, and immediately, because time is precious, never forget it.

Time is precious.

This the boy has never heard.

So far, time has simply passed by, gone through people and animals, and taken many valuable things with it along the way, but time itself is not precious, only life. She's sleeping, he said finally, after digesting this peculiar assertion; I think, he added hesitantly. The man took off his capote, lay it folded over his arm; beneath it he was wearing a blue two-button jacket, moulded tightly to his broad chest. A person is asleep or awake, there's nothing to think. He who questions never gets anywhere, never becomes anything. Run in and tell them I've come. It's unhealthy for people to sleep in broad daylight, I know my way to the parlour. Bring me coffee, black.

The boy hurried into the kitchen, there's a man who wants to speak to Geirþrúður, he said, I don't think he's fond of waiting long, he invited himself into the parlour and I'll be damned if I don't think it's Friðrik; he wants his coffee black. Helga took off her white apron; you don't think anything about Friðrik, she says, he just is, and everyone knows how Friðrik takes his coffee, the man owns everything here, in his own way; she'll be here in five minutes, Ólafía, the coffee, says Helga, but Ólafía is already brewing it, her hands slightly shaky.

It's perhaps going a bit too far to say that Friðrik owns us; if anyone does, it would be Tryggvi himself, the owner of the trade empire that dominates the life of the Village and the surrounding fjords; we must die to escape its authority, but Tryggvi spends the long winter months out in Copenhagen, with his Danish wife. Those who are able to do so flee the winter and the suffocating darkness, and all through the long winter months the responsibility for and control over Tryggvi's Shop rests with Friðrik, who seems to be everywhere, not leaving us any more than the air we breathe, whether we stand on the deck of a ship far out at sea, stoop over salt fish on the spit, sit on the loo.

Friðrik took the coffee cup without looking at the boy, drank the coffee quickly, though it must have been very hot; as if he didn't feel the heat any more than the Devil, thought the boy. I've heard of you, Friðrik said to him. Pétur is a good foreman and there aren't many people who leave such a position voluntarily. The boy said nothing, nothing came to mind, perhaps he wasn't expected to say anything anyway and Friðrik's presence oppressed him, his throat went dry and he thanked his stars when Geirþrúður arrived; she didn't greet them, merely said, this is unexpected, and Friðrik stood up straight, darkening the parlour. I need to speak to you. Of course, you hardly could have come for any other reason; the hoarseness in Geirþrúður's voice was conspicuous, a raven's croak in place of a heart. Friðrik ignored the possible derision in the reply, smiled, bared his rows of robust teeth, in private, he said tenderly. Geirþrúður stood beside the boy, who caught a faint whiff of dreams and night, there was a green tinge to her dark eyes; they resembled an ocean in which many had drowned. This is in fact my stepson, she said calmly, a smile, or a trace of a smile, coming to life at one corner of her mouth. If that's the way you want it, said Friðrik courteously, bowing slightly. Did Helga let you have the text? she asked, looking at the boy, who nodded; then go to the Café room and start working on it, now your education begins, you're to read it tomorrow evening.

At the door the boy turned around to look; Friðrik stood in the same spot, filling the parlour, Geirþrúður stood before him, her eyes full of drowned men.

And then he's sitting over English words, with a poor dictionary, pen, paper, it's snowing, the whiteness comes from Heaven, the sorrow of angels, but why are they sorrowful? *It was the best of times, it was the worst of times.* He's looked up the words that he didn't understand in the first sentences, feels a bit like a magician, albeit a failed one, with a broken wand, yet senses the magic and forgets Friðrik, forgets everything, really, he's going to visit a distant world, distant thought, distant experience, and sow seeds in the Icelandic language, perhaps grow plants and trees bearing new colours, different scents. He looks through the words and everything becomes new; it's probably they, first and foremost, that change the world. The English text fills two pages, a great deal of incomprehensible symbols as things stand, but after just over an hour's struggle he's conquered four sentences, has marched off into the incomprehensible and returned with thought and a hint of a poem, and he senses the silver inside him as he stoops over the words. So is this life, the existence that he has missed, yet without knowing it; to journey into the unknown, the incomprehensible, and return with a bundle of words that are all at once firewood, flowers, and knives? Silence over everything; there's only the snow that falls and the words that hold something mysterious, a message to the world.

Four lines in an hour is of course not much, but these lines are also wondrous, they resemble wings. Then he was interrupted; Lúlli and Oddur entered the Café. The men who shovel snow in the Village. It's their job, to attack the whiteness, and there's rarely a shortage of it here. They'd been at work since five in the morning, shovelling snow for four hours, started with the three big shops, would get to the smaller ones when and if they could, the cracks in life are reflected everywhere we look, even in snow-shovelling. They'd drunk coffee, eaten English cake, wet their index fingers and carefully wiped up the crumbs with them, watched the boy closely as he sat there hunched over his words, lost in the world behind reality. And there was something in his manner that caused Oddur to ask him to compose a letter for him, a sort of courtship letter, understood the boy; Oddur too shy or too breathless to speak clearly, and here, of course, hardly anyone speaks clearly about such things. But since the boy seemed to know how to hold a pen, would he be willing to write a letter on behalf of Oddur, a letter to a woman named Rakel? She, said Oddur, has dirty-blonde hair, strong arms, bright laughter, and when she blushes her ears move slightly, it's so beautiful, but naturally you won't write that, I mean, that she blushes. No, of course not, the boy had replied, not having the heart to refuse the request, nor the payment that Oddur promised; so proud was the boy that he simply said yes.

And now he sits alone once more, but finds it difficult to get back into the translation. The cheerful chatter of Lúlli and Oddur is carried in to him; he pushes away the English text, wants to put aside writing the letter for Oddur until later, needs to think it over, gather words, he reaches for *Othello*, be still, hands, and begins preparing for the evening reading, which will no doubt commence later than usual due to the meeting of the Craftsmen's Association. Opens the book, feels for the form of the words, listens for their breathing, perhaps Jens will listen to the reading, he took the post to Dr Sigurður at nine that morning, practically herded off by Helga. Took a sled and pulled the trunks behind him down the road, the snow soft, causing him to sink in places up to his waist, but the distance was short, two hundred metres, no mortal danger, far from it; Jens on the other hand had drunk unnecessarily much the night before and his hangover was excruciating for most of the morning. The boy sits over the book and for a long time no sound is heard but the beating of his heart. The snow outside is white, but some words have more colours than the rainbow.

IX

Sigurður invites Jens into the parlour; the doctor stands ramrod-straight, his back on the verge of arching backward, before the postman, who feels uncomfortable in such elegant surroundings. The parlour in the doctor's residence is smaller than at Geirþrúður's, but the furnishings are carefully chosen, dark and weighty, positioned so precisely that everything would be thrown out of kilter if anything were moved. Jens forces himself to stand still, had spent a good amount of time brushing off every snowflake before entering the house, the sorrow of angels had no business in such a fine parlour, two heavy paintings in gold frames, one of a majestic ship sailing a restless sea, whose perilous aspect, however, is diminished by the size and grandeur of the ship; such ships aren't seen in the fjords here, in comparison with them, our ships are mere washtubs. The second painting is of Jón Sigurðsson, standing with his left hand resting on a table, looking sternly at Jens; why does the hero of our struggle for independence have to be so serious, almost joyless? Jens has to work hard not to shuffle his feet, hang his head, droop his shoulders; the meekness of the common man isn't buried deeply in most of us. Docility seems to be innate to this nationality, like a chronic illness, dormant at times but always rearing up again, usually in the presence of wealth, solid furniture, strong and impertinent authorities. We're heroes at the kitchen table, docile in grand salons. Sigurður stands for some time before the postman, his well-groomed, aromatic hair and thin, straight moustache lending his stern face an air of weightiness; perhaps he's trying to cow Jens with his presence and the atmosphere of the room, but Jens manages to contain himself, he stands upright, it's a victory, because although Sigurður is not a great power compared to Friðrik, he is imposing; he's part of the powers-that-be. He's postmaster over a vast area, sits often on the town council, is the only pharmacist here, having just driven a competitor out of the Village using all the means at his disposal, and is a bookseller, to boot. Of course, this last position provides him little power or money; power and wealth have never gone hand in hand with poetry, and that's perhaps why it's so incorrupt, and sometimes the only reliable defiance.

Jens takes Sigurður's reprimands silently; he is three days behind schedule, actually four, because although he came to the Village the evening before, he's only just now delivering the post, which is, in the highest sense, unusual. Jens knows this as well as Sigurður does; and why didn't you come here first as your duty requires, and now as so often before you didn't cross the fjords from Arngerðareyri by boat, although it would have sped things up. Do you wish to compel me to submit a complaint? The weather wasn't exactly ideal for a boat trip, says Jens in a low voice, before reaching beneath his coat for the certificates from rather coldly, before entering his office to go over the post and compare it with the register of letters. Jens says nothing; this was an order, after all, not a request; of course he'll obey it, no need to give Sigurður reason to lodge a complaint. Jens lets little hinder him on his postal trips, confronting heaths and mountains in the worst of weather, even though common sense and others' persuasions try to stop him; but what would his life be if he lost his position? The postal trips give him a kind of purpose, they fill his life, are always something to look forward to, these long journeys out and back, and up to four times a year all the way to Reykjavík when he replaces the postman for the South. Yet it isn't easy to be an overland postman; certain of these men have lost toes, arms, horses, their own lives. It's difficult to redress such losses, and the pay is so low that it's hardly possible to go any lower, sometimes just barely covering the expenses. Jens has to pay for lodging for himself and his horses, food, fodder, upkeep of his clothing and horse tack, but what remains is always cash, cold hard bills, and there are terribly few here who are paid in them; most of us live and die without ever having a chance even to touch one. With cash comes a rare freedom, and there is also freedom in the postal trips. Anyone who has crossed the heaths alone on a tranquil summer night, in the company of the sky and the birds of the heath, has conceivably lived for something. Yet it's not such moments, as blessed as they may be, that Jens thinks of as he stands unmoving in the elegant parlour while Sigurður goes through the post, assisted by members of the household; their muffled conversation comes through the wooden wall, the large grandfather clock swings its heavy pendulum and Jens grows older with each swing. Nor does he think about the catastrophes that he's just escaped; about the cold that glued him to his horse and would doubtless have cut off its legs had the route to the Village been longer. No, Jens thinks first about his sister, as so often when man's corruption frustrates him, thinks of her cloudlessness and feels his black anger, almost hatred towards Sigurður subside, dwindle to nothing, even transform into foolishness that it's possible to shake one's head at, this hatred that the two men have shared from the start, we don't know why, except that Sigurður finds Jens arrogant, irresponsible and imprudent; the doctor is likely waiting for a good opportunity to lodge a complaint about Jens and have him stripped of his duty. Some think that he's gathering various details into a long report that will deal Jens his deathblow at some point. Yet Jens manages to push Sigurður from his mind, thinks first about his sister, her brightness, her cloudless happiness and trust in her brother, then of his father, that powerhouse whom life and time are slowly but surely bowing, yet who still manages to run his farm, those hundred sheep, while Jens is on his postal trips; little by little, however, the father and daughter fade from his mind, to be replaced by something entirely different. His entire body heats up, his blood runs quicker, even surges through his veins, yet he stands dead still, looks straight ahead, expressionless, as if thinking of nothing at all, as if just waiting for time to pass. There can be such a gulf between one's exterior and interior lives, and this should tell us something, it should teach

57

him; but missing someone can be a comfort, breaking up the everyday, and Kristján was in high spirits when he returned home, with a lot to talk about. But the years change many things. Men wanted to drink with him, the women eyed him; he was also handsome, and it can be so nice to look at a handsome man, the dark hair that reached to his eyebrows, the supple movements, and the obsidian eyes, most bewitching. Slowly but surely, these trips changed him, or perhaps he simply discovered new sides to himself and life; sometimes it was as if he were encountering his true self, that this was the real him, that existence should be this way: companionship, poems, stories, attention; not back-breaking toil on a barren hill, the gruelling struggle for life, grey banality. They had three children, one died just several weeks old; little by little, Salvör's skin lost its enchanting power and greyed. There came hard winters, dry, cold summers; the trips lengthened and it became more and more difficult for him to return, some-times almost intolerable. Mediocrity loomed over the cottage: Salvör's reprehension, Salvör's grey skin. On other farms, women lay in wait for him in the dark passageways; there he was another man, more of a man, and life had more colours. Existence split slowly into two different worlds and the distance finally became unbridgeable. On the one hand, happy times with people, drink, poems, stories, popularity, respect, and on the other, the weight that hung over the cottage, the damned barren hill and the raw, wet meadows; the cursed solitude, no joy. And the closer he came to home, the harder he drank, barely managing to stay up on his horse by the time he arrived. Life takes us in numerous and vomit, didn't move until he seemed to be asleep. Then stood up and spread a blanket over him. Looked long into his sleeping face, dark, haggard, but still handsome in sleep. Then she went to the children, who were both awake in their beds; a six-year-old girl with big eyes, a two-year-old boy who coughed and coughed. She dressed them warmly, tucked the boy into a blanket, whispered something to the girl, and then went out to find the horse. Had to search for a considerable time. Called out gently, whistled, but to no end; she found it dead a short distance from the farm, Kristján had killed it and dead horses seldom respond to whistles. But snow covered everything and it wasn't terribly difficult for her to drag the children away on the primitive sled. A dark, starry winter night, and a three-hour walk to the nearest farm; the girl held her coughing brother tightly and they never looked back, didn't even stop once to regard the flames. The fire gave off an astonishingly bright gleam, the sky over the farm was so beautifully illuminated, yet the buildings were small and cramped; this was twelve or thirteen years ago. Since then Salvör has worked as a maid on the farm that she came to during her night march, diligent but reserved. The housewife appreciates her industriousness and trusts her, but certain women still hate her and miss him, who could seem like a foreign fairy tale when he went from farm to farm, with his dark hair, his eyes black as obsidian and voice that made the women tremble. The younger child, the boy, didn't live long, the three-hour sled-ride in the frosty night was perhaps too much for him, even though Salvör had dressed him as warmly as she could. He died a few weeks later. The girl had been placed on

I hate men, she said, and kissed him. Men are beasts, she said, and started to cry, the silver-coloured tears ran silently down her cheeks and Jens wrapped his huge, heavy arms around her, stroked her reddish-brown hair, patted her and comforted her just as he does with his father when he breaks beneath the disappointments of life, old and worn. This shoulder's been cried on before, said Salvör. Yes, said Jens. Then can I trust you? I've never betrayed anyone. Why have you looked at me like that? You're beautiful, he replied, the only answer he could think of, because one doesn't think such things, simply looks and eyes have never had need of words. You're lying! No, you're beautiful, I think only of you, really, on my postal trips. Why don't you just take me now, here on the banks of the stream, and then pride yourself on it afterwards? Jens looked at her; at first he didn't know what she meant. Take you, he repeated, then the meaning suddenly came to him and he became so inexpressibly sad, as if melancholy itself had filled his heart; he had a lump in his throat and could say nothing, simply looked away and thought that now it was all over. She took his big head in her hands, regarded him, kissed both his eyes, if you still want to and if you dare, you can sneak into my bed in September. Why wouldn't I dare? You know that I killed my husband, many people wanted and still want to see me locked up, it won't be to your advantage to sleep with me. If I'm forced to choose between you and the world, then I choose you, said Jens; the midnight sun and her eyes made him a poet. Two months later, in September, she lifted her blanket for him to slip in under. That was nearly two years ago and now he stands erect and expressionless in Dr Sigurður's office, waits, listens to the heavy beat of time in the parlour and thinks of Salvör. They start by whispering, lay their lips close to their ears and whisper things, sometimes just beautiful nonsense and words that ascend to the sky like colourful balloons, sometimes he tells of his sister, something she'd said, so childlike and cloudless that he and his father saw everything in a new light, my father has grown so old, he whispers, something breaks apart inside him, he tries to compose himself but when she lays her head on his shoulder the tears start to flow, completely silent, those transparent fishes of grief. She tells of her days, far too joyless, tells of her daughter and repeats parts of her letters that she knows by heart; I haven't seen her in four years and it hurts so much that I would much rather be stabbed with a knife every single day. Yet Salvör won't tell him where she is; not until I trust you entirely, she says. But she tells of her dead boy, he'd already spoken his first words, had recently started to walk, though he was late to start due to his frequent illnesses, but he had a bright, pure voice, and then he died and it was her fault. They hold each other, two desolate skerries in the heavy current of life. They're naked and it happens very slowly. So slowly that it's beautiful. Salvör feels his penis swell slowly, even apologetically; grief, despair give way slowly, she licks his salty eyes and he runs his hands over her body, which has aged and had turned so grey that it was nearly dead when Jens touched her first.

Jens moves his right shoulder slightly, reflexively, in Sigurður's parlour; Salvör bites it so that she can't be heard in the silent family room, in the silence that is broken by snores and the mumbling of dreams. Entirely by accident, Jens had discovered the magical power of his fingers; they lay close together and waited for the darkness of the evening to put everyone to sleep, but of course it's impossible to be living and lie so close together and simply breathe, their hands had to do something and they started moving, all four, roaming about their bodies and quite by coincidence he placed his thumb and index finger between her legs, entered and found a place that made her gasp for breath in such a way that he could barely think of anything else over the next few weeks. I didn't know that place existed, she whispered hoarsely after the first time, and kissed the bite marks on his shoulder. What place? Where I went, whence I was coming, almost as if I were going through the horizon! Jen looked at her in surprise and she giggled, which she likely hadn't done in fifteen years, and then grasped his penis. Come, she whispered as she spread her legs, and I'll take you there.

It's a strange reality that man has invented; there is not a single word mentioned of Salvör in her husband's brief certificate on the impediments to Jens' postal trip. It says only that foul weather and impossible conditions delayed the journey of the postman, Jens Guðjónsson, and that the heath he is crossing is considered by everyone to be as good as impassable to someone on foot, let alone to horses bearing trunks. But nothing about Salvör. Not a word about her life, her sorrow, her despair, not a word about regret or what happens between her and Jens, yet we should

66

probably never write about anything but this: the sorrow, the regret, defencelessness, and what sometimes occurs between two people, invisible but stronger than empires, stronger than religions and also as beautiful as the sky, about the tears that are transparent fish, about the words that we whisper to God or someone who makes all the difference, about the moment when a woman directs a penis into herself and the horizon tears apart. We should never write about anything else. All certificates, all reports, and all the messages of the world should express only this:

> I cannot make it to work today due to sorrow.
> I saw those eyes yesterday and therefore cannot make it to work.
> It's impossible for me to come today because my husband is naked and so beautiful.
> I cannot come today because life has betrayed me.
> I can't make it to the meeting because there's a woman sunbathing outside my door and the sun is making her skin glow.

We never dare to write such things, never describe the electricity between two persons, and instead talk about price levels; we describe the appearance, not the rush of blood, we don't seek the truth, unexpected lines of poetry, red kisses, but hide our weakness and surrender in strings of facts, the Turkish army is mobilising, yesterday the temperature was two below, men live longer than horses.

*

Hm, says Sigurður after entering the parlour; he holds the certificates, reads them over in front of Jens, has read them thoroughly but tries to make Jens uncomfortable by reading slowly and suspiciously, Jens is completely calm on the surface, though his blood rushes with excessive speed through his veins, he hardly notices the doctor, so lost in his thoughts about Salvör, reliving the moment. Sigurður folds the certificates, puts them in his jacket pocket; I won't hesitate to recommend that you be removed from your position if you don't perform, rest assured, he says directly, coldly. Jens' blood slows momentarily, and then his hatred blossoms, pitch-black, like a memory from Hell. Sigurður sits down in the one chair that seems in some way designed for him; the doctor has a cigar, a rather large one, takes time to light it, disappears for a moment behind a great cloud of smoke. Jens takes the opportunity to inhale deeply, enjoy the aroma while Sigurður can't see him. I must ask you a favour, says Sigurður when he returns from the cloud of smoke, appearing not to find it a bit uncomfortable to have to ask Jens for something. Jens transfers his weight from his left foot to his right, looks suspiciously at the doctor, who sucks down new smoke, new pleasure, and then asks Jens to cover the postal route to the Vetrarströnd coast and the area around Dumbsfjörður fjord; you can reckon three to five days, Guðmundur is in bed with the flu and is going nowhere. Sigurður falls silent, smokes, acts as if Jens isn't present, yet waits for a reply. Jens tries to ignore the enticing cigar smoke and to think clearly. Weigh and assess; choosing is torment. He would prefer to say no, set off for home tomorrow, his father will be worried if days pass with no word from him, and Salvör will be agitated; nor does he like the idea of burdening the old man with too much work, the little that he can endure nowadays; time is digging away at him rapidly. On the other hand, he'll earn a few extra krónur for the trip and his horses would be entirely rested by the time he returned; nothing is as bad for a horse as exhaustion, it does them in, turns a good riding horse into an old jade, and what can Jens do without horses, what would then become of the postal trips? He transfers his weight back to his left foot; but why is Sigurður asking him to go, is there more to it than meets the eye? Perhaps Sigurður knows that Jens isn't very familiar with the area; he's been there once before in the summer, but what of that? The landscape here in summer is entirely different than in winter; sometimes it's as if each is in its own hemisphere. The route is likely hellish after constant snowfall, relentless wind, only to be ventured by highly experienced travellers, who certainly aren't found around every corner now, truth to tell, now when so many men belong to ships' crews. That's why it's natural for Sigurður to ask Jens to go. Still, is there something more to it? Perhaps Sigurður is betting that due to Jens' unfamiliarity with the route, he'll deliver the post late, thereby providing the doctor a place to strike? Anyone making this journey has to cross open fjords by boat a total of four times – of this, twice over the wide, dark blue Dumbsfjörður – and four times over perilous heaths, one of them practically a mountain that most days reaps storms. But if he succeeds, delivers the post well and briskly, despite his unfamiliarity, he'll be in a better position with regard to the

X

It's snowing. The snowflakes fill the vault of the sky and pile up on the world. The wind is gentle and the drifts hold their shape, the surface of the sea is calm and ceaselessly swallows the snow. But the depths are still restless following the previous days' storms, a restlessness that makes things difficult for boats and ships. Like man, the sea has a sensitive quick and is long in recovering from an assault. It's rarely possible to judge by appearances, neither the sea's nor a person's, and therefore it's easy to be deceived and possibly pay for it with one's life or happiness; I married you because you were so gentle and handsome on the surface, but now I have no happiness; I went to sea because it was tranquil on the surface and now I'm dead; I weep on the seabed among other drowned men and the fish swim through me.

The snowfall is so dense, writes the boy, *that it connects Heaven and Earth. The snow now falling to Earth was perhaps in the vicinity of Heaven a few minutes ago. How long does it take to descend from Heaven to Earth? A minute, perhaps? For some, however, an entire life doesn't suffice, seventy years, to ascend from Earth to Heaven. Perhaps Heaven exists only in dreams?*

The boy puts down the pen, half frightened by the final sentence. Instinctively closes his eyes and imagines his sister, recalls how she giggled when he played with her, and for several moments it's as if she's still alive. Her eyes, full of trust and joy of life, little space for much else in the eyes of infants, they have no room yet for shadows, but then death extinguished her eyes, they are gone and will never be seen again. Is Heaven just a dream? And then where is his sister now, if that proves true? Her name was Lilja. He has to force himself not to write her name across the page. Lilja, after the poem that the monk Eysteinn composed to the glory of Heaven many hundreds of years ago, many hundred thousand lives ago, the poem of poems, for which everyone would have wished to take credit.[4] Lilja was the only name possible as far as her parents were concerned; his sister was their hymn of glory, with such a pure countenance and clear blue eyes and bright personality that old folk went out of their way just to get a chance to touch her; it was like touching innocence itself, before sin entered the world. *Lilja is so mischievous*, says one of the letters from his mother that the boy keeps in his room, worn from repeated readings, *that sometimes she becomes an unbearable, yet rather charming imp*. Are Heaven and the next life perhaps like dead gods which only exist if someone believes in them?

If so, then the boy is Lilja and his parents' only hope.

If he doesn't believe in them they will fade and turn to nothing; Lilja's blue eyes, eternally inquisitive and eager, will merge with the emptiness, become a vacuum that sucks in all life, all memories. If he dies too soon, without leaving anything behind,

4. The monk Eysteinn Ásgrímsson (d. 1361) composed the well-loved religious poem *Lilja (The Lily)* in the mid-fourteenth century.

an imprint, a sign, goes through life without placing his mark on it, he will fail them, fail their dreams and hopes. It's so simple; and there we have something of the essence of life, something of a reason: to experience everything that Lilja was deprived of. Learn everything that she missed.

She is so inquisitive that some flee at her approach. Not everyone can tolerate it when a child asks questions that force us to re-evaluate our own lives. Why do you exist? Why are you like that? Why are you angry? Why do you look at my mummy so much? How far is it from here to God? What's in my poo? Why do you smell so bad? Where do my dreams go when I wake? These are the questions your sister asks everyone here on the farm, day out, day in.

There was much in the letters that the boy didn't grasp when he was a child, especially in the last of them, much that is only now opening up to him, as if his mother had had a suspicion of the end and written the letters with it in mind. These were thus letters to the future, to him in the future that she'll miss, she and Lilja. Enthusiastic words, but saturated with painful sorrow, only so delicate that it's barely noticeable. These words are boats that ferry his mother's life, the lives of Lilja and his father, away from oblivion and absolute death. And it's up to him not to let the boat wreck and the cargo sink unobstructed into the dark sea. Him and no other. Not Egill, his brother whom he hasn't seen or heard from for years. There's something that tells him, perhaps his mother had insinuated it in her letters, between the lines, so much is possible to fit between the lines, that Egill will save nothing from oblivion.

But what can he do?

He looks down at his hands, they're empty, and man's arms are just worm-eaten planks of wood in the face of time, which grinds life beneath it and consigns it to nothingness.

My sister's name is Lilja, he writes, immediately following the sentence about Heaven. *Dear Andrea* is written at the top of the page. He's going to encourage Andrea to leave Pétur, abandon him, start over, begin a new life, it's so simple, the answer is clear, he's almost embarrassed to point it out to her, as if he's belittling her intellect by writing down what is so obvious. Leave him. But it's not until the words have taken shape on the paper that he realises their gist. Written words can have more depth than spoken ones, almost as if the paper releases an unknown world from its shackles. The paper is the fertile soil of the word. Because where can Andrea go? And how is she supposed to live? He looks around as if in search of the answer, but sees only the empty tables, empty chairs, the snow outside linking Heaven and Earth and somewhere in the snowfall is the sea. It's both fascinating and frightening to take a boat to sea in such weather. The world appears to vanish with the wind; nothing exists but the heavy snowfall, the boat and the sea around it. The snow silences everything, it's as if it carries the silence within it, or as if the snowflakes carry it; between two snowflakes is silence. But how is it possible to take one's bearings, find the fishing banks and then the way back, he never understood this and always feared deep inside that they would drift slowly away and when the snowfall finally lifted, all the mountains would be gone, it would

74

just be the openocean, rising waves, a darkening sky, and the end of the world.

My sister's name was Lilja.

It's his task to see to it that she's not forgotten, that her short life be given purpose, yet he's never been able to tell anyone about her except for Bárður, and now Bárður is dead and perhaps remembers nothing more. Besides, what use is it to say a name out loud if nothing else follows? Some people talk and talk, expand their existence in words and we get the feeling that their lives are somehow larger, and greater, but these are perhaps lives that in fact become nothing as soon as the words stop buzzing. I have a brother somewhere, he writes, whose name is Egill, like the poet.[5] I haven't seen him since we were children. He was always so unsure of everything, and mainly himself. I should find him.

Why is he writing this to Andrea? She has no interest in his insignificant concerns. Why is he wasting paper on himself? Andrea needs help, not complaints from him. I should probably offer to marry her. Of course! And even take her to America. A shame how old she is, flashes through his mind, like malevolent lightning, probably more than forty years old! He grabs his hair and pulls hard. It isn't particularly fun to sit here and think of Andrea as an old woman; not to find it natural to marry her. Now he can't continue his letter, not while he thinks like this; it will contaminate the words. He looks at his pen and hopes for support, a way out; of course it would be best to start on the letter

5. A reference to Egill Skallagrímsson, the renowned tenth-century Icelandic Viking and poet.

for Oddur. But no, it's impossible, it won't work, he needs to be happy to do so, like Oddur. The sun needs to shine through the words, they must sparkle with a pure joy of life; how can he conjure up such a thing? Is it possible in general, because where should he put the shadows in the meantime, who will keep them? No, now he'll just finish the letter to Andrea, damn it, she needs him, she's alone in the world, but how did it cross her mind to marry Pétur, anyway; what did she see in that damned clod who's as salty as the sea, gloomy and sombre and probably never says anything beautiful to her, never says anything beautiful in general, his heart isn't a muscle, it's a piece of salt fish. Of course she should leave him!

Andrea, he writes, but then hears someone coming from within the house. It's Kolbeinn, with his hesitant yet stubborn gait, supporting himself with his cane, they're inseparable, the lifeless supports the living, if only the same applied to us. The old skipper sniffs the air and turns his nose towards the boy, as if smelling him. What are you doing? he asks in a gruff voice. Oh, you know, answers the boy. What? says Kolbeinn, as if he'd never heard these trivial words, oh, you know, before. Writing a letter. Is there reason for that? I don't know. What? I think it matters. For whom, you? No, for the person who receives it. Well then, that's something, barks the old man, feels his way forward with his cane and sits down by the window; so I have a better view, he mutters, but then withdraws into silence, says nothing even when the boy asks if he wants coffee, sits at the window and looks out into the impenetrable darkness that never leaves him, not in this life, except in deceitful dreams. He sits completely motionless, looking as lifeless as the cane leaning against its owner. The skipper's body is as dense as stone; he's a head shorter than the boy, amply so. His shoulders appear to have been pulled up, or his head to have been driven further down into his trunk. People shrink with age; it's time that does this to life, the tremendous weight that compresses a person. You can grow shorter by many centimetres in your final years; if you lived long enough, several hundred years, time would simply erase you, compress you into nothing.

The boy looks back down at the letter; words are the only thing that time seems unable to step over lightly. It penetrates life and life becomes death, it penetrates a house and turns it to dust, even the mountains give way in the end, those majestic piles of rock. But some words seem to tolerate the destructive power of time; it's so strange, they certainly erode, possibly lose their sheen somewhat, but endure and preserve within them long-gone lives, preserve vanished heartbeats, vanished voices of children, they preserve ancient kisses. Some words are shells in time and within them is perhaps the memory of you. Andrea, he writes, time can be so cruel, giving us everything only to take it away again. We lose far too much. Is it because we lack courage? Mother said that the courage to question was the most important thing a person can have. I don't know how this can be, but it's as if I'm always understanding her assertion better. I question everything. So is that why I know nothing? Yet I don't want to lose this doubt, though it's sometimes like a wicked person within me. The way to a secure life and numbness is not to question which he said that he was thinking of me as a pastor but also as a friend, he cared for me as the widow of his friend; to think of a priest letting his pen lie like that for him. And as a friend he wished to point out to me that with my lifestyle I degraded other women. The noblest role of a woman, blessed by the Lord, is to be a wife and mother. And I slight this with my lifestyle. Nothing less. A beautiful lifestyle makes us beautiful, an ugly one ugly, that's the way the letter ended; am I ugly? she asks the boy. No, he replies. Am I beautiful? Yes, replies the boy; yet my life isn't beautiful, she mutters, pouring another shot and emptying it as quickly as the first. Doesn't Þorvaldur just want to have his way with you, he's had trouble with his horniness for ages, says Kolbeinn. Yes, naturally he wouldn't have anything against it, the poor fellow, she says without changing her expression, but first and foremost they want me to get married.

The boy: And for what?

Geirþrúður: Maybe they're just romantic.

Kolbeinn: There's nothing of the sort in them; they just want to lord it over everyone, and anyway it's all in their hands.

Geirþrúður: Friðrik said I was a discredit to the community with my lifestyle and habits; he said I was a bad example. Get married, he said, a woman isn't meant to stand alone. He was very nice about it, but of course it wasn't a request, it was a command.

The boy: And what . . . what are you going to do?

Kolbeinn: You have a pistol. Use it.

Geirþrúður: That would undeniably be invigorating.

Kolbeinn: I'll marry you. Though I'm of little use anymore.

Will you marry me? she says, looking at the boy with her dark eyes, those two dark suns. No, you need a man, says Kolbeinn, that's how you are. Well, that excludes the both of you, she says, her smile rejuvenating her for a moment. Why do you need to get married? asks the boy, blushing, since she no doubt noticed what he was looking at before. Why did he have to look?

Geirþrúður: By law, a woman can only be a man's equal if he loses his mind or commits a very serious crime.

Kolbeinn, almost heartily: Or loses his sight.

Geirþrúður: If I marry, and then presumably someone who's acceptable to them, my husband will take charge of everything I own. Or so says the law; and aren't we bound to heed it? Strictly speaking, I couldn't even go to a bakery without getting his permission first. So there'll be a great deal to look forward to, that is, if you marry me. Besides all the other things that can't be discussed.

Kolbeinn: I've never liked Friðrik. He was a little shit of a child and his father not much better. But they're bloody strong.

Geirþrúður: The male is strong, males are stronger, you have the physique to prove it and you use it when necessary. In that way you gain the assurance of the oppressor.

The boy: I'm not strong. I've never been strong, and don't want to be.

Geirþrúður: I know; why do you think I've taken you in? You two are as far from being men as is possible. One blind, the other having come from dreams.

I haven't come from dreams, mumbles the boy – because whoever comes from dreams must be as transparent as a June night.

Such a one doesn't look at the glen between two breasts. He doesn't wake up in the middle of the night after a coarse dream, wet and sticky.

Kolbeinn: I was a man in my day; I could even be a damned rapscallion.

The boy: But you never married.

Kolbeinn: No, I read too much.

The boy: What?

Kolbeinn: It didn't inspire confidence, reading. And I ended up blind. But you need to get yourself a woman, then you wouldn't be so bloody idiotic and erratic. You need to become a man. But can't you marry one of those foreigners of yours, Geirþrúður, they've done you well in bed, why not get a little more use out of them?

The boy stares at his lap. There are only two, Kolbeinn, she says, both married and living abroad, which is why I trust them. Then you have to marry a sluggard, says Kolbeinn, rubbing his cane, someone you can control easily; you'll hardly have any trouble finding one here.

Go find Jóhann for me, says Geirþrúður to the boy, and he stands up so quickly, relieved to be given a job to do and to get away, that his chair topples over. Are you going to marry him? he asks like an idiot, instead of keeping quiet and getting out of there when he has the chance. She laughs briefly, pours a third shot; he's my steward, that's enough. Besides having no inclination for sex, the bastard, says Kolbeinn.

Geirþrúður: Of that, we know nothing. But the worst thing I could do to myself would of course be to marry a man I'm fond of; then I would be defenceless. I should maybe marry Gísli; there's plenty of misfortune in him already.

Kolbeinn: Gísli! He's never had the guts to be himself, that's why he's hardly anything. Friðrik controls him with his little finger.

What have you got there? Geirþrúður asks the boy, looking at the densely written sheets of paper on the table; it's not your translation, you've hardly done much? What translation, when will it be read to me? asks Kolbeinn, his head doddering with impatience. No, says the boy, this is a letter. Letter, echoes Geirþrúður, who has come over to the table, may I read it? she asks, picks it up before he can say anything, she's so close that he can smell her aroma. He's never written anything like this before, and now it's being read. I'm here too, says Kolbeinn loudly, after several minutes pass in complete silence, and he raps the floor twice with his cane; aren't you going to read it to me; damned darkness, he then growls when no-one replies, lifts his cane and waves it as if to divide the darkness enclosing him. Wasn't Andrea your housekeeper at the fishing huts? asks Geirþrúður, putting down the three sheets. He nods. And she doesn't feel well? No. Nor do I feel well, says Kolbeinn loudly.

Geirþrúður: Only he who questions lives, that's quite well-put. Finish the letter, then come to the kitchen, Jóhann can wait until then, and then we'll get someone to deliver it to the fishing station. Kolbeinn, she says, and the old man gets up.

The boy listens as their voices fade. Only he who questions lives, and what of it, what's he going to do with this woman? he hears Kolbeinn say; is the boy's only inclination for words?

He hunches over the paper and writes:

> *The way to a secure life and numbness is not to call into question one's surroundings – only he who questions lives. Andrea, leave Pétur. Stay and you'll never forgive yourself. Go, and you might discover life again, stay and you'll continue to die.*

He doesn't think, his heart is buzzing, he feels it, it fills his chest. The pen darts over the page. Words can be bullets, but they can also be rescue teams. The boy hunches over the paper and dispatches the teams.

Then he shakes his tired hand and reads the letter, his face soft but resolute with deep concentration; time hasn't yet marked it with its knife. The boy reads over what he's just written, and the words are bigger than him.

A few minutes later he has come out, with the letter in his pocket, a one-króna coin, and two fragrant loaves of bread in a sack. Go to Mildiríður, Helga had said, after she and Geirþrúður read the letter, her son Simmi will deliver the letter for you. But don't forget to stop at Jóhann's, and send him here.

The snowfall is less dense than this morning, he sees the world through the snowflakes, the leaden sea that rises and falls, a huge creature following the boy with half-shut eyes as he trudges through the drifts in the direction of a little house by the bay, or bight, below the church field. The house is sagging and leans forward as if a giant passed by and kicked it out of boredom. He stands in a deep drift and knocks cautiously on the door a few times, the snow floats down from the sky, lands gently on the ground, melts on the surface of the sea. The door opens and an aged face appears in the gap, wrinkled and hairy like a mouldy fig, and not much larger either. Mildiríður? he asks hesitantly; she nods her head. I need very much to send a letter to the fishing huts of the brothers Pétur and Guðmundur; Helga told me . . . Have you come from Helga, my dear boy?! Blue, slightly cloudy eyes peer at the boy, her voice is weak and broken by age and a toothless smile brightens her figgish face.

The house is so small that it barely fits the two lives that vegetate in it; the boy stoops reflexively and looks at the man lying in one of the bunks, a stone oven near the wall and two stools, nor could much else fit therein. Daylight trickles in through three small membranes; caul in place of windows and rags stuffed into the spot where the chimney meets the ridge, to keep the cold away and the snow outside, no doubt, but then the stale air has nowhere to go and lies heavy and stagnant on the boy, who tries to breathe through his mouth, impatient to go back outside. Simmi is sleeping, tearing the air with his snores, his face puffy and coarse; his large, twisted mouth, flattened nose and slanted eyes give him a threatening appearance. He has a black cap on his head, the threadbare bedcover has slipped off him, revealing his short legs and hairy belly. Simmi, dear boy, whispers Mildiríður, standing bent-backed over her son, a young man has come with a letter for you to deliver. She nudges her son gently, and he grumbles and waves her away. Mildiríður looks at the boy, tries to straighten up but it's time that has bent her back so mercilessly, and who has the enormous strength needed to push back against it? He'll wake soon, she says, and smiles again; would you like some coffee, my dear? She doesn't wait for a reply, but starts busying herself at the oven. The boy straightens up carefully, leaving no more than five, six centimetres between the top of his head and the grimy ceiling. Simmi mumbles and squirms; it's not always easy to abandon one's dreams. The boy has seen him before, from a distance; he's sent willingly and untiringly between fishing stations with various trifles, limping along like the offspring of a common seal and a sea monster, always with his hood pulled down over his eyes, no matter what the weather.

The coffee boils and the aroma blends with the stench inside. The boy reaches into the sack; this is from Helga, he says, holding out the bread, and the old woman says oh oh oh, strokes the bread lovingly and blesses Helga at least seven times. Simmi opens his eyes wide, sniffs the air and springs to his feet, then spies the boy and comes right up to him, scrutinises his face as if needing to feel it with his dull, slanted eyes, a smell of urine and filth strikes the boy's senses, and the coffee's no good. Simmi takes a long time eating, finishes off one entire loaf, gathers and eats the crumbs slowly, sighing and panting with contentment, then suddenly farts loudly and burps, his eyes beam, but the boy has become so impatient that he has trouble standing still. Finally Simmi's ready and is given the letter, holds it tightly with his

85

which was, however, not far enough, although they could see in each other's eyes. I managed to bid him farewell, she says to the boy, stroking the back of his hand as if it were he who needed comforting. The men soon rose to the surface again. There was air in their skin-trousers and they surfaced upside down, their legs stuck up out of the sea, their heads down, and the sea rocked them in that way for hours, like strange seabirds, and Simmi laughed so much that he had to sit down. It's difficult to hate the person whom one loves, she says to the boy, of course it's the most difficult thing in the world, but then one gets over it, and forgives everyone. Except for oneself.

The wind is blowing as the boy sets out again. Breaks away from those eyes, smile, sorrow, the words of blessing, and struggles over the churchyard, is driven somewhat off course, has to manoeuvre around big drifts, and once the wind blows him into the arms of a big man who turns out to be Jens; I didn't know that puppies were let out in such weather, says the postman, and he shoves the boy aside and is gone.

XI

Somewhere out in this storm Simmi hobbles along in the direction of the fishing station, the letter under his coat, the sentences that were written to change life, that's the way we must always write, and the grease in his clothing spreads to the envelope, it'll be spotty when Andrea receives it; what letter is this? asks Pétur, suspicious, apprehensive, just a letter, she says haughtily, and then he grows fearful, wants to take the letter from her but dares not, looks at Einar, who's too slow to hide his sneer; there's always someone who takes delight in others' misfortune. She'll read it, thinks the boy, but then what? Will his words go out into this storm and return with Andrea? Won't he then be automatically responsible for her, perhaps forcing him to sacrifice something of himself to help her? What is responsibility; to help others so much that it damages one's own life? But if you don't take the step towards another, your days will ring hollow. Life is only easy for the unethical; they do quite well and live in big houses.

Evening falls between the mountains. The boy helps with cleaning up after the meeting of the Craftsmen's Association, which went smoothly. Only two who vomited, only one who passed out, and one other who went home with a broken nose;

88

important meetings, said the chairman to Helga, they bring us together, it's the solidarity that counts, otherwise the nobs march over us and trample us into the shit. You're quite good at that yourselves, it seems to me, she said. What nonsense, replied the chairman, without the fellowship we'd be defenceless; Friðrik fears us, and not just a little – but your Kolbeinn went somewhere with Ási, probably to a hotel, I'm told the old man enjoys his drink. What does he mean? asked the boy when the chairman was gone, a bit unsteady on his feet but so pleased with himself that he tried first to hug and caress Helga. Kolbeinn can't handle his drink, which puts him in bad spots; we'll have to go fetch him later.

A hard wind is blowing. It whips up the drifts, shakes the world, and the mountains rumble heavily. It takes the boy and Helga just under half an hour to come down to the hotel, ordinarily a five-minute walk. The weather changes everything here, the north wind and cold make us huddle in our homes and increase the distance between people. Indeed, there's no-one out but them, and what business does a person have being out in such weather, other than to die? The ships have doubtless sought shelter beneath the rock walls, where they might expect less violent assaults when the wind blows in this direction, and the fishing boats that are still out on the sea try to fight their way towards land, which, however, is visible nowhere; it's gone, the world is a white, formless whirl-wind, with perhaps dozens of men struggling to row at this moment, listening for the breakers that announce land, but which are also the final and most perilous obstacle. They fight against a superior force, unprotected in open boats, fight for themselves, fight for those waiting on shore, wives who dare not sleep for fear of seeing their apparitions in dreams, drenched with seawater; well, that's the way it went, pray for my soul because I yearn to be brought from the sea up to Heaven; now I'm dead, so you no longer have to curse me, you're free, congratulations; my love, my heart, I'd give my life for dry socks, but simply have no life left to give.

And somewhere there are people who must venture out into the same storm to feed ever-hungry sheep, bleating and chewing their cuds, dreaming of succulent grass and an occasional hand-some ram.

The boy is familiar with all of this: the dream of greenness, going to the outbuildings in every sort of weather, the wind on the verge of tearing off his head, risking his life for hay, and he's gripped oars or gunwales with a death-grip and listened for the sound of the breakers, that dark rumbling holding both life and death, the heavy roar cutting through the howling wind, full of promises and threats: come to me and I'll crush your boat and drown you like hapless mice, or allow you through to get on with life, if you still wish to call the brief moment that you're here by such a big name. But those who make it through the breakers are also safe. Waiting for them is solid ground and the everyday with its comforting words, dry socks, warm embraces, clear children's voices, betrayal and banality.

The boy struggles to catch his breath and withstand the wind, walks quickly back down the corridor and turns a corner to the right. The boy looks inquisitively at Helga. Daughter of Ásgerður and Teitur, she says, you two are the same age, the poor dear is terrified of men. As old as me, scared of me, says he, hardly knowing which of the two is more surprising. You're a man, says Helga, as if revealing a previously unknown fact, but Hulda isn't as homely as she appears; never let appearances deceive you and lead you astray. Hello, Teitur, says Helga to the man who comes to them quickly, holding up his large hands apologetically. My dear Helga, he says, forgive me for making you wait, but Friðrik and his family, along with some others, are having a meal here, and you know that one can't run out in the middle of a conversation with him. I should have let you know about Kolbeinn, of course; but he's just in the barroom now and in excellent company. I, and we all, have kept a watchful eye on him, and Hulda was going to take him home. You can count on us. Kolbeinn won't be wandering away from us again, like last time; but tell me, what young man is this with you? he asks, leaning forward to get a better look at the boy, his smile displaying the rare benevolence that makes the world a habitable place. The Village would certainly be bleaker if Teitur and his wife Ásgerður weren't here; the hotel is located at Central Square and had started deteriorating by the time the couple bought it twenty years ago. They'd acquired a bit of wealth operating fishing boats and put everything they had into refurbishing the house, which was no small task; it's a large, two-storey house with a cellar and a spacious garret that serves as the apartment of the hotelkeepers and their daughter Hulda. It went very one in everyday life appears not to touch them. Those who have the privilege of crossing the paths of such people momentarily perceive the purpose behind everything. The only real shadow in the couple's life is Hulda's sadness and loneliness, this weight that she carries within her, this dark block of stone that she hides from them as best she can, though they wake at times to the sound of her crying in the night. The poor dear will never marry, say the women here, and perhaps there's something to what they say. At a glance, the girl's a bungled piece of work: emaciated, lacking hips, flat-chested, long-necked, not to mention buck teeth, awkward hands, diligent hands; she derives satisfaction from work and enjoys playing chess on calm, dark winter days with her father, who stands before Helga and the boy and asks out of curiosity, but with obvious tenderness, what young man this is, and leans forward to get a better look at the boy. This is my and Geirþrúður's boy, says Helga, we're going to educate him; he's far too dreamy for fishing. Education, excellent idea, says Teitur, looking inquisitively at the boy, squinting as near-sighted folk do; almost anyone can work in the fishing industry, go to sea, we have quite enough of such people, but your type is far too rare. We can have Hulda teach you English, that is to say, if you choose – the company would do her good as well. In any case, I'm very sorry about what happened to your friend. That was a great tragedy.

It's this word, *tragedy*, that prevents the boy from immediately grasping the gist of the sentence, but then it dawns on him that the hotelkeeper knows the story of the waterproof, of the line of poetry that separates life and death, and perhaps he's also heard of the great march with the poem on his back. The story has spread around the Village, the boy is aware of people's glances when he goes down to the shop or runs an errand for the house, and it gives him the feeling that he's transforming into a character in a story.

Where are you now? asks Helga, taking him loosely by the arm and following Teitur, who has set off down the corridor. The boy follows them; the corridor is dimly lit but is brighter at the other end. Teitur turns left into an open room with several tables and stout chairs; three men are sitting there at a big table. The boy looks to the right and stops in his tracks when he spies Ragnheiður's bare shoulders and white profile through a large, double glass door, spies her high cheekbones that resemble a glacier planed down by the winds.

He hasn't seen her since she stuck a wet, glistening sweet in his mouth.

She's holding a fork.

Her brown hair is tied up in a bun but one single lock dangles at her cheek. A single, brown lock silhouetted against her white, incredibly smooth skin. He looks and he looks and gradually the Earth's rotation slows, slows until it stops. Hangs unmoving in the blackness of space and all else grows tranquil. The wind becomes transparent air, the blowing snow sinks to the ground and falls silent, over it a black sky with glittering stars, as old as time.

He didn't know that it was possible to stop the Earth's rotation by looking at a single lock of hair dangling against a white cheek.

He didn't know that this same lock of hair could cause him to sense the dawn of time.

He didn't know that shoulders could be so slender, and as white as moonlight.

She doesn't look at him, she isn't aware of him, but the woman sitting at the end of the table, perhaps her mother, regards the boy coldly, deliberately, and when he discerns the little muscles twitching around her mouth, he hurries after Helga, giddy, lost; when his head clears he finds himself in the chair next to her. They're sitting at a table with Kolbeinn and two men. How long have I been sitting here? thinks the boy, lays his hands on the table but instinctively yanks them back when he sees a single, deathly pale finger in a glass cylinder in front of him.

Fingers are rarely bored.

From time to time the boy regards them jealously, how they extend from the palm and stand close together, except for the thumb, which keeps itself apart from the others, cocky, a bit lonely, yet an inseparable part of the whole. Most often the fingers are grouped by five; ten when the hands are laid together, but the finger on the table is poignantly alone, a very long way from its brothers. Teitur brings two plump glasses, nearly half full of a heavy, yellow liquid, and places them in front of Helga and the boy. You know the watchmaker, Ási, says Helga, nodding in the direction of a slender, handsome man sitting opposite them to the left; and this is none other than the schoolmaster, Gísli Jónsson, a famous man here between the mountains, she says, meaning the man directly in front of the boy. The schoolmaster is an imposing man, stout and stocky; his puffy, ruddy face is completely whiskerless, which may explain why there seems to be a hint of vulnerability in his countenance. Gísli greets them by nodding his head slightly, then reaches for the finger and sticks it in his jacket pocket. To me it borders on the perverse to go around with a stranger's finger in one's pocket, says Ási, his eyes unsteady with drink; and a dratted foreigner's to boot. The human soul is home to many things, says Gísli. You haven't seen a finger before? he asks the boy, who has difficulty taking his eyes off the jacket pocket. Yes, but only in the company of a hand and other fingers, he answers quietly, as if from a distance, and then the schoolmaster gives a quick laugh, extends his large hand, spreading out his ten fingers; it's true what you say, they have company! He turns his hand over, as if in amazement, looks again at the boy, leans back as if to regard him better, isn't this? . . . asks the schoolmaster but can come no further because Helga says only, yes, it's him. Remarkable, mutters Gísli, truly remarkable, absolutely remarkable, and fascinating to a high degree, yes, and truly . . . different. He runs his index finger quickly over his chin. Did you know, my boy, he then says, that there is a French poet, or there *was*, of course long dead like all decent men, who ordered us with unusual force and authority to become enraptured, continually drunk, with wine, virtue, poetry; then we would be alive, then we would have *lived*. I try at times to live according to this order. At times, and I don't give a single damn what others say about it; I'm absolutely my own boss, and now I wish to toast you and your friend; his memory shall shine eternally. Gísli stands up, holding his cognac glass, stands up carefully and has to struggle to find his balance on this globe that revolves far too rapidly in space, but

Village. Thirty ships, that's approximately three hundred fishermen, many of them from elsewhere, meaning quite a bit of action when they're made ready, most at the same time. Teitur is happy that the bustle is behind; it's certainly profitable, yet entails long and difficult nights, noise, commotion, coarse days. Men in groups far from their homes lose so much, the group dynamic is bad for them, strips them of their grandeur; they become vulgar, and for a time it wasn't safe to let Hulda go anywhere in the hotel unaccompanied in the evenings; some of them harassed her, even savagely, Teitur once had to tear a sailor off her, piss-drunk and behaving like a rutting bull, had torn down his trousers and pressed Hulda, white with terror, up against the wall, rubbing his hard, swollen penis against her, this organ that can be beautiful but sometimes seems more like a horrible message from Hell. What will become of Hulda? She's unbearably shy of all men, yet it's only drunken sailors who seem to pay her any attention, will I never be a grandfather, thinks Teitur, and everything turns grey and sad for an instant. He runs the palm of his hand distractedly over the table, opens his eyes and meets those of the boy. Peals of laughter can be heard from the dining room, voices muffled by the glass door, it seems my big brother's having a good time, says Gísli pointedly, pulling out a deck of cards. People who play can avoid speaking of delicate subjects and can escape from life momentarily. The boy is content to observe, reaches for his glass, has just begun to accustom himself to the heavy drink but the glass is so bulging that he needs to lean back and when he does he sees Ragnheiður; she's wearing a blue dress, half hidden behind the doorpost and signalling him to come, clandestinely yet with great impatience. The boy stands up hesitantly; the others seem not to notice anything. And he goes to her.

I thought you were never going to notice me, she whispers, taking hold of the boy and pulling him into a corner where no-one can see them. She's wearing a blue, sky-coloured dress, one of the gods has torn a piece from the sky, wrapped it about her, the sky lies tight against her body above the waist but flares out slightly below it. She pulls him into the corner, coming so close to him that he feels her breasts, they press against him, perhaps completely coincidentally but perhaps not at all, and they're hard and they're probably rather large, yet he isn't certain, he knows so little about breasts, but it would be incredibly nice to feel them again. Her hair is put up in a bun, he looks at her soft neck, at her bare shoulders, there must be happiness in having such shoulders. We don't have much time, she says softly, she's trapped him in the corner so that he can't go anywhere, nor does he want to go anywhere, they're waiting for me, I said that I just needed to go to the loo, to take a shit, she adds, looking defiantly at the boy. What are you doing here with Helga, I thought you two preferred not to go anywhere? I'm just, he says, hardly hearing himself over the heavy murmur of his blood, his pounding heart, I just came with Helga, and, um, we were . . . were looking for Kolbeinn, he mumbles when he notices Ragnheiður's growing look of impatience. I know, she says, seemingly on the verge of stamping her foot. What can he say to calm her, what words might possibly appease this woman, this girl, who has eyes of mountains? Why do you stare at my shoulders like that? Her flint-coloured eyes pierce the boy, though they aren't too severe at the moment and her lips aren't shut; her lips are red, they're thick and they gleam with moisture and those eyes are of mountains.

The boy: Behind the mountains is a great light.

I'm going to Copenhagen soon, she says, glancing downward for an instant. She has long eyelashes, two fans lying over her eyes. I'm staying the next two years with Tryggvi and his wife in Copenhagen. The fans are lifted; and just as well, she continues, you could completely lose it here, in this *backwater*, where nothing happens and there's only vulgar sailors, while overseas there are *museums* and *boulevards* and throngs of people in the streets just *life*! I don't understand how people can bear to hang around here.

Well then.

So she's going.

Alright.

Away.

Over the sea.

Incredibly far away.

Which is just fine, and safe journey! What does it matter to him? He has no interest in her, doesn't know her at all, not a whit, she's from another world, far far away from his, an ocean between them whether she's in Copenhagen or here.

And yet. She's leaving. With those eyes. And those shoulders! She's going.

And leaving the mountains behind.

And me at their feet.

And that's why somewhere out in the night is sorrow, on its way to me with a loaded rifle, to shoot me like a dog, he thinks, convinced that the cynicism of existence would have the last word. Why do you say nothing? she asks him sharply, again seemingly on the verge of stamping her feet. And stop staring at my shoulders! See how silly you can be!

The one who's left behind beneath the mountains with their plunging slopes can in fact say everything, simply because he has nothing to lose, and of course nothing to win either. I say nothing because sorrow is out there in the evening and is on its way here with a loaded rifle, and I look at your shoulders like that because they're more beautiful than moonlight and I wouldn't be able to describe them, even if I lived for ten centuries, and I . . . the boy stops because the words have suddenly abandoned him, an entire language has vanished, leaving only silence behind. There's hardly any space between them now. They're so close that they breathe precisely the same oxygen, divide it between them, and she has those shoulders and looks at him and breathes, just breathes him in and all the world's words are gone and the boy thus does the only thing that it's possible to do: obey the commandment of the heart.

His lips hover in the air for a long time. They float through the sky, leave the atmosphere and travel a very long time through the darkness of space, finally landing softly on moonlight-white shoulders. Then he draws his lips slowly along the surface, up the neck and to the earlobe, which is white and hard and soft, he hears her breathe, feels the palm of her hand on his stomach, she grasps his head, moves it down and kisses him and her lips are warm and they are moist and they are and they are and they are and they are.

Then she lets go of his head, turns around, walks briskly to the dining room, opens the door, a few words slip out; she goes in, shuts the door and the words die on the floor before the boy.

XII

The next day is nearly calm and the wind, as transparent as time, is gone; it vanished with the night and left behind an apologetic breeze.

The boy is slow to wake; he half dozes. People think little as they wake, they just sense, and are therefore close to being dreams, but he knows that wakefulness awaits above the surface like a bright noise, murmurs something, tries to change blood into sand, make himself so heavy that he sinks again. Sleep is a dark refuge, and he sinks.

They hadn't been sitting very long at the hotel. The boy travelled these approximately four hundred thousand kilometres to kiss shoulders, kiss an earlobe, and was then kissed himself. When his head cleared he was back at the table, next to Helga, who put down the cards and said, well, we're leaving now. No, no, no, said Gisli, who seemed frightened, don't go right away, you just can't, no no, Ási, help me to stop them, we still have so much to talk about this evening, and the entire bloody night is still ahead! The words aren't going anywhere and there'll be other nights, said Helga. We don't know that, said Gísli, one's final evening comes at some point and then it's too late to talk. I'll take the risk, said

Helga. Ási prepared to stand, someone might be waiting up for him at home, but Gísli held him down forcefully; stay, he said, it hurts so much to be alone, let's talk, Ási, talk and talk until we don't know who we are, what we're called. Do you think, Ási, that God needs you when you're dead?

They took a long time walking from the hotel, the storm had subsided considerably, they could walk upright but Kolbeinn adamantly refused to accept help, shook off Helga's arm and walked by himself, slowly, feeling out the way with his feet at every step, they on each side of him, prepared to grab him and doing so thrice. Which do you think took my sight from me, God or the Devil? he asked the boy after he'd fallen for the third time and Helga had brushed the snow off him; I don't know, replied the boy, but hopefully you'll end up in the same place as it. Then the old wolf fish gave one of those hard, hoarse laughs of his, most resembling a sad bark, and allowed them to support him the rest of the way.

Geirþrúður was waiting in the parlour, the boy was supposed to read from Shakespeare; take me away from this place, said Geirþrúður, handing him the book. And the boy did so; he took them all away, himself included, away from Ragnheiður, the lust, the kiss, the sensitivity, the regret, he read and the evening passed, night approached, while the heavy clock stood speechless out in a corner; now I'll stop time, Geirþrúður had said once, and since then time hasn't passed in any palpable way in this parlour, the pendulum hangs motionless, like a condemned convict upside-down. He read, he took them away and Kolbeinn sat motionless in his darkness while Shakespeare's words entered it like glowing torches.

How can I please thee, madam, what ails thee? the villain Iago asks Desdemona, who is so beautiful in her misfortune. *I cannot tell,* she replies,[6] which is a good reply, because what do we want, why are we fearful, whence come these hidden, cruel aspirations, where is life taking us? I cannot tell, she replied, the truest words, we fumble our way through life and then die into the unknown. I cannot tell, replied Desdemona, and was going to say something more, even though she'd likely said everything; but then someone was heard entering the house with a great deal of commotion, Helga opened her eyes; it's likely Jens, she said, the boy let the book drop, his finger resting on Desdemona's reply, prepared to read onwards, and the postman staggered into the parlour, white with snow. Jens stood there swaying and looking around, as if surprised to see them, astonished to be inside, turned around as if he wanted to ask, where's the blowing snow, where's the wind? Bumped his foot against a chair, lost his balance and fell, a boom resounded throughout the house and there he lay. Dead drunk. He'd lingered long at Sodom, with Marta; Ágúst lay ill in the little room adjoining the Café. Jens had decided to drop in on Guðmundur, the reserve postman, and was on his way to the man's house when the wind blew the boy into his arms. Wanted to get information that could make a crucial difference in bad weather up on a mountain, on a risky mountain path; what

6. The original in William Shakespeare, *Othello*, Act IV, Scene 2, reads: "Iago: What is your pleasure, madam, how is't with you? Desdemona: I cannot tell."

perils he might encounter, what peak would tell him of the approach of storms, what farm would have the best advice, which routes were best to take and which to avoid. But the human world is never logical, is seldom sensible, and is overflowing with all sorts of impurities. The reserve postman is in Sigurður's good graces, which sufficed to cause Jens to decide, at the last minute, to avoid him and go straight to Sodom. Sat there across from Marta, watched her smoke, watched as she read a book about Napoleon that Gísli had loaned her, watched her drink beer. Marta is sometimes quite careless about her appearance and seems insensitive to the hunger in men's eyes – yet some nights she's like a roar. Jens had drunk, had spoken briefly to Ágúst, asked whether he could borrow his dory tomorrow, but when four patrons showed up he went home to Snorri, fled the company, and sat for a long time with the merchant, drank too much there, finally tottered up to Geirþrúður's house and lay there dead-drunk on the parlour floor. It took them quite some time to get him into bed. Heavy to carry him, at least a hundred kilos and exhausted from drinking. But they finally managed it, and Kolbeinn leaned up against the wall, old, breathless, worn. What ails thee – if we only knew. We hardly know why we ask, just know that something ails us, that we don't live as we should be living. And death awaits us all. Now we'll go to bed, said Geirþrúður.

Daylight wakes the boy.

The morning light descends into the dark abyss to fetch him. He sits up and blinks, as if to ascertain whether he's still alive, stretches his young, supple body, goes to the window, pulls back the curtains, opens the window, sticks his head out to rinse off night and dreams completely, the day is nearly calm. The wind is gone and has left behind a gentle, immensely polite breeze. The boy enjoys feeling the cold breath of air on his naked skin, breathes in the morning and the light as deeply as he can, the houses opposite are white with snow and the world is peaceful. Perhaps the spring will come after all; perhaps it will manage to thread all those fjords south of us, vastly deep and dangerous, and reach us before it's exhausted. The boy leans out and looks to the left, the sea is grey and innocent-looking and seems not to have anything on its conscience. Vetrarströnd rises white as a glacier from the grey sea. Two windows on the doctor's residence are open wide; all the post that Jens has brought has doubtless been sorted and put in bags, to be delivered to the surrounding countryside, a task for the deputy postmen, they're five in number and take variously difficult routes. The boy looks slowly to his right and sees Ólafía inching her way through the snow towards the house. He shuts the window, dresses hurriedly, rushes downstairs and manages to open the door before Ólafía knocks on it. He receives a smile in return and life can certainly be beautiful, we just have to know how to accept it.

Brynjólfur arrives around nine. *The Hope* is to sail today. Snorri's ship, which some call the *Disappointment*. Long since prepared for departure but the storm has delayed it, the world vanished from us for an entire week, the gloomy weather took it and only just returned it this morning, so white and pure and the breeze passes between the houses like an apology. Brynjólfur's business is, on the one hand, to say goodbye to his wife, and on the other to invite the boy to attend the launch. The boys, he says in clarification, but by the boys he means the crew, a ten-man group of rough, weathered men, most of them around sixty, their faces like old rocks and their words like salt from the sea; the boys, and in fact I as well, would feel better if you would attend the launch, says Brynjólfur, but then he sets eyes on his wife in the corridor, stops, doesn't know what he should say. It's you, he finally says and she nods, between them a deep ravine eroded by disappointment, drink, the incomprehensible mercilessness of everyday existence; they each stand on their own brink and look each other in the eye. So we're finally sailing, he says in conclusion; be careful, she says, and means it.

Be careful.

Two words that fall like silver over the chasm separating them and quiver for several moments between the brinks, but when he hesitates, mistrusting their weight, the silver dulls, sprinkles into the depths and is gone.

The boy goes and gets his overclothes, doesn't even ask Helga, even though he's leaving in the middle of things, no-one hesitates at such a proposition, refusal would foment unrest among the sailors, even dread that something dark and grim awaited them out at sea; no catch, accidents, death. A sailor with such a suspicion or fear in his blood surrenders sooner to the vehemence of sea and sky, and that surrender can call down death over the entire ship; those who live at the end of the world drop like flies face of life? Ragnheiður is speaking to a tall, rather broad woman, it's Lovísa, her paternal aunt, the wife of the district administrator Lárus; the shop clerks and customers remain at a suitable distance. Lovísa speaks loudly, as those do who have no reason to lower their voices; she complains about the weather, and about how few ships have come so far this spring, if it's possible to call this spring! And she's right; is it possible to talk about spring when the land is silent beneath the snow, when the frost polishes the sky and it becomes ever bluer and colder above the clouds? And it's also true that few ships have come; hostile winds blew so long, the ships were driven here and there over the vast sea, some sank, others sought shelter in distant fjords, only steamships made it here without excessive hindrances, the last one was here a week ago, its holds full of salt, no salt fish without salt, no life without salt fish, or, at best, only half a life. The steamer stopped only a few days, its skipper stayed in the hotel the entire time and drank toddies and rum there with Gísli; we know this heavy-browed, harsh skipper, know him more or less, in any case he's been sailing here for twenty years, first on a sailing ship, now on a steamship, the black smoke can be seen from quite a distance; as if Hell were coming to fetch us, Gísli had said to Þorvaldur when they met by chance a short distance from the church and saw the black smoke ascending from the ship as it cut through the waves. I repent, contrary to you, and therefore have little to fear, Reverend Þorvaldur answered his brother drily. The skipper has brought modest gifts for members of the distinguished families; chocolates and novels for Lovísa and her sister, a red brooch for Ragnheiður, an American pistol for Friðrik, while Gísli received a book of poetry in a gold-tooled, red binding. Only dead poets are published like this, he muttered, fingering the book; the skipper asked, what? Only dead poets are golden, explained Gísli, but then the skipper took out another book; you're probably right, he said, but there's certainly no gold lacking in this one, either! Gísli leafed through the book, an illustrated volume in a beautiful, blue binding; I hope they're not cold, he muttered, glancing quickly over several illustrations of half-naked women.

One of the clerks attends to the boy's purchases; he's given up on waiting for Ragnheiður and has no mind to waste any more time in the shop. The clerk finishes quickly and the boy hurries out, in fact flees, in a manner. Shoulders of moonlight, yes, but the moon is far away and its surface is assuredly lonely, and she's the daughter of Friðrik, the daughter of the powers that be, there's nothing good that can come from there, he thinks, so absorbed in swearing her off, denying the moonlight, that he doesn't hear the footsteps and is startled to feel his shoulder gripped hard. You were supposed to wait, she says, breathless, sharp. I didn't know that, he mutters, immediately feeling weak-nerved, his heart instantly beating harder, pounding against his ribcage. They stand opposite each other, less than an arm's length between them; he listens to his blood. So you've met Gísli, she says.

He: Yes.

She: He's very learned.

He: Yes.

She: He's a drunk. And weak-kneed. That's because too much

113

poetry makes people soft; they become unfit, weaker, that's what my father says and you know who he is.

He: Poetry is the world behind the world. And it's beautiful.

She: Gísli only does what he's told. You simply don't know anything about him, and you simply don't know anything about what matters, have no idea what it might be. And you don't know what's necessary.

He: Writing is better than salt fish. Also better than a steamship.

She: My father says that people like you are past praying for. You turn into wretches and starve to death if no-one helps you.

She shivers slightly; the air is cool and she's wearing only a thin jumper over her dress. Her red brooch gleams. Poetry can also be dangerous, he says, maybe because of how she shivers, maybe because his mind turns to a deadly poem and the final words of life out on the sea, on board a coffin, nothing is sweet to me, without thee. But then she comes so close to him that it seemed she might embrace him, which of course she doesn't do. This summer, she says, I'm going to ride in sunshine. Which should I be then, the horse or the sunshine? he asks. It isn't summer yet, she says, it isn't even spring.

Helga is cutting Kolbeinn's fingernails when the boy comes into the kitchen, she herself has just come in from outside; her skin is still ruddy from the cold. The skipper holds his hands out far, as if to deny them; did the launch go well? he asks. Yes, though it pitched a little beyond the harbour. The sea keeps the weather in it a long time, says the old man. Yes, says the boy.

embers hiss softly as the fire burns upward, her skin appears smooth around her blood-filled lips but wrinkles extend from her eyes, deepening as she squints. Yes, but it's the language of authority and I've got to get a grasp on it if I'm going to survive, she says, and the hoarseness has returned to her voice, the raven's croak. Do I need to understand it? he asks, looking at Geirþrúður as if asking for permission to avoid doing so, and she leans back in her seat, puts down the more than half-smoked cigarette, lifts her arms, fiddles with her hair; only if you want, authority belongs to men and you're a man, despite everything, though there's probably more Heaven in you than masculinity. I'm not at all heavenly. I'm speaking in metaphor. But what about Kolbeinn? He saw little until he lost his sight. Do I need to tear out my own eyes in order to see? That would be a good start. Are you unhappy? asks the boy, without thinking. Geirþrúður props her elbow on the table and rests her delicate chin on the back of her hand. What is unhappiness? she says; I've been loved twice, is that often? Is it possible to count the kisses, or the betrayals, and the times when one feels something that could be happiness? Seven thousand kisses, twelve happy moments; is such a thing often or seldom, and what is happiness and what are kisses? It's possible to kiss a person a thousand times and yet she's never kissed. Sometimes I think that humans are condemned to unhappiness.

Happiness exists, he says obstinately, like a child. The sound of Helga's voice reaches them; don't pay too much attention to what I say, says Geirþrúður; the world is more complex than one person. Gunnhildur and Jón the Joiner are happy with their son, at a glance there's no special reason for their happiness, yet with just one look at them it's as if all grief becomes a misunderstanding. Happiness certainly exists, isn't that right, Helga? she says, as Helga enters with a big tray of coffee and bread, Kolbeinn following along behind her, supporting himself on his cane, trusting it with his weight; it's easier to trust a lifeless thing than a person, and one doesn't have to put much effort into doing so. Is what right? asks Helga, putting the tray down on the larger table before starting to transfer the cups over onto the smaller one in the inner parlour. That we aren't condemned to unhappiness. Everyone is his own judge, says Helga; have you spoken to him?

Geirþrúður: We've been speaking continually.

Helga, transferring the bread to the other table: Yes?

Geirþrúður: About kisses and unhappiness and the language of authority.

Helga: Then let's get to the matter at hand.

They've moved into the inner parlour, taken seats around the dark table, where they sit in the evenings and the boy reads, where it's also further to the windows, a bit further to the world. We were thinking of commencing your education today, begins Helga; I went this morning and spoke to Hulda and Gísli, she's going to come this afternoon to teach you English, he tomorrow, to start his lessons on history, Icelandic, and literature. I'll then give you some instruction in mathematics, as long as I can; is that alright with you? Good, then it's settled, she says, after he ekes out a nod; there's nothing else he can do at this point.

*

Your father's only regret, says one of the letters from his mother, some of the letters now so tattered from reading that he'll have to start making copies of them, otherwise these important messages from the past will be lost. *Your father's only regret, and perhaps mine as well, was a lack of education, though I as a woman naturally had little or no chance of any education worthy of the name. When your father was twelve years old, it looked as if his dream would come true, to some extent. The parish priest volunteered to take him in as his pupil for two years, or longer if his performance warranted it. Two days before leaving, your father long since having gathered together everything that he wanted to take and was allowed to take with him, fitting it all in a bundle that he could carry easily beneath his arm; and he could hardly sleep for the anticipation, your grandfather fell off his horse. He was on his way home from town, the poor man, excessively drunk, as he was sometimes. The horse shied, your grandfather fell off and could never get to his feet again. Lay helpless in bed for over a year, and then died. Your father was the eldest of the siblings and just barely managed, and by sacrificing his education, naturally, to keep the family together until your grandmother died, when your father was a good twenty years old, the household was in debt and he was too old for school. Drink deprived me of learning, he used to say. Liquor is a bloody menace, it's true, and you should be careful with it, but without it your father and I would hardly have met. What kind of life would that have been? I loved your father so indescribably much, more than life, and we were going to make sure all of you, including Lilja, received an education, even if it were to break us.*

So it goes:

A horse shies, and that's why he's born.

But there will be minor changes to these plans, says Helga, as if from a great distance. Changes? asks the boy fearfully, visibly agitated. Yes, changes, or rather, a delay; the boy is to be sent on a journey, out to the end of the world. Where Iceland ends and eternal winter begins. Snorri had come earlier, looking for Jens, who had spent the previous evening with the merchant, after having been at Sodom. What business did he have at Sodom? Helga had asked. Probably the same as everyone else, Geirþrúður had replied. Yes, Snorri agreed, but also to ask for the dory and for Ágúst to row him over to Vetrarströnd. For some reason Sigurður had convinced Jens to go there, and even further north, to deliver the post, or had tricked him into doing so. Tricked? asks the boy. Yes, presumably to get back at him, says Geirþrúður.

Helga: Are you certain that's the case?

Kolbeinn: Sigurður's a beast, like all of those bigwigs. Otherwise he would never have been accepted as their brother-in-law.

Helga: There's no need always to believe the worst about people.

Geirþrúður: But it's often difficult to avoid it. It may well be that the world is good; humans are not.

But why should I go with him? the boy asks. Jens is afraid of the sea, says Helga, he would never make it alone over Djúp in the dory, he would go mad with fear, that big, strong man. And then he would have to traverse Dumbsfjörður, as well. He needs to

119

have someone with him who can row him over, keep a decent pace with him on the trek, and last but not least, who will not make light of Jens' fear of the sea. You know the sea; you can walk. When do we leave? As soon as possible, says Helga, as she leans to one side to look out of the window; the sky is still heavy with clouds. Before it starts snowing again, and maybe blowing, she adds. Have you spoken to him about it, that I come along? asks the boy. No, says Helga. Will he agree? asks the boy doubtfully. It's not up to him. People don't get very far when they're asleep, he needs to be woken, says Geirþrúður, but then a heavy thud is heard and Jens scrambles up off the floor of his room.

He dreamed that something dark was pushing him over the edge of a precipice; he fought back long and hard but his strength finally failed. He started falling into the vacuumous black depths and heard the thundering of the sea below; he falls but then wakes on the floor. Looks around, astonished at the blueness surrounding him, panics momentarily; I'm at the bottom of the sea, he thinks; have I drowned? Yet this isn't the sea's blue death, but rather the blessed light of the sky; that's how hard it can be to distinguish between them.

So that's how it is: the space between life and death is so small that it can fit in one word. And that's why you must be eternally careful with words – at least one of them is bearing death.

Death Brings No Contentment

It all started with death; it can hardly be more backwards. The sky can be bluer than all that is blue and we were of the belief that death would finally bring us there, but years have passed and we've gotten nowhere, attached as we are to the Village; we died, but instead of leaving we became trapped between life and death like flies inside a partition, if you listen you might hear a weak buzz.

Death brings no contentment; if such a thing exists, you'll find it in life. Yet there's nothing as underestimated as life itself. You curse Mondays, rainstorms, your neighbours; you curse Tuesdays, work, the winter, but all of this will disappear in a single second. The plenitude of life will turn to nothing, to be replaced by the poverty of death. Awake and asleep, you think about the little things that lie far from the essence. How long does a person live, after all; how many moments does one have that are pure, how often does one live like electricity and light up the sky? The bird sings, the earthworm turns in the earth so that life doesn't suffocate, but you curse Mondays, you curse Tuesdays, your opportunities decrease and the silver within you becomes stained.

We died, or simply stopped living; we transformed into invisible shadow-beings and our bones moulder in the soil. Years have passed, and decades, and no-one is aware of us. The ravens notice nothing; they flap black and croaking through us without knowing it; it isn't fun when a big, black bird flies through you, leaving nothing behind but a hoarse croak. We're an aberration, a misunderstanding, flies trapped between worlds. At first we sought relief in the bitterness; there isn't much that nourishes a person like bitterness, nourishes and gnaws and grinds apart, and we sought to console ourselves by taking delight in the misfortune of your life, the mistakes, the waste, in your eternal defeats in the face of lust. Bitterness and malice, what else besides these two sisters is found in the Devil's spit? Someday we'll tell you what happened, how we managed to wash the spit off, we'll tell you of the moment when something resembling a crack opened between us and you. It is perhaps a hallucination, but through it we whisper poems and stories, joy and despair, hope and hopelessness.

The Journey:
If the Devil Has Created Anything in this
World, Besides Money, It's
Blowing Snow in the Mountains

I

Words seldom suffice to describe the wind here. Jens and the boy got a shovel from Marta; they shovel the snow off the dory and the wind blows around them. There's a north wind and everything's white, even the sea appears white, everything except for the cliff belts on the mountains and the shadow in Jens' eyes. They're silent, the three mail bags lie in the snow, each weighing around twenty kilograms, mostly newspapers, the *Parliamentary Times* and a few letters. Helga had provisioned them well; you're responsible for him, she said to Jens, and therefore take account of the weather, don't go rushing out into whatever it might be. Jens sat sombrely over his porridge, hardly a word could be pulled out of him, said little when he was informed that the boy was coming with them, just nodded and with that the matter was settled.

And they shovel; there's a heap of snow on top of the dory. Marta stands between the house and the boat and watches. Maybe you'll have good weather, Helga had said after they'd dressed themselves in the entry; wool trousers and skin-trousers, a pair of thick sweaters, Jens in a heavy parka, the boy in a leather jacket, a pair of wool socks and new boots from Tryggvi's Shop. Jens opened the door; a bit of a gentle wind, the clouds light grey and seemingly harmless, Kolbeinn stepped out onto the porch and sniffed the air; good weather, I hardly think so, he said, and went back in the house, just try to come back so that you can finish reading *Othello*, he told the boy. The wind had started to make its presence known before they made it over to the next street, as if it were waiting for them, and was blowing hard by the time they came to Sodom. They shovel, the boy's face stiffens immediately but Jens acts as if all is normal, maybe the cold doesn't bite him, hardened by the years, the weather, and innumerable trials. Kirkjufjall Mountain rises to the sky on the other side of the channel named Rennan; the shadow of the mountain can be heavy and suffocating here. The mountain is approximately three kilometres long; they'll miss it when they round it and row out onto the shelterless Djúp, that vast fjord.

Marta has moved nearer the house, where the wind isn't as persistent; she's cold even though she's wearing the thick over-coat that a foreign sailor had given her the previous autumn. They finish shovelling snow off the boat but it takes time to free it, frozen fast to the earth, as if it doesn't want to go. Except that it isn't a dory but a little rowing boat; the boy is somewhat startled to see how small it is. Jens tosses the three postbags into it, he has the postal trumpet around his neck, in a leather pouch; they straighten up and look towards Vetrarströnd, look out over fifteen kilometres of sea. The seashore is completely white; heavy grey clouds lie over it and further out they see Dumbsfjörður, nearly merging with the distance, and the greying daylight. The boy clears his throat and says, well, because well is actually a good down twice to amuse them, yes, one does bear responsibility for these young souls. You know Kjartan the Frenchman, in Vík? he then asks Jens, who merely shrugs his shoulders. Well, what of it, you know a priest when you see one, and these pages here are for him, a mélange of Heaven and Hell, hopefully you'll guard them with your lives. Gísli holds out the package, Jens steps forward to take it; and here's your payment, adds Gísli, handing the postman a slender silver-coloured flask, my close friend of many years, but sometimes friends have to part, that's the sorrow of life. Jens says nothing to this, but takes the flask and sticks it inside his parka. Be careful, says Marta unexpectedly as they prepare to push off, doffing her hat momentarily, as if to empha-sise the words. Her black hair blows down in front of her sharp face with her slightly slanted, dark eyes, and they both hesitate, as if to contemplate this unexpected warmth in life, or to welcome it and perhaps bury it at the roots of their hearts in order to keep it warm in the cold into which they're heading. Then they simultaneously grab the boat's gunwales, and it slides so easily into the sea that they nearly topple over. They step in slowly, so as not to capsize the boat; the boy sits on the aft thwart, Jens on the forward one, it simply happens automatically, and the boy is quicker to put out the oars; his hands are steady, but Jens is stiff, he's a postman, not a sailor, yet the journey begins and all four blades are in the water, the two of them bend forward, lean back; the boat crawls off against the wind and they feel the sea beneath their feet. They move slowly away from land; Gísli and Marta stand side-by-side watching them. Jens looks up briefly to see Ágúst appear in the doorway, gaunt and pitiful, pallid from spending all his time inside. The hotelkeeper raises his hand, so slender that it resembles a talon, moves it slightly to bid the men farewell, or else to grope for them.

II

Just over three weeks since he last went to sea, and touching the oars brings it all back, the sixereen and the fishing station, Bárður and the life that's gone, the eyes that dulled and changed into two frozen puddles. He squeezes the oars, kicks his feet, leans well forward, then back, keeps his back straight and thereby achieves more power, which they certainly need; the north wind blows almost directly at them, but at least their bare flesh and sensitive eyes face away from it. Marta and Gísli are gone, there's no-one out in front of Sodom, the building grows smaller, they move away from the Village. With difficulty. This will be a strenuous fifteen kilometres and will become even more difficult when they crawl out of the fjord and onto Djúp, where the sea will deepen, the wind grow stronger, the waves grow larger. And an old, familiar fear wakens within the boy; just a thin plank beneath his feet, above metre after metre of cold sea; more than a hundred when they reach the middle of Djúp and row over the waters of Djúpálnir.

They row, inch their way out from under the shelter of the mountain, inch their way out onto the heavy, leaden sea, hesitantly, so hesitantly. The wind is now at a slight angle, the waves are an ever-changing, growing landscape around the boat, they rise and fall, cold blue with a touch of green, not terribly large seen from the land, not much larger seen from the deck of a ship, but those who sit in a rowing boat cannot avoid seeing the high seas in these waves, these big waves heave themselves higher than the boat and momentarily shut out the land around them; it's incomprehensible, really, that the two men are able to stay afloat. "Boat" is also far too big a word for what they're in, being not much larger than a medium-sized bed; if one wave were to break over them it would be transformed into a deathbed. They row in rhythm; two men stick four oar blades into the sea and lay into them with their weight and all their strength, yet they hardly budge an inch. The sea lifts the boat and they catch a glimpse of where they are, before sinking again and losing sight of most everything but the waves. Damn it to Hell, thinks the boy; he looks up now and then and sees that they're putting distance between themselves and Kirkjufell, albeit unbearably slowly, yet doing so; which, however, means that the sea is deepening beneath them. Sitting behind him, Jens breathes heavily; they haven't spoken a word, yet it would be good to talk now, words are often excellent, they connect people, alleviate loneliness; you aren't as poignantly alone facing the sea. The boy looks over his shoulder as he leans back, is going to say something, anything, just to connect with another human, something about the wind, something about the sea, about the exertion; he looks over his shoulder but immediately looks away. Jens' face is deathly pale and his eyes are two tiny black stones staring vehemently at the boy. This big man who fears no storm, who's

Human life is a vague tremor in the atmosphere; it passes by so quickly that the angels miss it if they blink. Jens stares straight ahead, moves like a machine, doesn't take his eyes off the boy's slender back and tries in that way to deny the pitch-black, insatiable sea. Their mittens are drenched, their faces are wet with seawater, stinging from the salt. They row, are swept forward and back, their lower backs ache, they work like mad. Is time passing? Are they moving? The boy is panting by the time he gives in to the temptation of looking over his shoulder, and hardly believes that they're approaching Vetrarströnd, it must be a lie, a hallucination, wishful thinking! A short time later he looks again and the shore has moved even closer; yet they've been borne well off track. They'd planned to land at the little fishing village of Berjadalseyri, but now they would need to walk a brisk ten kilometres to reach it; that is, if they reach the shore. Waves break over the boat, Jens gasps for breath and soon the bottom is filled with five centimetres of seawater. Jens starts retching, he vomits without letting go of the oars, vomits over his thighs and lap. When next the boy looks they have only a short distance to go; we'll make it, he thinks, but then it starts snowing. First just one or two snowflakes that blow in his face, as if by mistake, then the whole sky has turned white; yet behind it is the shore, it awaits them like a reassuring embrace. We're going to make it, we're practically there, damn it, shouts the boy triumphantly over his shoulder; but Jens starts, pulls in his oars and jumps overboard in one continuous movement.

Are you mad?! screams the boy when he realises what's

happened, throws himself to the side, thrusts his arm into the cold green sea, manages to grab the postman's parka, on his way down to the bottom of the sea, pulls him up and holds him there until Jens grabs the gunwale, spitting and gasping, then reaches for the oars and rows. Despair grants power, he feels the strength well up in his arms and Jens shouts when his feet encounter resistance, he lets go and paws his way or half swims to land, totters drenched to his bones up the frozen, slippery beach, straightens up, shuts his eyes to relish better having land beneath his feet, then sinks to all fours and vomits.

They're safe. Have even landed in a decent spot; few big rocks and the boy is able to drag the boat up the beach, it's good to have a foothold, good to feel land beneath both feet, free from the sea that has nearly vanished in the falling snow. Jens squirms to his feet, stretches, tall, broad-shouldered, strong yet shivering, the freezing cold has penetrated to his skin and somewhere within is a heart that's vulnerable to frostbite. They hurry to take care of the boat, load it with stones, weigh it down, the boy finds good rocks but Jens vanishes into the snow and returns with a boulder, more or less, hardly under seventy kilos, puts it in the boat and goes after another, works frenziedly to keep himself warm, works frenziedly to turn back into a man; be careful not to break the boat, says the boy when Jens comes with his second boulder; no no, he replies, putting it down gently, as if it were a pebble. Stands up straight and they look for a second in each other's eyes, completely by accident, and then the postman says thanks. The boy says, it was nothing, and the postman says, yes, quite. Why did you jump overboard? Thought we'd landed, replies Jens, I don't like the sea. You're soaked, we need to get you inside, says the boy. They finish loading the boat; Jens hurries, he doesn't want to die like this, wet with sea and shame, takes two postbags, the boy takes the third and the leather pouch holding their provisions and dry clothing, which he ties on his back. Then they set off into the snowfall in search of a house.

Their only two options are left or right; if life were only so straightforward, so decisive. They can't take a direct route, a sheer mountain slope rises before them, followed by unforgiving heaths; they can't turn back because of the sea. They head left, to the north-west, in the direction of the village, a collection of fishing huts and modest houses; there's even a chapel, because what is man without the Lord, or rather, what is the Lord without man, and waiting there is a horse belonging to the deputy postman. Likely around ten kilometres to the village, says the boy to Jens' back; the wind and cold blow around them, the snowfall thickens and evening descends. For the last three weeks the boy has often stood at the window in the garret and looked over towards Vetrarströnd; from a distance it resembles one continuous glacier and it's difficult to imagine that people reside there of their own free will. But what is free will and what man is free? Around three hundred people live on the thirty-kilometre-long strand; three hundred human beings who have fixed themselves onto the few grassy berms at the feet of the rocky slopes, some with several animals but mostly living off the sea, the mountains white all year round, the snow never disappears completely and hasn't done so for seven hundred years, even in the best summers drifts lie in the gullies and hollows, and then autumn arrives with new snow.

And now he is walking here.

He walks and nearly falls onto the frozen beach.

They move upward, free themselves from the smooth, slippery ice, only to wade through snow. Jens leads the way, walks quickly, tries to walk off the cold, takes out the flask without slowing down, takes a big drink, twice, holds it out into the falling snow and the boy has to jog to grab it, Jens takes a third drink but can't escape the chill, can't escape the cold that's started to paralyse his muscles and is heading for his heart. He glances to the side where the sea pants in the snowfall and drowned men plod along the seabed abreast of the two men, sucking the salt from their lips. The boy follows and misses Bárður, but man can't always allow himself to regret and cry, sometimes he just has to live, focus on that and nothing else, keep death at a distance, that black being sitting eternally in ambush for us, except that here at the end of the world it's probably pale as a corpse and therefore blends in with the snow. I'm not going to think of death, but rather focus on walking, keeping myself upright and not falling, he thinks, but then he nearly trips over Jens, who's suddenly lying in the snow, as if hit by a bullet. The postman squirms silently to his feet and trudges on, even speeds up, perhaps in the hope of walking off the exhaustion that he feels following his fall, as if part of his strength and will were left behind where he fell. But he soon stumbles again, manages to get up, walks, falls a third time and then lies there, his muscles no longer obeying. The boy helps him to his feet, Jens hisses something incomprehensible, presses on, and falls a fourth time. And lies there. I need to think, he says into the snow. The boy tries to pull him up but lacks the strength. Jens, he says, but receives no answer. And there the boy stands. It snows, and so it goes: First Bárður froze to death, and now this giant of a man is going to go the same way. The boy sinks to his knees, at a loss. *It has snowed a great deal, to everyone's chagrin except for your sister. She got Sigmar to make two snowmen; one of them was you, the other your brother. Now they're with us, said Lilja. She wanted so much to sleep outside with you; I carried her in sobbing.* He's forced himself up onto all fours and has started rolling an ever-growing snowball around himself. Jens looks up, manages to lift his head, that heavy chunk of ice, up from the snow; what the Devil are you doing? Making a snowman for my sister, replies the boy. Bloody hell, says Jens. Now Halla and his father have started looking towards the north, hoping to see him returning, two individuals whose entire existence depends on him. He stands up stiffly, ponderously, and walks off. The boy isn't able to finish his snowman and they trudge on through the dark, against wind, snowfall, frost. The snow piles up on them, they keep going, step-by-step, cold but undefeated. Then Jens falls for the fifth time. Perhaps because the land has started to rise; not much, but enough. It snows and snow blows over them, blows down from the mountain in enormous amounts, blows violently, it's nearly impossible to breathe and Jens gropes feebly for the postal trumpet, tries to free it from his shoulder and hand it to the boy, opens his mouth to say something but his tongue is frozen, because first it's words

139

didn't look so serious. But of course it's very difficult not to be able to bark, the dog hops to the side and gulps several mouthfuls of snow to restrain itself. The farmer stops at a white tussock, extends his hand and as if by magic a dark passageway opens before them; are you an elf? mutters Jens, almost unrecognisable behind the frost and rime.

The passageway is narrow and Jens has to traverse it unsupported, which he does, but when they reach the kitchen he sinks to the floor and simply lies there. The postbags, is all he says. I'll fetch . . . them, replies the farmer, glancing at a woman standing there; she nods and appears to understand everything. The kitchen is dark and rather constricted for the three of them, especially when the woman kneels by the stone oven and starts blowing to rekindle the fire; the oven is still warm following supper. We had some trouble, says the boy, moving nearer the oven, moving nearer the heat, moving nearer life. Yes, says the woman, glancing up at him, otherwise you'd hardly be here. He doesn't look good, did he get wet? she asks, looking at Jens, and then at the boy. Our boat nearly capsized, says the boy, and Jens was cast overboard; this here is Jens, he adds, nodding towards the postman. The woman looks again at Jens, and then continues to blow. The boy leans up against the wall, discerns a vague sound coming from it; mice, no doubt, there are plenty of gaps between the stacked rocks, some of them useful for storing small items, including children's milk teeth, in order to ensure the children's longevity. He leans up against the wall and watches the woman work on the fire. The women here at the end of the world know

142

right cheek in the light of the fire, her left in the partial darkness; she's both radiantly young and dark with age. Then it's as if she comes round; she stands up, kneels near Jens, puts her hand in beneath his frozen clothing, feels the icy cold; help me take his clothes off, she says, and Jens raises no objection as they start pulling off his half-frozen garments. Three children's faces appear, six eyes round with curiosity; back to bed, orders the woman, seemingly seeing the children despite having her back turned to them. Then Jens is entirely undressed, he's naked, this big man, no-one has seen him like this for many years, except perhaps Salvör, in the secretiveness of the family room and thrice in the light of summer nights. Stout arms, strong legs, broad and muscular shoulders, and now as feeble as an old man. Together they help him into the family room; it isn't as warm as the kitchen. The farmer reappears and Jens murmurs something, naked and defenceless, the children's faces watch from one of their beds and one of them, the youngest, starts coughing; first two abrupt coughs, as if to rid itself of phlegm in its throat, but then the cough grows stronger and becomes so unbroken that the child can't breathe. Mummy! shout the other children but the woman has already slipped out from under Jens' arm, which would have sunk to the floor like a sack if the farmer hadn't grabbed it. She takes the child in her arms, lays it over her shoulder, the child's face is red but its lips are blue; she whispers something, strokes its back firmly and the coughing subsides, it can breathe again, its life didn't go anywhere. The woman puts the child down gently, turns back to the visitors and the six children's and two dog's eyes watch as Jens is laid in what must be the couple's bed. You need to lie next to him, she tells the boy; must I? he exclaims, almost aghast. He needs the close warmth; it's the only way to take the chill from him; people have died for less. The woman looks sidelong at the boy, as if expecting a response; he regards Jens, trembling beneath the cover, his eyes closed, his face deathly pale. Then the boy starts undressing; the cold has killed far too many in this country. The couple goes into the kitchen, the children and the dog continue staring at the boy, the youngest coughing again, its siblings sit up but lie back down when the cough subsides, and then the boy has also removed everything but his underpants, doesn't take them off, oh no, out of the question, he's supposed to lie up against Jens, one never knows what direction dreams will take, and some of them have a noticeable effect on the male physique. Just think of the humiliation if he dreamed of Ragnheiður so close to the postman, as he dreamed of her the other night, following which he had to go down to the cellar and wash his underpants, in among dying mice. He feels almost ill at the thought, slips hurriedly under the cover alongside Jens, resists, with difficulty, the temptation to take a better look at the books above the headboard, which likely number around thirty, and instead wraps his arms around the big trunk, gasps for breath when he feels the cold, almost like hugging a corpse. He doesn't move, focuses on driving the chill from this bulky body, so focused that he hardly hears the energetic whispering of the children and the cough that the youngest is constantly trying to stifle, it isn't dark in the family room, nor is it bright. Three oil eyes, holds its younger sister, trembling from stifled coughing fits, in its arms. Is the big man going to die? asks the little boy, perhaps six years old and also with brown eyes. Hopefully not, says the boy. That's good, because it would be hard to carry him away from here, you would have to help mummy and daddy. No-one's allowed to die, the younger girl manages to say before a coughing fit rips apart her voice, and this time the cough doesn't ease up until her father comes in, takes her in his arms, lays her over his shoulder, strokes her back firmly; then the coughing slackens somewhat, she can open her eyes and she takes a good long look at the boy, her lips nearly blue; she also has dark brown eyes, reminiscent of summer.

The boy mustn't go to sleep yet. He must eat, and preferably Jens as well; warm porridge, cod heads boiled to mush and mixed with rye-meal and milk. The boy eats quickly, his body demands it, but Jens just mumbles and can't be gotten to eat, curls up in a ball, sinks back into sleep and searches there for something warm, something that's glowing and can drive the chill from his bones, the cold kiss of the sea. He sinks into sleep; at its bottom roam drowned men, ceaselessly humming his name.

Outside in the snowfall it is evening, and night is approaching.

The cow moos, not loudly but long; where is the light? it asks again. Not terribly much goes on in a cow's head, just a few sentences repeated continually, but cows ask about things that matter, and it's generally calming to sit with them, invariability makes them happy and happiness is a treasure that all men search for relentlessly. The children are now in bed; they get to sleep in the same bunk tonight, thanks to us, thinks the boy, and their energetic whispering doesn't stop until their mother starts telling them stories of a land where there's always good weather; even the rain is warm, and most everything is good except for a witch and her gang, who want to steal children and do terrible things, they're red as hate and their eyes burn; their hands are long, razor-sharp claws. No-one in the story is allowed to die, says the younger girl. The mother's quiet voice fills the family room and the children listen, the dog listens, the cow in the barn listens, as do the farmer and the boy, who breathes through his open mouth. Then the story is finished, no-one died, that's how stories can be superior to life; the lamps are extinguished and the darkness snatches up everything. The dog lies down, curls up in a ball, whimpers to itself a bit and is eager to sleep. Dogs seldom dream difficult dreams; they simply dream of good pieces of meat, the blue sky, soft hands and running. Neither household nor weather make a sound, but then the younger girl coughs. First half stifled, softly, as if she's trying to suppress the cough, hold it down, which is a hopeless fight, and then she coughs and coughs, remarkable that such a great cough can fit inside such a little body. Someone sits up in the darkness, says something, the cough dwindles little by little but is a long time in leaving completely. The farmer starts crooning; his voice is completely free of hesitation, is as soft as lukewarm water, gladly will I follow thee:

> Gladly will I follow thee,
> Father, to glory thine,

Saved shall I ever be
With thy hand holding mine.

Sleep comes slowly over these human beings beneath the snow, inside the underground house.

With thy hand holding mine; our hands have been outstretched for decades but no-one has taken them, neither God nor the Devil.

The boy is falling asleep. There he lies, nearly naked, up against the big body of the overland postman, with whom, as of yesterday, he'd hardly ever spoken. He holds tightly to the cold body, cold from the kiss of the sea, the cold is in his bones and it sometimes brings death. No-one is allowed to die in stories, yet the kitchen walls hold the milk teeth of a young girl who died just over a year ago. The boy thinks about his sister; he remembers how she laughed, and then he sleeps.

Sleeps in a family room on Vetrarströnd.

From a distance it resembles one continuous, lifeless glacier. Yet here he is, and a dog breathes on the floor and people in beds, there's a cow in the barn and somewhere beneath the snow are two sheep sheds with sheep. That's how it was: sometimes life isn't visible until you've come right up to it, and that's why we should never judge from a distance.

He wakes to the aroma of coffee, and is alone in bed. Continues lying there as the dreams evaporate from him, ascend to Heaven where angels read them, but hopefully just for their own amusement, not to write them down and read them up on the final day,

149

to the disgrace of most men. Then he sits up and looks around. Jens is sitting in the bed opposite; so he's alive, the train-oil lamp in his chest is still shining. Their eyes meet but they say nothing; words can also be so uncertain, with such a gulf between them and what moves inside of you, that distance has often given rise to bad misunderstandings, even destroyed lives. That's why it's better sometimes to say nothing and rely on one's eyes. Jens is going over the postbags; the three children sit as near to him as they dare, the dog on the floor in front of him, watching closely, his eyes fixed on the postman, who rummages in one of the bags and then pulls out, like a bashful magician, a white, empty piece of paper, lays it on the bed and says, you can have it. The children don't move, stare at the paper, have never seen such a white, empty piece of paper before, until now have gotten to draw or write in the margins of the rare letters delivered there, perhaps sketching little animals in the corners, but here they had an entire page, an empty page, it's probably possible to put all of life on such a page. And then there's the other side as well! Yet they're much too astonished to say thank you, so the dog goes to Jens and sticks its snout in his big palm. Yes, yes, says the postman embarrassedly, and the boy puts on his clothes.

They're served porridge and coffee. The farmer says nothing, stares down at his lap for the most part; he's short, thin. The woman comes from the barn, bringing warm milk, straight from the udder; the cow moos after her, where's the light, where's the spring, wasn't there once green grass? The boy eats slowly and reads the titles of the books over the bed, Páll Melsteð's *History of*

Mankind, Vídalín's Sermons, the *Passion Hymns*, four old Icelandic sagas, several poetry collections.[7] He puts down his bowl, reads in two books, seeks out poems, seeks out what can enlarge the world, moves his lips as he reads, looks up and meets the eyes of the woman, who stares at him so firmly and peculiarly that he feels shy, puts the book back in its place and goes to the door, the passageway low and narrow, opens out to the day so white with snow that his eyes sting, has to blink them for a good long time to accustom them to the light. Nearly calm, and cool, the clouds hang heavily over the world, barely holding themselves up and resting here and there on the mountains, the sea leaden and breathing heavily. Is it snowing? asks Jens from within the passageway, and then he comes out, stretches, squints. No, not one single snowflake, says the boy, even triumphantly, at the same time as the first flakes of the day float down from the clouds. I'm better off saying nothing, mutters the boy, before heading back down the dim passageway.

And then they're prepared to depart.

Their clothes are dry; the woman has dried them on the stove and the stone oven, her name is María, like the mother of Jesus who is said to have freed mankind, though it seems not to be particularly free right now – who reshackled us? But Jesus' lover

7. The Icelandic historian and parliamentarian Páll Melsteð (1812–1910) wrote several textbooks on the history of mankind. *Vídalín's Sermons*: A popular collection of sermons for home reading, written by Jón Þorkelsson Vídalín (1666–1720), scholar, preacher, Latin poet, and bishop of Skálholt. The *Passion Hymns* is an enormously popular collection of hymns to be sung during Lent, composed by the poet and clergyman Hallgrímur Pétursson (1614–1674).

was also named María; it's a rather big name. She hands the boy a creased piece of paper; we have an account with the shop in Sléttueyri, she says; sometimes they have books. I don't know when I'll get there next, would you perhaps choose three books for me that you like, preferably poetry? Do you think I can choose correctly? he asks. I saw how you read, she says simply, moistening her lips with her tongue; they're chafed, as if time has gone over them with rough sandpaper. She doesn't take her brown eyes off the boy's face; choose something, she says a bit hoarsely, that is . . . different, which . . . where the words don't sit still on the page but instead fly to the sky and give us wings, even though we might not have the sky to fly in. Yes, María, he says, because he wants to say her name; it's a big name. The farmer, on the other hand, is named Jón, it's not a big name and is so common that it actually stopped being a name a long time ago. Yet this Jón is happy not be named more; the name doesn't attract attention to him, for which he's eternally thankful. Stands with his hands in his pockets as they bid farewell and thanks, leans up against the wall as far from the fickle oil lamp as he can, but then María lights a kerosene lamp, perhaps desiring to say farewell with dignity and even provide better light for the children, who sit enthusiastically over the paper, too important a moment to let pass by in the half-light of the train-oil lamp. They disagree on how best to use the paper; write verses, poems, draw something, maybe a little of each, their mother suggests, and then the younger girl is going to say something, but her cough interrupts her once again. Jens places some money on the couple's bed, for the room and board,

152

says he, and they both look away, because it isn't easy being poor. Then they've come outside, but the boy feels as if he's forgotten something, goes back in; the children, hunching over their paper, immediately fall silent when he appears, and he lays a one-króna coin on it. Don't waste it, Helga had said, nor has he done so.

IV

They're on their way. Out into the snow, and the wind has of course woken, has begun amusing itself by shifting snowdrifts, transforming the landscape, filling the sky around them with blowing snow, making things difficult for people, and animals; where's the light, where's the spring, and wasn't there once green grass? The boy turns back to look at the farm; who knows, maybe for the final time, this turf house containing five lives, no, six; we'll count the dog, and then let's say seven, why not count the cow, seven lives; how will things turn out for them, how will life go for all those dark-brown eyes, and wasn't that cough a very bad one? He turns to look, with these questions, and this fear, but the farm is gone. They haven't gone far, but the blowing snow takes every-thing with it, the farm has vanished entirely and he will perhaps never see these people again, or the dog, or the cow that he's in fact never seen, only heard its insistent questions. They trudge onwards and see nothing but snow. And the boy sees Jens' back, as he leads the way; straight on, it's easy to find one's way here despite being completely blind, with the mountain on one side, the sea on the other; the middle road is the right one; not up and not down. Ten kilometres, Jón had said, and he took his time saying it, especially to get past the "k"; he didn't look up in the meantime, dug his hands into his pockets and seemed fragile as he leaned into the shadows. Some people are closed shells, grey and nondescript on the surface, easily judged, but then there's possibly a glowing core inside that few come to know, sometimes no-one. But ten kilometres. That's at least three hours in these conditions, this weather, four not out of the question. The bag rests heavily on the boy's shoulder, Jens carries two and seems not to feel anything; he simply trudges on intrepidly, people let surfaces deceive them and that's why big, sturdily built men appear unconquerable. The boy needs to use all his strength not to fall behind; sometimes he becomes lost in his thoughts and momentarily loses sight of Jens. The wind is once again from the north, blowing polar cold over them, blowing over the mountains that rise on their right hand, the snow blows over the crests and down upon the few farms that scrape by at the shore, over the two men who stumble onwards, the one in front looking straight ahead, the one behind mainly keeping his head lowered and thinking about *Othello* and *Hamlet*, muttering words from these works; it's good to move his lips, that way they won't freeze into one. There are words, he says to the snowstorm, that enlarge the world and change the human landscape, but then he finds himself thinking only of Ragnheiður. About her grey eyes, but unfortunately much more about the breasts that he once got a good feel of, yet certainly not good enough; he moves the palms of his hands reflexively in his thick woollen mittens, how does one touch breasts and what does one do with them? Mankind is constantly reminded of his own insignificance in the face of the big questions. The boy has forgotten all about the possibilities of words when he bumps roughly into Jens, who's standing still, looking around. I see something, whispers Jens. What? I don't know, something that moved. What? Damned if I know, a shape or something; just caught a glimpse of it, then it was gone. They both look around, tilt their heads, try in that way both to protect their eyes and to see better, let their gazes slip in between snowflakes, into the gusting snow. Was it . . . was it living? asks the boy, suddenly hesitant. Aw, hell, whispers Jens in return, don't be such a bloody big baby. It's not my fault there are ghosts! Jens makes no reply to this last comment and they look around, the sea is panting somewhere behind the snow. There! says the boy, pointing at a shape that vanishes the same instant. Hello! shouts Jens, and shortly afterwards a voice replies, reticently, helloo! They don't move, see nothing but the sea, wait, the boy moves his lips but then the voice calls out again, are you living or dead? Good question, mutters the boy, but Jens calls back angrily, bleeding hell, of course we're living! The shape moves closer, slowly but surely, and takes on human form, albeit white with snow; the face, red with cold, thrusts itself into theirs and the lips say, no need to be angry, I was just asking; but who are you, anyway? The postman, replies Jens. Yes, now I see the bags; the man peers at them and discerns the postbags covered with snow. You aren't on the customary trail; and where's Guðmundur?

The man is a farmer from the shore, a neighbour of Jón and María, three kilometres between their farms and several thousand tons of snow. Jens has produced the flask; they all take a drink, the boy included. The farmer takes quite a big sip, yet feels dejected; he's lost one of his sheep sheds, that's why he's out in this relentless storm, he'd built a sheep shed last summer beneath a cornice, which perhaps wasn't clever, he readily admits; the shed housed forty sheep, have they heard any bleating coming up through the snow? No, says Jens, and the farmer asks again, because not only does it hurt to lose one's sheep shed, it's downright humiliating. I should go and get Jón's dog, says the farmer hopelessly, and is nearly blown over by the strong wind gusting down the slope. We might be able to help you, says the boy; that would be good, replies the farmer appreciatively, even appearing more cheerful. They stand there in a semi-circle, exchange a few words, the aggressive, gusting snow forces them to look down; it's best, says the farmer, that we head this direction, because . . . he walks off, pointing straight ahead, the wind cuts off whatever he was saying and his outline immediately turns hazy in the snow, as if he were dissolving. Wait! shouts Jens, and they hurry after the farmer, wade through the snow, but the farmer has vanished into the whiteness, as if he were a hallucination. They stare at each other, look around, several times cry out ho! are you there?, and the wind replies perkily, yes, I'm here! They wait, they listen, and they grow cold. Was he alive? asks the boy hesitantly, but Jens shakes himself; María hadn't managed to dry his clothes fully and yesterday's chill spreads, as if it had nestled in his bones and were now on its way to his veins and organs. We have to keep going, he finally says, and that's what they do, plunge through the snow, sermon is white and cold. It's a church, says the boy, as if he's made an important discovery. Yes, is all that Jens says, and he's right, there's a church here, in among fishing huts and small houses, a turf church with seats for twelve people, which is appropriate, considering that there were twelve apostles, no church should be bigger. The priest in Vík comes here twice a year and talks about God, but never in the dead of winter; at that time only the snow says mass from the pulpit, and the wind from the roof. The church tolerates the tempests from the north-east poorly; the windows often break, the roof sinks beneath the weight of the snow, and in winter the building most resembles a blind old man whom time is on the verge of swallowing. But certainly, the ways of God are impenetrable; if they hadn't stumbled onto the church by chance, if the boy hadn't toppled head-first off it and they hadn't called out for each other like lost souls in an immense world, they would have possibly roamed between the fishing huts in search of the light that the fishermen mentioned, growing ever colder and more tired, the postbags heavier with every step, each minute; Jens' heart would have begun to grow weary, the attack of the frost heavier; the winter and the whiteness would have led them astray, they would have wandered out of the sparse village and died of exposure. But the church topples the boy; Jens and the boy call out to each other and shortly afterwards a man has come to them, and the man is none other than Jónas, the Postmaster of Vetrarströnd and head of this fishing village. I didn't recognise the voices, he said, after showing them to his home, a short distance from the church, they saw

160

enthusiastically as they eat, as they nourish themselves and take pleasure in feeling their bodies warm up by the stove. He sorts the newspapers and scrutinises the addresses written on the letters that come up from the bag, mutters the names of the addressees, not many letters, in fact just six, and one of them tells of a death, another of a betrayal. The third: I miss you and miss you and miss. The fourth tells of troubles breathing and burnt porridge. The fifth: the children are difficult, Siggi is a slacker, and when am I going to get a letter from you? The sixth is so overjoyed with life that Jónas clearly feels his fingertips quiver.

But then they've finished eating, their bodies have warmed up and Jens wants to depart, to make it down to Vík before night. In this weather? exclaims Jónas, so flabbergasted that he has to stop in mid-sentence, likely the tenth story that he told them as they ate and warmed up; are you so certain that the heath and the mountain care for company today? Jónas is short; he reaches just up to Jens' chest but stands regularly on tiptoe, just for a moment, as if to add to his height, as if to say to the world: I'm actually this tall. Ingibjörg is sitting by the stove once again; she took her seat as they stood up, and now nods when they thank her for the food, but doesn't look at them, moves as close to the stove as she can and absorbs the warmth, with which life is perhaps a little too stingy. The boy covertly regards her sullen expression. Her eyelids have started to droop over her big eyes. Jónas talks, he talks and talks, the heath this, the mountain that, he wants them to stay the night, sleep off the storm, yes yes, we should be able to find some-thing to talk about, there are a lot of stories in the world, there was, let me tell you, a woman here in these northernmost parts who needed to get some medicine, her husband had such a terrible toothache that he could do nothing but lie in bed, his face swollen, yes, couldn't really lie there either and there were no men around, they were all at sea and their children were young and there were ten of them, the oldest eleven or twelve years old and the youngest aged accordingly, you see, and the weather was gloomy, the worst sort for ascending mountains, freezing cold and the woman with milk in her breasts, hopefully you know what that means, a woman with milk in her breasts doesn't do well in the cold, she had to be careful and it's a huge mortal danger to be up in the mountains in the dead of winter, you see, at least a fifteen-hour hike to the doctor, and hold on a second, then . . . But Jens immediately took advantage of Jónas' hesitation, this chink in his tightly packed stream of words, and said, we're leaving, we mustn't dally, and where's the horse?

The woman is dozing next to the stove as they leave.

V

You must believe us when we say that the heaths here can be lovely in the summers, and downright beautiful with snipes in the air, raindrops on the grass, a brook running silently between grassy banks, tussocks all around like sleeping dogs and every sound tending somehow towards silence. He who traverses the heaths on a calm summer day in sunshine might feel as if he's come to Paradise. There's also the tranquil, dreamy winter nights beneath the moon and thousands of stars that twinkle like old poems over the land, but such weather and such goodness belonged to a separate existence, a separate solar system, as Jens and the boy walked away from the fishing village and felt the land rise gently beneath their feet. The boy often sees nothing but snowflakes, occasionally his own arm and the rump of the grey horse that Jens is leading there in the storm, the precipitation, the snow that the wind ladles over them, they squint and have to turn their heads to gulp air, because man needs to breathe, otherwise he dies; the basis of existence is no more complicated than that. The mare, ten years old, wasn't a bit appreciative of the men dragging it out of the stable, away from its hay and out into this storm. A bit sullen, the grey, Jónas had said. And what's the mare's name?

I told you, The Grey, and she knows the heath, the mountain, and the weather here, you should pay her heed and wait until tomorrow. But Jens said nothing; just fastened the postbags to the mare, and then Jónas, the Postmaster of Vetrarströnd, was forced to watch as they left, unhappy about losing the company; what was he to do now, how can one make time pass, his wife sleeping inside, perhaps preferring to keep company with her dreams rather than her husband, who stood and watched the snow and wind swallow men and horse. Stood there with so much discontent in his mouth that he had to open it to relieve the pressure.

I would rather be driven here and there by the storm than by his stories, Jens had told the boy, and then they say no more, separated by horse and falling snow as they head up to the heath, which lies seven hundred metres high, the main route between Vetrarströnd and Vík, they hike upward for so long that one might think they were on the road to Heaven. But of course they aren't on the road to Heaven, but rather up a rough mountain, only to descend again as soon as possible, press on and not stop until they reach the parsonage in Vík. They could possibly have followed the shore, stepped their way through the rocks beneath the dizzying cliff walls, but then the sea would doubtless have splashed over them and drenched them and the cold seen to the rest, or a heavy cornice would have collapsed over them, broken and smothered them; it's better to cross the heath, that damned mountain pass, yes, says Jens, they've stopped to catch their breath a bit, sheltered more or less by a big rock, have been pushing on for more than three hours, against the wind that rages around them like a white shut up inside until it calms down, locked up as is done with crazy people. Núpur is the mountain here, lads, it's none other than the mountain, it's a lookout for Dumbsfjörður, sullen in summer sunshine or winter storms. Those who attempt to cross the heath from here, in blinding snowstorms like this one, and who head too far to the north-east once they're up there, instead of turning in time straight north, yes, those, my lad, suffer the same fate as the farmer whom my cousin searched for, along with three others: they walk off Núpur and fall! You can't see a thing in storms such as this one, that I can tell you, neither your own nor anyone else's ass, everything's white and there's no difference between sky and land, let alone if it's blowing, as it's doing right now; at such times people wander about, disoriented, lost, until they walk heedlessly over the brink and fall. And how far a fall is it? Seven hundred metres down to the beach, a freefall straight into the sea, if it's high tide, otherwise onto the rocks. The boy shut his eyes for a moment. Unless you land on a ledge, said Jónas, and he opened his eyes again. As the farmer did; he plunged off the brink but landed on a ledge several metres below, landed in snow, a downy soft drift, unbroken. Was saved! said the boy happily, glad that life, despite all else, should be merciful, even here, in this part of the world. Saved, yes, one might say that, but only to starve or freeze to death on the ledge; the egg hunters found him there the next spring; the birds had eaten from him a bit, blessed man, but the package that he'd brought with him was quite undamaged, a parcel from the priest in Vík, a translation of a French story and a letter to Denmark, the birds have no interest in poetry and such behind mare and man, it's so obvious that the heath cares nothing for them, Jónas was right, it cares little for company at the moment. The snow falls thickly, the wind blows it into drifts and although it's freezing and the snowcover hardens the higher they tramp, the snow doesn't harden quickly enough to hold up men and horse; they sink constantly, sometimes just several centimetres, which is difficult enough and frustrating, while sometimes their legs simply vanish entirely and the men sit there stuck, forced to use all their strength to tear themselves free, first one leg, then the other. Yet the men have little excuse; they have only two legs and a vertical shape, as if their bodies are part of an eternal tug-of-war between Heaven and Hell; they also have hands to use to free themselves. It's different for the mare, The Grey; she has four legs, slender relative to her bodyweight, which rests evenly on all of them, they slip down easily and she lies there on her belly, completely stuck. Then Jens has to pull, and the boy to push, both sinking and stumbling, and the mare struggling; it's bloody difficult but they manage it in some bizarre way, the mare is freed – only to become just as stuck again a few steps later. The wind rages, now we're having fun, it howls around the men and The Grey, who's ceased being hostile towards them, it's too tiring; neither the men nor the beast can afford such a luxury as hostility, they can't afford anything but grinding onwards, fighting back, reaching deep inside and finding the strength, finding a reason to continue, finding a way to stir up their thirst for life. The men are wet with sweat that changes into an icy skin each time they attempt to catch their breath, making it easy for the wind like an empty bag. Alright, alright, says the boy bewilderedly, stop it, but Jens doesn't stop, he even shakes the boy harder, says something, perhaps, people don't die when they're with me, but it's very difficult to comprehend words when one is being shaken so frantically, and is also completely unbearable. All of this, the snow, the mountain, the wind, is absolutely unbearable, so unbearable that the boy is filled with rage, is absolutely brimming with it, he tears himself away and then strikes out at Jens with his fists clenched in his mittens, twice, thrice, four times; Jens is able to avoid the blows but The Grey stares at the two men with her big eyes, apparently thinking something that isn't in their favour. Then the boy's fury leaves him, just as abruptly as it came, and Jens says quite calmly, we're going on, you're not lying down again. No no, says the boy just as calmly, as if they're two people having a chat out on the street, far from the danger, the storm, the precipice. And they plod on.

Dusk will surely overtake them soon. The night will surely find them up there; at least the sky appears to darken a bit around them, unless it's just fatigue that makes everything darker, and they press on without thinking, but why do that, anyway? The world is so painfully simple up here; one loses all one's grief, uncertainty, guilt, shame; in fact nothing ails the boy, except of course fatigue and the persistent fear of the precipice. He pushes the mare firmly, prepared to throw himself backwards if the earth gives way; twice Jens and The Grey appear to evaporate and he stiffens in his tracks, even feels as if he can hear the sea many hundreds of metres below, senses the dark pull of the precipice, good to know about the hut, nothing like it, except perhaps belief in God and Heaven during the tribulations of life. He who has faith is never broken, he who has faith has his own refuge, a promise of shelter gives one immeasurable strength. But how far is it to the refuge – and now we ask in minutes, not metres, the measurement of distance is of course useless; five hundred metres can mean from ten minutes up to four hours; do we still have half an hour or six hours to go? Hopefully not six hours, because then one might as well just lie straight down and die, give up, merge with the whiteness and vanish into the stillness. Half an hour, at most, shouts Jens, coming so close to the boy that he sees two small, black spots on the postman's face: his eyes, grimly black, and they both dive into tugging the mare up one more time, removing the mailbags for the hundredth time to lighten her load and either drag or shoulder the heavy bags until the mare is free once more, refasten them in the hope that she won't sink again, ridiculous optimism, of course, but perhaps justifiable because the powers-that-be have taken sides with them, rewarded them for their perseverance, they've come so high, so close to the sky, that an icy crust has formed over the snow, just beneath the newfallen snow. Albeit only a thin crust that at first holds only the men; the mare continues to sink and is stuck twice as fast as before, they have to go down on all fours and break the snow crust around her to prevent its edges from injuring her legs, but it's so indescribably good to be able to walk on the earth without sinking at every step that they feel downright happy; the wind blows over the world and changes the snowfall into sleet that scratches the skin; the men are forced to look down, as if humbly, but their relief doesn't leave them and the icy crust strengthens and soon holds both horse and men, now they only need to be careful not to let the relentless side-wind harass them off the right path. The boy looks up now and then, checks whether the mare is still in front of him, whether he still has a glimpse of Jens, but then looks down again before the sleet hurts his eyes. And finally The Grey lifts her head and whinnies softly. Jens looks back and the boy discerns something resembling a smile behind his icy mask. It's the refuge. They're saved. So there is justice in this world.

Blessed be they, those kindly men who were so concerned for the lives of their neighbours that they built the refuge, this universal shelter, here at the summit, all the way up against the sky where the winds are so severe that the snow seldom manages to bury the hut or hide it from humankind. Of course it's entirely white with snow at the moment, yet they see it clearly, glimpse its gable between the icy downpourings, there behind the blowing snow, a façade with little windows, as if the hut were peering into the storm in search of lost and terrified souls and calling to them. It's not big, of course; it would actually be more appropriate to call it a shed, but here it's equivalent to a palace. They make it beneath the gable, to shelter, and there feel their fatigue; it hits the men like the blow of a fist, they gasp for breath and everything goes momentarily dark, as if they've used the very last drops of their strength to reach the house, to reach shelter, and damn it'll be good, almost absurdly good, to go in, lie down, nibble at their provisions, listen to the storm rage against the house, powerless and furious at having lost the men and the mare. But now they need to go around the corner and find a door, the hut's merciful embrace. The wind is waiting for them around the corner and it grabs them immediately, wanting to fling them out into the blue, but they refuse to be blown away from shelter, happiness and rest; we're saved! shouts the boy perkily into the wind when he spies the outline of the doorposts, and he longs most of all to embrace Jens and the mare and call them beautiful names. No, we're not, says Jens; he needs to say no more, they aren't saved at all, the wind has long since ripped the door off the hut, torn it away, and all three of them, men and mare, stare into the refuge, which is a little over half full of snow and ice; it's turned into an icebox and will save no-one from the weather, but is assuredly an excellent place to store meat and dead men.

They move back to the sheltered side; so this is the way it is: they can choose to remain here, try to wait out most of the fury of the storm and possibly freeze to death, die here up against this hut with all their memories, all their dreams of a better and softer life, with all this post for which they are responsible, or else keep going and attempt to reach the village alive. But first they eat. Eat from the provisions that Helga prepared for them less than forty hours ago; there's energy in the frozen meat, they bite and chew and absorb the energy. The Grey sticks her head between them and has a bit of bread. The men say a few words but The Grey is silent, her eyes half shut. The wind blows, it howls and they're in the only shelter in a vast area, scanty cover for two men and one horse, the men need only reach out with their hands to feel the violence, the polar wind that seems vexed at all that lives. Damn, says Jens, taking out his flask.

Damn: because the door blew off the hut and it's full of ice and death.

Damn: because the storm is so severe that it's hardly possible to stand upright in the open, let alone walk; but that's what they need to do if they're going to make it to the village.

Damn: because they're seven hundred metres high.

Damn: because he's thirsty from the meat and the difficulty. Thirst is the worst enemy on these journeys. It's intolerable to find oneself in the midst of winter, with frozen water all around, yet still be parched with thirst. It's possible, of course, to crunch ice between one's teeth, but that grants only temporary relief, deepens the chill substantially and leaves one as thirsty afterwards as before.

Damn: because he's ominously cold; he hasn't managed to warm up properly since leaping into the sea, his cowardice let the cold in, a deep-rooted cold that no-one can dress against, the only thing that works is to keep oneself moving, struggle through snow and wind. The longer that he sits here, the more difficult the cold becomes; half an hour more, forty minutes, and he's dead, or as good as dead.

Damn: because now he's not only responsible for himself and the post, but also for another man's horse and this boy who crouches at his side, staring out into the darkness, pale with cold and fatigue.

Damn: because on top of all this – seven hundred metres high,

177

cold, fatigue, thirst, responsibility, the boy opens his mouth and starts to talk. Those who talk a lot aren't good travelling companions; they're quick to give up.

He talks about his sister. Her name is Lilja, which is a beautiful name, for sure. No, her name was Lilja, she's dead, which is of course regrettable, impossible to deny that, but who isn't dead? Then the boy starts to talk about his father, he's also dead; he talks about his mother, she as well, damn these people are fragile; so there's no-one alive? Finally he stops, which is good. But then asks out of nowhere, do you live alone? Me? says Jens inquisitively, as if there were anyone else who might answer. Yes, you. No. Oh, I thought so. You thought so? Yes. Well then, says Jens, in not an entirely unfriendly tone; this boy has lost so much that it's hardly possible to treat him badly. So you don't live alone? No. That's good. What do you know about it? I think it's bad for people to live alone, I think it doesn't do them good, the heart needs to beat for others, otherwise it grows cold. Oh, well then. Do your parents live with you? What does it matter? asks Jens, hardly feeling sorry for the boy anymore. I don't know; everything, I suppose; it means there's a lot of people alive. My father lives with me, says Jens, dissatisfied with having said too much, but then he just makes matters worse by adding, as well as my sister. So there's three of you, says the boy, ridiculously happy, how old is your sister? Her name is Halla, says Jens, and only because he longed to speak the name, feel the warmth, the innocence. Halla, says the boy slowly, it's beautiful. Those who speak on such trips should stay down on low ground, says Jens, standing up; he feels the stinging chill throughout his body but tries to ignore it, grabs the reins and steps out into the wind.

Or in into it. It's blowing so hard that common sense dictates crawl-ing; humans have the advantage over horses in being able to lie down and transform themselves into snakes, yet Jens won't stoop so low and takes on the storm upright, the horse following behind. The boy follows hard on the mare's heels, where he's sheltered slightly; the fatigue that had faded to a small degree thanks to the tiny cover and the food returns and makes his legs twice as heavy; the wind rages, the cold spreads over his face, slips through his clothing and stiffens everything, his muscles, thoughts, memories. Yet not everything is against them; the snow here is so hard that it supports them all. Who knows, perhaps they'll make it down to the village, down to inhabited land, down to the community and parsonage of Vík.

Life, in any case, is rather simple. Those who put one foot in front of the other, and then vice-versa, and repeat it often enough, finally reach their destination – if they have a destination at all. This is one of the facts of this world. But for those who are up on a heath, in a blinding snowstorm, dead tired, thirsty, the cold pressing slowly but surely towards their hearts, for them the facts are like any other twaddle. Because, you see, they've been cross-ing these heaths for a thousand years, generations have come and gone down below, wars have been fought out in the world, coun-tries created and dissolved, whelps have leapt into the air and come down as half-blind dogs and someone has bent over them with a sharp knife. The entire time, they've plodded onwards in blinding snowstorms, one mare and two men, three creatures on their way to a place that constantly seems to be retreating. But the difficulties and the hopelessness have united them; a strong line runs from the man in front, passes through the mare and is tied to the young man trailing. The evening has deepened all around them but the line holds them together, and at one point they find decent cover. The boy sighs but Jens does not; instead he struggles for some time to pull out his flask, takes a big drink, hands it to the boy, the mare is between them and gets nothing. Then they listen to the wind raging around the boulder, waiting for them. How old is she, your sister, Halla? asks the boy as Jens takes his second drink, and maybe it's because of the liquor, the cursed liquor that has made so much in life ugly, or just hearing the name Halla here, deep within the storm, far from others, that he answers; she's twenty-eight, as if it's any of the boy's business. And she never married? What? says Jens, offended. She's never married? No. Oh? She never will do. What makes you so certain of that, it's hardly possible to say such a thing, one never knows what the future will bring. She's an imbecile, says Jens sharply. That's a pity, I'm sorry, says the boy, as if Halla's existence were sorrowful, a sheer disappointment. A pity, says Jens, and sorry for what, damn it, what do you know about her?

The boy clears his throat, gathers courage, your father, he says; he's an old man, says Jens, setting off again before the boy is able to stand up.

*

180

at Vík, which serves as both post office and temporary lodgings for the postman, where hay for the mare, water and shelter from bad weather await; no no, says the farmer at the door of the house, half asleep, it's night in human habitations; they were in the wilderness, within a dark storm, time there is not the same. The farmer has sleep in his eyes, they detect a slight movement in the vicinity of his pupils, where his dreams are evaporating. Their knocking on the door woke the dogs, which tore barking down the dim passageway and woke the household. Yet the dogs don't venture out into the storm, but sniff curiously in the direction of the two men and the horse; outlines of several faces appear further down in the darkness of the passageway, a knocking on the door at night is big news and one should never sleep through it. This isn't Vík, says the farmer, half smiling at the idea of this crossing someone's mind; what was I supposed to be then, the priest? he adds, obviously finding it difficult not to laugh; this is so funny, absolutely absurd and the dreams are gone from his pupils, he's wide awake. But the two men and the mare between them appear not to be particularly amused, perhaps God has completely forgotten to give them a sense of humour; they look sullenly at the farmer, the men stand with their legs spread wide as if they're afraid of losing their balance; they're covered in snow and ice and are unrecognisable, although the farmer doesn't know them anyway, has never seen them, but he does recognise the mare; yes, now he recognises the horse, those contemplative eyes; isn't this The Grey? he asks, and the bigger man nods his head. So you've brought the post; what have you done with Guðmundur? He's ill,

A beautiful name? says Jens pointedly and derisively as they head back out into the storm, due north, as if their task is to discover the source of winter and place a huge stone over it. Sometimes it's hardly possible to live in this country, the cold shuts something inside us, the harshness of the conditions makes us coarser, constrains the joy of life – makes it seem as if we need to take a run-up to enjoy life. The horse plods through the drifts with its ears perked; yes, I find it beautiful, replies the boy, staring straight ahead, as focused as the gusting snow allows. Then they've reached a churchyard, having crossed the river that bends just below them without noticing it; so much is hidden from us in snow and frost, almost the entire earth, in fact. Who would suspect that in the summers an amiable and dreamy river runs here between grass-grown banks, with northern phalaropes floating on its surface, terns screeching in the air, trout gaping in pools and crowberries darkening in the sun? The parsonage is a stately wooden structure, not an underground house like Svörtustaðir; it rises somewhat high over their heads and the roof disappears in the dark storm. Jens pounds on the door, instinctively pounds it hard because the cold has started to gnaw its way towards his heart, as if a levee has suddenly broken. He pounds hard on the door, using the remainder of his strength to make his blows audible within. He pounds again but receives no response. Maybe there's no dog in the house to bark, damn it, mutters Jens, and he sways, places his arm over the mare and doesn't even look up when the door finally opens, hesitantly, scarcely halfway; a man appears in the doorway, reluctant to open it fully and thereby let

184

the storm in. Postman Jens, his companion, and horse, says Jens without looking up, his voice hollow and flat. And the priest responds, because this is indeed he, Reverend Kjartan, Kjartan the French, that's what I like, post and company; great is the mercy of the Lord!

VI

A man can stand upright a long time if it's a question of life and death; the will to live is almost immeasurable and Jens has been on his feet this entire trip, seven hundred metres upward, up into snow and frost, heavy wind, towards a threatening sky and then down again, sinking into the whiteness at every step, pulling the mare up from depressions, as thirsty as if in the desert, weary after the long postal journey from Dalir, the gentle countryside where his father is bowing to time and his sister is a bright summer day; when is Jens coming? she asks thirty times a day, forty times a day, and her father looks apprehensively out into the storm that's swallowed bigger bites than one postman; this entire way Jens has stood on his feet, unbowed, only supported himself on the mare the final kilometre, when the cold of the sea inside him stripped him of all his strength. But they've come to a house; not to their final destination, of course, existence isn't so generous, but to a place to rest, and for this reason it's not entirely vital that he stand upright, it won't be certain death to relax for a brief moment. Jens lets go of the horse, strokes it, thanks it, goes up to the house, slowly but perfectly straight-backed, steps into the stillness and then it's as if both legs have been shot out from under him and he

186

is nothing but a shapeless heap on the floor. Damn it, where's your dignity; aren't I more of a man than this? he thinks. The boy has entered and knelt down by Jens before Kjartan realises what's happened; he'd been so sincerely relieved and grateful to the night for sending him company, but then one of the men is lying as if dead on the floor; in no way fit for conversation. Kjartan grows suddenly angry, but then regains his composure and feels responsible; these men have in all likelihood brought the post over the heath, and done so in this weather. God help us all, says Reverend Kjartan out loud, yet involuntarily; the days have unfortunately passed and lie far distant when he believed sincerely and with pure faith that man could expect help from God. Jens tries to curse, but it turns out to be little other than an indistinct murmur; yet he does manage to mutter, see to The Grey, loud enough for the boy to hear, before falling silent. The storm pummels the house and a bit of it is sucked in through the doorway. Kjartan looks down at the men. He hadn't been able to sleep, which is nothing new; sleep eludes him far too often; it seems not to matter how tired he is when he lies down, as soon as he shuts his eyes he's wide awake. He tosses and turns, reels off prayers and old rhymes, tries to calm his mind and entice sleep to come to him, most often without result, all others sleep while he's awake, deprived of the succour of sleep, deprived of God's mercy, and rightly so, he mutters; he roams about the house or sits in his study, seeks company in books, letter writing, translations, sips of liquor, and those moments can also certainly be fine, yet it's rather dull to sit alone like that, evening after evening, night after night, year after of sleep and everything becomes gentler for a moment and it's easier to live. He simply places his hand firmly on her shoulder, presses once, presses twice and says, some men have come, they're battered, cold and wet. And it takes no more; the woman opens her eyes, her name is Anna and she's awake.

Once she thought that life would be different and much better. It was also good to be young and married to Kjartan; scholarship, Copenhagen, a trip to Paris, Berlin, conversations and words that enlarged the world and made the stars brighter, few more eloquent than he, more handsome, few as sparkling, they had their moments together that still shine, even now, but rather dully under the dark weight of the years. They'd planned to live in Vík temporarily, several years at the boundary of the world, but it had been twenty-two years now and most of the sparks they shared were extinguished, yet Anna always seems to expect the best in this life, her uncowed optimism stuns Kjartan at times. What's the real difference, he thinks, between optimism and idiocy? He watches her blink her eyes and immediately notices a touch of an involuntary smile at the corners of her mouth. She looks towards him standing in the doorway and squints.

It's growing ever darker around her, her sight is failing; eyes that fade. At first the mountains opposite the farm, steep and imposing, were hidden in a haze; then Maríufjall Peak itself, which towers over the house, the church and the churchyard, began to vanish, the mountain that the Irish monks blessed more than a thousand years ago, the only Christian mountain in this area. Some days it looks as if it's made more of air than hard stone, as if it's on its way to Heaven; it was a sacred mountain in Catholic times and fishermen still invoke it in times of peril, in the anguish of death call on the mountain that has appeared to many men through dark storms and saved them, as if it has gone to sea to retrieve terrified and fragile human beings. Maríufjall vanished from her sight just over a year ago, and last summer the tussocky ground around the farm started to fade; she barely sees the birds any longer, they've transformed into song. But she discerns her closest surroundings and can distinguish people's outlines, if they remain still, and she can perceive the silhouette of Kjartan from a few metres away. It must be night by now, she emerges from such a great depth, a deep dream. His bed is in the little space just off the bedroom, it's been many years since they lay together, she hardly remembers any longer how it is to feel the warmth of human flesh. But she believes, can't help but believe, that sooner or later the world will brighten, that the fog will be lifted from her eyes, the darkness will dissipate around Kjartan, that one night he'll come and lie with her, flesh will find flesh, lips will find lips, souls will find souls.

She dresses quickly. Sleeps naked despite the cold in the wooden house, the cold passes through the walls but she is hardy and sleeps naked while others tremble in their beds, wrapped in clothing and blankets. Kjartan gazes at her body, the small breasts that he once desired, composing for them two sonnets, one for each breast, believing at the time in mercy, himself and the world, at that time they were round and firm and so warm, now they're just empty sacks and her lean body is worn down. Kjartan leans falling; as if, while walking in darkness, she fears the bridge at the end of the world. Yes, and a cold horse, says the boy, hearing the priest shut the door. The horse will be seen to, says Kjartan from the stairwell, on his way up to fetch a farmhand, who comes down the stairs, a middle-aged man, short but stocky, still dressing, his face puffy with sleep; without a word he goes out to tend to the horse, brings The Grey to shelter, gives it water, hay, relieves it of its worries. My name is Anna, says the woman to the visitors, as she walks right up to the boy, her eyes wide open as if she's flabbergasted at the world, her face round and her nose very small. At first glance she doesn't appear beautiful; her wide-open eyes give her an almost idiotic appearance, but there's something deep within them that causes the boy to feel as if she isn't looking at him, but rather in him, investigating his kidneys and heart. The boy stands completely still, hardly daring to breathe or blink or glance to either side, inhales her warm, gentle breaths, discerns the priest behind the woman, leaning against the wall and watching, his expression impenetrable. Someone is heard coming down and going into another part of the house. I see so poorly, says Anna apologetically, and have to come very close to people to distinguish the details of their faces, which say more than most people realise. Of course many people find it uncomfortable having an old, partially blind woman in their faces, but I prefer the truth to courtesy; by the way, you needn't be ashamed of your face, she adds, and then kneels next to Jens, touches him, feels how cold he is, slips her hand beneath his shirt to feel his skin and starts giving orders. Speaks in concise sentences, saying only what needs to be said, resulting in everything going quickly and flawlessly; shortly afterwards the boy is sitting up next to the stove, has removed all his clothing and put on dry clothing handed to him; he slurps warm coffee, while Jens sleeps naked in bed. Recovered his senses on the floor and managed to make his way unaided up to the bedroom, but not much more; he lies there in bed nearly unconscious, stones are heated and placed under the covers with him, placed like warm thoughts into the bed. Then he's brought wolf-fish soup, warm and powerful, it has the potential to raise men from death; I'm not so pitiful that I can't feed myself, says Jens, taking the bowl from the housemaid, his voice sounding as if it has come from the bottom of the ocean, up through a surging sea, the housemaid remains seated on the side of the bed, gazing at this big man whom the night and the storm brought them, at his thick blonde hair, his unkempt beard, semi-dark eyes, huge nose. She sits with her hands in her lap, resting them; she's pulled the cold clothing off him, cold and frozen, rubbed life and heat into his legs, had to rub them a long time to Jens' muttering, her young and calloused hands stroked his legs to just beneath his groin and in those three or four minutes that the two of them were alone in the room she could touch what she dared and wanted to touch, the man was practically unconscious and it's hardly a sin to touch, it's hardly a sin to feel life; she did so out of sheer curiosity. He was also chilled to the bone and her stroking had no visible effect for quite some time. Many are the human desires. Jens finishes his soup, hands her the empty bowl, says thanks, their eyes meet for one second. I need to rest now, he parish, a world that can hibernate for months at a time beneath a heavy burden of snow, doesn't want to let him go. Hardly anyone comes here during the winter months, except for people from variously distant farms, bringing the corpse of a relative or remains of a pauper, some old person who hardly leaves behind a name, let alone a memory. But it's all the same: his farmhand has to dig graves for them, break through the frost that sometimes extends an ungodly distance down, finding it difficult not to curse the dead roundly for dying at this time of year. But otherwise noone comes here, except for the deputy postman Guðmundur, and though he brings them news, papers and letters, he himself has little to tell, stuck in his banal complaints, completely apathetic regarding poetry, deep thoughts, capable at most of reciting a few verses and ballads that seldom surpass the level of drollery, and are more often stupefying, depressing doggerel. Kjartan tried once to talk to him about Søren Kierkegaard but could just as well have tottered out to the sheep shed to chat with the sheep, or worse, the rams that know only how to chew their cuds and to look forward to the rut. A dangerous man, Kierkegaard, says Kjartan to the boy, who naturally can't restrain himself, although he's tired, from reaching for book after book, and had tried to fumble his way through the start of a work by this Dane. Why is he dangerous? asks the boy, looking up from the book. He threatens to change us, he makes us doubt, he forces us to reconceive the world, and such men have always been considered dangerous. We prefer agreeableness to provocation, abstraction to stimulus, numbness to stimulation. That's why people go for ballads, rather

Kjartan runs his hand over the two piles of paper on the desk: one, translations of a French writer, the other, fragments of the story of life. Fragments of life in this place, says Kjartan, before telling the boy about Svörtustaðir, about happiness and kisses; it takes time, and the storm and the night lie over the house. He then sighs and asks the boy to hand him the postbag with all the post for his parishioners. Let's have a look at what the world sends us, he says, removing the contents of the bag, emptying it completely; that's one less bag to carry. Kjartan's face brightens when he sees the package from Gísli, touches it gently, almost amorously, somewhere upstairs Anna sleeps, in her dreams she sees perfectly and she hasn't been touched for many long years. He lays the package aside carefully and inspects the other material that emerges from the bag, there are newspapers, a few parcels for people in the parish, a letter from an old friend of Kjartan's, a priest in the East. Egotistical bastard, mutters Kjartan, having forgotten the boy's presence; a letter from their son that he also sets aside, yet not with anticipation, he livens up when he sees an advertisement for two vacant pastor positions, Staður in Steingrímsfjörður and Höfði, his back and shoulders straighten reflexively but then slump again immediately as he reads on and discovers that the deadline for application in both cases expires in just under twenty-four hours; messages travel long and arduous roads to their destinations here at the end of the world. He stands up awkwardly, goes to the window, it's night outside and the weather is gloomy. Go to sleep now, he says into the night, I'm going to wrestle a bit more with Maupassant and have a look at the parcel from Gísli. Forgive my bosh just now, I'm growing old and have taken to spouting rubbish, not everything went as it perhaps should have gone. The boy stands up carefully, uncertain whether his tired feet will support him, which they do, the certain knowledge of the coming rest gives them strength; he turns around at the door, looks at the shelves full of books, full of words that can open new worlds, new skies, but Kjartan stares out into the night. You can see how a person feels by what he or she looks at. I thought, he says from the doorway, too numb with fatigue to be shy, that one couldn't be unhappy surrounded by so many books. Kjartan turns around and gives the boy a long look, but says nothing.

Jens wakes him the next morning.

It's difficult to tell what hour it is; the windows are covered by little curtains, besides being half blind beneath masks of ice. It takes him time to wake fully; Jens is saying something about Dr Sigurður and the boy asks, what? I'm not going to give that man his satisfaction by delaying any longer; we're going, sticking to plan. Jens speaks quietly but his voice is strong, devoid of all frost. The boy's clothing dried during the night and he dresses, nothing is heard from outside, perhaps the storm has abated. Perhaps the wind has finally given up blowing people off this land. The farmhand and a maid are outside tending the livestock, the two men are given something to eat as the priest's wife describes her son's letter to the housemaid Jakobína; his name is Sigfús. Kjartan is nowhere to be seen, I wonder if he's sleeping, thinks the boy as he devours his diluted *skyr*; he eats heartily, needing the nourishment, and drinks coffee, fills his body with the warm drink, ahead of them is a long journey and bitter cold. The men say nothing, the boy is too shy, Jens because he prefers silence to most everything else, silence is shelter, it is peace. Then Kjartan steps in from outside, stamps to shake off the snow and brings the morning cold in with him. He pours a cup of warm coffee, the settlement here would have been deserted for certain if it hadn't been for coffee, he says with a smile, as if glad. You're not taking the sea route today, by the way, he says, and stops smiling. Is that so, says Jens, after making the others wait for these three words. No, Kjartan had gone down to Svörtustaðir and the skerries at the verge of the harbour were clearly visible.

Anna: Well, that's that.

Kjartan: Exactly, that's that. When these skerries emerge from the sea, you can forget about sailing over Dumbsfjörður; it would be a grave blunder.

Jens: A grave blunder?

Kjartan: A grave blunder. No-one sails at such a time, except of course men who are incredibly weary of life.

Jens: Is that so.

Kjartan: That's how it is.

Jens: Indeed.

Kjartan: There we have it; and not any other way.

Jens: So we'll walk.

Kjartan: I hardly think so.

Anna: No, no, stay here and gather your energy today and

tomorrow, if necessary. The lads will ferry you over when the weather permits. Bring these men something good to eat, Jakobína. Anna looks in the direction of the housemaid, her eyes two tarnished pearls. The boy gulps his coffee to burn off his fatigue; he would have preferred to sleep longer, Jens sits with his head bowed but looks up when Jakobína returns with flatbread and butter; she's tall, her movements are strong and graceful, her brown eyes meet those of the postman, she places the tray between them, brushing, as if by accident, Jens' hand, which rests solidly on the table. A hand that touches another hand in this way is saying something, Jens knows this but dares not respond. Anna doesn't see what passes between them; she sees so little with her tarnished pearls, and Kjartan seems lost in his thoughts. It's a bad idea to go now, says Jakobína, sitting down at the table, opposite Jens, it's already dark and the outlook is bad, we'll help you make the time pass, we can do this and that, she smiles without taking her eyes off Jens, who looks away, as if out of cowardice, then straightens, quickly; thank you very much for all you've given us, but now we're leaving.

What nonsense, says Kjartan.

But Jens is immovable. His big hands are wrapped around his coffee cup; this broad-shouldered man, with stern, grey eyes over a stupendous nose. Jakobína gazes at him a little longer, indulging herself; her hands resting on the table hold the memory of his nakedness in their palms. Well then, says Kjartan, sighing, so you're leaving.

Anna: It isn't wise.

Jens: I know little about wisdom.

Anna: But I think you know enough.

Jens: A man simply does what a man has to do.

Kjartan: Difficult to argue with that.

Anna: That's not for certain; but will you prepare some provisions for them, Jakobína?

I would very much have liked to have you here, to tell the truth, says Kjartan; monotony has killed more people than me, and you must know that it's no joke to travel in these parts in bad weather; it's still dead of winter here. He rubs his eyes, as if to wipe away his fatigue, his ever-present fatigue, his insomnia; he'd managed to doze for two hours before dawn, sunk into a deep sleep before something woke him suddenly, like a cold knife wound in the vicinity of the heart; *doubtless the misfortune, doubtless the guilt rearing their heads*, he'd written in a letter to Schoolmaster Gísli, nearly nodding off as he wrote. *My soul is covered in barnacles and will soon sink into even more darkness. That's how it is. Have you read this Norwegian, Knut Hamsun, whom my colleague to the east writes about, in between bouts of self-aggrandisement? I've hardly slept, not properly, for weeks. It wouldn't surprise me if the Lord were punishing me, and I certainly merit it. But who is this boy who has come with the postman? Was he sent here by God or the Evil One? You should hear what he said: I thought that one couldn't be unhappy surrounded by so many books. Dear Gísli, how are we treating our lives? And ourselves? I'm awful to my Anna; it's been so long since I held her, sometimes I find her body ugly and that strange optimism of hers makes her either an imbecile or a saint; I obviously can't bear either. Oh,*

I've seen a better, more beautiful servant than me, my old friend!

They have more to eat. They're full, but pack it in. Eat, now, says Anna, her clouded eyes roaming around the room. Yet I don't understand why you want to leave. People do what they have to do, says Kjartan; they've always done so, though of course there's little sense in it.

Anna: Yes, that's right. For ages men have rushed off, made haste to die, leaving their women and children destitute. They forget that life is beautiful and that one should attend to it, first and foremost. Or do only that.

Kjartan: Life is, of course, full of variety.

Anna: On the other hand, I think that men are irresponsible and preoccupied with themselves, and it's we women and children who must bear the consequences of it. But have more to eat now; the Lord wants the best for all of us.

Jens clears his throat and says, almost apologetically, we'll be careful, but we must hold to our itinerary and deliver the post; that's what I was hired to do.

And then they're ready.

Neither word nor wisdom can stop them; they bid farewell to the household with handshakes, Anna runs her hands over their heads before they put on their hats, she has to stand on tiptoe to reach Jens' head. The farmhand is to accompany them but leads them first to the building holding The Grey, who stands up when she sees Jens and the boy, seemingly completely prepared to go with these men, storm and trial had united them; but no, unfortunately, says Jens, you must remain here, but we'll come back for you, after two days or so. Jens is generally more talkative to horses than men; the horses, of course, understand not a word and thus never answer, but they have big eyes and at times it's as if they contain the truth of the world. The boy wraps his arms around the mare's big head and she blinks.

The weather is calm; only light precipitation. Snowflakes drift around them, bearing the stillness between them and there's really no use in talking. The snowfall isn't dense; they can see the mountains that surround the bay. Maríufjall to the left, hardly more than four hundred metres, but so steep and tapering in some places that it resembles a giant sword. To their right stand four adjoining mountains, similar in appearance, with black ravines between them, dome-shaped and seemingly full of rage, as if at some point four giants thrust their heads violently out of the earth and turned to stone. The boy listens to the silence between the snowflakes, enjoys it, but unfortunately not for long; the farmhand wants to talk, he's chatty, these are proper mountains, lads, he says, waving his arm to the right. And then tells a four-hundred-year-old story about a priest.

It's in the parsonage's records, says the farmhand, Kjartan read it to us this winter, a long-forgotten story that he managed to dig up in that incomprehensible delving of his. Well, at least it's led to something. This priest was considerably vexed by these four mountains, The Heads, as we sometimes say, and set out from his farm early one summer morning with four other men to consecrate them. Climbed the first one, then had himself lowered on a rope, bringing with him the consecrated water and the word of the Lord, sprinkled water on the cliff face and blessed what we call the forehead, but came back up with a strange expression on his face. Yet he went straight on to the next one, so fast that his companions had trouble following him. Went down, then several long moments passed in silence, the sun shone and a gentle breeze blew. Lower a good knife to me, lads, they then heard him call, very calmly, which they did; tied a piece of cord around it and lowered it. Shortly afterwards he tugged on the cord and they pulled up the knife, covered in blood. The farmhand stops, waits in the silence that the snowfall carries from Heaven to Earth, waits in heavenly silence, and finally the boy says, reluctantly, yet knowing that he can't avoid it, covered in blood, what? Yes, my lads, a bloody knife comes up. Naturally they're startled and shout down to the priest, but receive no answer. So they start pulling, at first determinedly, then frantically, but have to work very hard, as if the priest has suddenly put on a ton of weight, or else as if something were pulling back, but finally he comes up over the edge, startling them so greatly that they lose their grip and the priest plunges and is torn apart on the rocks many hundreds of metres below. Jens and the boy say nothing, just keep walking among the snowflakes and silence, and then the farmhand adds, in a more sombre tone of voice: The priest had cut his own neck, from ear to ear; his neck was wide open, it was like an infernal smirk.

The snowfall grows denser, drawing a curtain over the mountains that killed the priest many centuries ago. I suppose they just threw the poor fellow right off, says Jens brusquely. Could them and they'd had rough going, wound up in sheer hell. A man from some cottage or other had died; there are one or two of them there in every bay or little fjord and it's hardly possible to get from one farm to the next in the winter, hardly in the summer either, that lot hunker down on their farms and can't go anywhere, know nothing, never hear any news and are hardly anything themselves, and then some of them get in the habit of dying in the dead of winter, which should be prohibited, naturally. Because they've got to get the remains to a churchyard, though some don't feel like messing about with such a troublesome task and store the bodies as long as the weather's freezing, for months at a time, even, which I find downright sensible; the dead person hardly makes a fuss over where he lies. But this man had lain so much emphasis on being buried in consecrated ground that folk hardly dared otherwise than to ensure that this was done. So men were gathered to transport him here. I don't know how familiar you are with this place, but up there to the north it can take quite some time to gather five or six men of suitable age to transport a corpse, up to a week, even. Finally they'd come together at the cottage, but just as they were leaving, a blizzard hit, naturally, and lasted for three days; they'd come a long way in draining the household's provisions before it finally subsided, and then they got going. Hazarded taking a shortcut over the glacier. Bold men, I must say, or naïve, because although there's nothing more beautiful than the glacier under clear, bright skies, there's little as menacing in dark storms. And up on the glacier another storm hit, but they'd come so high that there was no chance of turning back. For hours they mother's pleas that her husband not take him up to the heath in uncertain weather. On the other hand, Jens and the boy should be in no real danger, or Jens anyway, so deeply experienced, having crossed fiercer heaths than these, and in worse weather and made it out alive from all of them, not due to his sense of direction, perhaps, which is just average, but due to his strength, stamina, stubbornness.

The land elevates slightly, the snowfall intensifies, they gain occasional glimpses of the outlines of the mountains, like dark shadows. Yet the snowcover is navigable, surmountable, they rarely sink deeply and the boy arranges the postbag, nearly full with letters and newspapers, *Ísafold*, *Þjóðólfur*, news that ages with their every step. He hasn't started panting, not significantly, yet feels tired from lack of sleep. The snow piles up around them, continuous snow from ground to sky, the snow connects air and earth, there's no difference between them any longer, everything merges and they can expect to meet angels bustling about in eternity. Time passes around them, seconds, minutes, and then hours. Their legs move instinctually, not knowing any differently, nothing else comes to mind and they meet each other briefly at every step; oh, it's you, says the left foot to the right, happy to have the company.

Jens leads.

It happens quite automatically, the stronger man leads the way and breaks the trail that the snow covers over quickly, in only a few minutes it's as if they were never there. Jens carries the heavier bag but doesn't feel its weight; he wanted to carry both of them but the boy wouldn't hear of it, I'll take it when you're tired, Jens had said, bluntly and calmly, that's just how it was, that's how it would be, but the boy swore under his breath and muttered to himself, be careful that it doesn't turn out the opposite. Big words, too big, bigger than him and now as the land rises and the conditions grow worse, it would be quite nice to be rid of the bag. He looks down and tries to think of something remarkable, something big, utilise the time in that way and forget the toil, let his mind control his body, not the other way round. You're different, Kjartan had said, meaning it as a compliment. Is that right; shouldn't he then be able to think of something remarkable, something big, and think it continuously, not let his lack of focus ceaselessly tear it apart? He starts thinking of poetry and it goes well to begin with, but then he just thinks of Ragnheiður and only of Ragnheiður. About the heat that he felt when she came up close to him at the hotel, the combination of warmth, toughness and suppleness that's found only in the human body, the best and most dangerous in this world:

> Press close to me and we'll no longer feel cold.
> Press close to me and our loneliness will be relieved.
> Press close to me and everything will be beautiful.
> Press close to me and I shall no longer fear death.
> Press close to me and I'll betray everything.

The land no longer rises, they've reached the crest of the heath, leaving around five kilometres down to low ground. Just maintain a fairly straight course, though the boy doesn't understand how Jens will manage it in this blinding storm, which isn't very dangerous, though, as long as the wind doesn't pick up. There are no birds here, no foxes, hardly a field mouse, there's just the two of them, the snow and possibly a dead farmer with a teenage boy in his arms; he'd wrapped them around the boy, pressed the young, ice-cold body to his own and muttered, forgive me, can you forgive me, and tried to hold the young life tightly enough, but they both died, far from their kin. Dying is cold, says the farmer, having suddenly come up next to the boy, the teenager silent by the farmer's side, they walk lightly in the snow, leave no footprints behind; it was my fault, says the farmer as they dissolve.

And then it starts blowing, of course.

The calm had only been momentary, just long enough to allure them further up the heath. At first gentle gusts of wind, apologetic and muttering, no no, we don't mean any harm, just keep going, you're perfectly safe, don't pay attention to us. The gusts swirl the snow, as if in a supple dance that grows more rigid, little by little, grows faster, wilder, until they can no longer tell the slightest difference between blowing snow and falling snow; this has become far too familiar, damn it, swears the boy, but Jens trudges onwards, untiringly, never glances back, a distance of ten to fifteen metres between them and increasing gradually. It's not very nice of him, mutters the boy, who feels fearful but is too stupidly proud to shout, instead tries to speed up but stumbles, almost as if someone has tripped him, lies in the snow, looks up and sees Jens disappear into the storm, or behind it; on the other hand the farmer and the teenage boy have returned, they stand over him and their frost-covered eyes look down at him, three are much better than two, says the farmer. I'm not going to die here, damn it, hisses the boy at the snow, and he tries to wriggle to his feet without touching the two men, which is difficult; they stand right up against him, dead men are drawn to the warmth of life. The farmer has come so close that he can't come any closer, his right arm hangs powerless at his side and looks as if it's missing a bit at the front, but the left reaches into the boy, gropes its way along like a blind snake in search of a living heart; we aren't so bad, he says and searches, and the heath is beautiful in good weather. I'm supposed to live, pants the boy, trying desperately to twist away from the cold, dead hand; what is this? growls Jens, having thrust his paw through the farmer's chest, are you going to take my hand or just die there in the snow?

Then it happens; they start descending. In calm weather they would soon look down over low ground, eight to ten farms lined up along the Dumbsfjörður shore, housing fifty, sixty, seventy lives that come and go, come and go, they would see fjords cutting into the land on the other side; deep, ancient wounds, and adjacent to them short valleys and then heaths, even more heaths with white sheep bones, dead people, dreamy lakes and lovely tussocks. They would catch glimpses of individual farms on the grassy patches found there, some with cliffs towering over them although they're located as close to the shoreline as possible. It's a long way between farms and the land route is seldom passable except in midsummer, and then people are generally so burdened with work that they can't go anywhere; they toil away at gathering hay for the livestock, go out fishing when conditions allow it and drown when someone cuts the line. Jens shakes his right hand now and then, a bit as if it's growing cold; are we in any danger of falling? shouts the boy, justifiably assuming a precipice somewhere ahead; we'll find out if it happens! Jens shouts back, his first words in a long time, or since he went through death to help the boy up, their first communication and it's like this; a worried question and an evasion. Icelandic life in a nutshell – we're completely incapable of expressing our feelings among others; don't come near my heart.

The two men plod onwards, and downward.

Distance themselves from the dangers of the mountain, draw closer to death by sea.

The wind abates little despite their descent, but the snow becomes softer and more difficult. Jens seems confident of the route, which isn't terribly complicated, as long as the strong wind blows diagonally at their backs they're heading in the right direction. But what damned direction? The boy shouts but receives no answer, shouts for Jens who's probably lost his ears and has started to pull ahead once more, the boy can't close the distance no matter how hard he tries, at least fifteen, twenty metres between them and increasing gradually. Couldn't they get a boat on some farm, get someone to row them over Dumbsfjörður? Of course it wouldn't be a very popular idea in this weather, the sea malicious and completely blind, but Jens pays in cash and some here have lived long without seeing, let alone having, such a phenomenon. In the worst case they could take lodging with someone, wait out the worst of the tempest, but now they're actually moving further away from Langifjörður with every step, and lengthening the sea voyage. It was a bad idea to leave Vík and it's foolish to continue pressing on here by land, the only thing that they're approaching is the glacier, which lords it over all else in these parts; it awaits them behind the storm, rises high and fills half the sky; he who goes too near it will lose God. And perhaps Jens is trying to do just that, to lose God, or why would he trudge on like this; sink into hollows, break his way out of them, lose the boy, appear again; the boy is drenched with sweat from the exertion, and tumbles over into a hollow. When he manages to dig himself out, Jens is gone.

Yes, fine.

It was bound to happen.

Just perfect.

Hopefully he'll be buried in snow and the Devil will take his remains at the first opportunity. The boy looks around but sees nothing through the blowing snow, the snowfall, knows nothing but his own fatigue; for that matter he could be standing next to a house without knowing it. I'll just keep going and try to find a farm before dusk, he thinks, and is starting to feel quite hungry; how good it would be now to be able to pay a visit to Helga's kitchen. And then, quite unexpectedly, so unexpectedly that it's almost a shock, he feels regret, even considerable regret. He has to stop, stands unmoving, leans into the aggressive wind. Did he have to come all the way out here, over a gloomy fjord on a rowing boat with a terrified companion, over two heaths and then lose his way in a blinding snowstorm with a godless glacier behind the storm in order to discover this: that he feels almost fine in Geirþrúður's house? At least fine enough that he can feel regret. It's a completely new experience for him to regret the loss of what hasn't disappeared into eternity. This new regret is easier and there's light in it. But regret over what? The people, the selfsame trio, the security, the possibilities that can come with living in that house? All his life, ever since his father died, he's been leaving, has never known where he was going but his dreams are about this, getting away. In this lay hope, and reason to keep himself standing upright. Getting away from the fish, the hardship, the haymaking, the incessant, destructive everyday toil, the constant grind that rips people apart well before their time, takes the gleam from their eyes, the heat from their touch. Getting away before it's too late. He's lived now for three weeks in a house where all the rules are somehow turned upside down, and he's supposed to begin his education when he returns, if he returns. The boy fights against the wind just to stand still as he tries to come to grips with this, go over the last weeks, the books that he'd got to read, the conversations, the peculiar, almost dangerous carelessness in some of their attitudes, the foreign skipper whom he saw his first morning in the house, Geirþrúður's lover, Geirþrúður herself in the bathtub, a bit old yet entirely different than old, and the mornings with Helga and Kolbeinn, a little more than three weeks of new life and it's only now, with innumerable mountains between

VII

Jens had found them a building, an intact building with an attached door, walls, and roof; it's an indescribable luxury. Simply open the door, step or stumble in, shut it and they're perfectly sheltered. A medal for those who constructed a building here, and put a door on it to shut out this beastly weather. It's indescribably good to be able to breathe normally, not to have to gulp air furtively so as not to get snow in one's mouth, amazing to hear one's breathing again. Jens stands erect but the boy is on his knees, it was of course he who half stumbled in. The building isn't large, just big enough to house the twenty sheep that stare in consternation at the two men who have started scraping snow and frost off themselves without a glance at the sheep, as if they aren't aware of the forty eyes staring at them. The sheep are so startled that they don't even dare bleat. No-one ever comes here, except of course folk from the farm, the few souls that the animals know like their own snouts; two new men is therefore tremendous news. Fear and curiosity shine from forty staring eyes, and finally one of them can no longer resist, simply cannot restrain itself, opens its mouth and bleats. One single bleat, an exclamation, actually, and then the others have to do the same, naturally.

Several seconds later the noise has grown deafening. Twenty sheep that bleat and bleat as if a terrible catastrophe is imminent; they stretch their necks, bleat vehemently and overwhelm the sound of the wind itself; they've huddled together as far towards the rear of the pen as possible, while behind them, partitioned off in its solitude and lifelong grumpiness, is a large, silent-as-stone ram that acts at first as if it has no interest in the sheep or this visit that the storm has brought them, but in the end it's smitten by the sheeps' hysteria, opens its big jaws and starts to bleat. At first softly and to itself, but it soon loses all self-control and adds its deep, dingy, surly bleat to the panicked, loudly bleating choir. Then Jens takes one step in their direction, says curtly and gruffly: shut your mouths! And no more is needed. They shut up, the ram as well, its lower jaw sinks, its mouth hangs half open with fear and its big horns have become so sadly heavy on its head; it's never good to be alone, even if you have horns. It's dead quiet inside, just a single brief, fearful bleat that one sheep lets slip, completely by accident, otherwise complete silence; that's how influential words can be, if they're spoken in the right way. But the wind, of course, takes no account of what is said in buildings and continues to rage. Twenty sheep and one ram stare at Jens. The boy looks over the group, says, damn it, then lets himself sink onto a pile of old hay in the corner, where he intends to remain for the next decade or so.

And he could have fallen asleep quickly, fatigued after staying up so late with Kjartan, weary from the hike and the labour of the last two days, if Jens hadn't started pacing the last few steps that the space allowed, having taken off his cap and mittens and laying them on a rock, with a black-browed, threatening expression. What does the boy know about this Jens? He pretends to doze but leaves his eyes open slightly and watches the big postman storm back and forth, feels a tinge of fear when he sees the fists clench, big as a baby's head, the sheep don't take their eyes off the postman but the ram looks down and thinks that now it would be fun to butt someone. Then the sheep start chewing their cuds. There are few things more soothing in this world than watching a sheep chewing its cud; the boy looks, then shuts his eyes and starts humming something, extremely softly, almost silently, a few notes that soon become a charming but slightly sorrowful melody, become the signal for departure that Benedikt blew their final night in this world, before they ran the boats down the beach, out to sea and rowed off towards Bárður's death. Andrea had stood on the shore and watched them recede; what is she doing now and where is Bárður? Where do those who die go; is it possible to come there, does a new dawn await us there behind all the storms, behind life, behind death, a new dawn, a gleaming horizon and fragile melody to soothe our pain after life? He's started to sink into sleep, which is like sinking into a heavy, warm lake, a tranquil lake, but then his right leg is kicked, the shroud of sleep is torn, he's back in a dimly lit sheep shed, the wind whining outside and Jens standing over him with clenched fists. What? mutters the boy, but Jens bends down, yanks him up like chaff and pulls him close, the boy feels the cold of Jens' icy beard, sees the little veins in the big nose and looks straight into the angry mention; things just happen and people are different, why mention it? They look at each other, two or three metres between them, forty-two eyes that watch them. I haven't thanked you properly for what you did, declares Jens, bluntly, calmly. It's unnecessary, says the boy, feeling it safe now to scramble to his feet.

The boy: And in return you've also saved my life; thrice in fact.

Life? says Jens, as if he's never heard this mysterious word before. Yes, it was impossible to avoid it, you were lying in the snow, it's not a matter of saving, it's just getting you to your feet. Besides that, you were lying there because I didn't pay attention to you. But what I wanted to say, was thank you for what I mentioned earlier, and I apologise for my behaviour, it was shameful, having left you behind twice, but now we must part. What? exclaims the boy, thinking that perhaps the wind's howl had distorted what Jens said. Part? Yes, because this is how it's supposed to be: Jens is going in one direction, the boy in the other, that's called parting, and before that people should exchange farewells. Farewell.

Jens: I'll take your bag, of course.

The boy: I don't understand this.

Jens: I'll help you find the farm belonging to this building; you go back when the storm subsides and return The Grey to Jónas and the boat to Ágúst and Marta; take someone with you, at least over the heath. You can row over on your own, can't you?

Yes, is all the boy says, relieved not to have to go any further in this ridiculous weather, relieved not to have to spend any more time in the postman's company, though the word *company* doesn't suit Jens at all; he'll have to settle for it even if he's forced to stay one or two days on this farm, whatever farm it might be; perhaps it'll be unbearably boring but perhaps not, one never knows what awaits in unfamiliar houses, banality or adventure, perhaps bright eyes and poetry, and who cares even if it's tedious and banal, it takes more than two days of tedium to kill a man. Jens has placed both bags over his shoulders, there's something tranquil about this big man, he looks over the sheep and the one ram, which all stare as one at the two men as if expecting something imminent; something unspoken. Why? asks the boy as well, and the postman's calmness vanishes. I'm going to walk, he answers curtly, looking sternly at the boy, as if daring him either to say nothing, or to protest.

The boy: Walk; do you mean all the way to Langifjörður?

Jens: Yes.

The boy: It's a long way.

Jens: Three days; is that long?

The boy: A boat could shorten it by two days.

Jens: Two days; what's that?

The boy: Don't you need to stick to your itinerary?

Jens: I need to stay alive.

The boy, hesitantly: One boat trip shouldn't be so bad, we'll get a bigger boat and wait until the storm subsides. Every farm here has a boat.

Jens: The sea is unnecessary. We're land animals.

The boy: Then we'll just forget about the sea.

Jens: What "we"?

The boy: Oh, we two.

Jens: You're alone, I'm alone, so there's no "we" in any of this. Now go; you'll find the farm yourself, it's impossible to be with a person who talks so much.

The sheep and the ram look at them, breathe rapidly, their breath steaming. I'll follow you, says the boy, completely out of the blue and quite absurdly, because why should one follow a sea-fearing and possibly mad postman out into this storm, thread their way around fjords, cross heaths and gullies as they cover the dozens of kilometres between farms, precisely zero advantage, but numerous disadvantages. Yet for some it's natural to make decisions concerning life or death without thinking; it isn't sensible, but perhaps they're less likely to moulder away. Sensibility can be detrimental to life; it can easily suffocate it. Jens says nothing, so the boy adds, I won't be a burden, but I can't promise to keep silent, and besides, talking to you is such fun.

And then it happens.

Jens laughs. Not much, of course, and neither loudly nor long, but he laughs; the laughter is unforced but a little rusty from disuse, and the sheep immediately stop chewing their cuds; soon afterwards, around five of them spread their hind legs and urinate. The men watch them, and then it's their turn to urinate. There's a difference doing such a thing inside a house as opposed to standing half bent in miserable weather and maybe drenching oneself with urine, shaking with cold, which is so quick to slip in through unexpected gaps. Two men standing side by side, urinating, sometimes feel united; for a moment or two they have something in common and maybe say something that they would never have said out loud otherwise.

Jens: I need to think.

The boy: You need to think?

Jens: And for that, it's best to be travelling, walking.

The boy: Some people find it good to sit as they think.

Jens: I don't put much faith in such things, there's something unnatural in it; the only sensible thing is to walk, and preferably for many days.

The boy: And why do you need to think?

But then they've finished urinating, the vapid smell of urine fades almost immediately, taking with it their sympathy. That's my business, says Jens, shaking out the last drops. You're absolutely right, admits the boy, adding that he also needs to think; I don't know why I'm alive, really. Jens glances at the boy, shakes his head slightly, takes out some of their food, hands some to the boy, then shifts the postbags on his shoulders and starts for the door. Wait, says the boy, having climbed into the pen with the sheep, which huddle themselves, terrified, into one corner. What are you doing there? asks Jens impatiently, and the boy says nothing, removes the grate penning off the ram, grabs it by the horns and drags it over to the sheep, puts one of them in its place, puts the grate back in its place, goes back over to Jens with a pleased expression and giggles softly to himself when he sees the ram standing there looking extremely insulted in the midst of the sheep. Why did you do that? asks Jens, his finger on the door latch. Surprise is healthy, says the boy. They step outside and the storm snatches them.

*

Two thinking men travelling in such weather; it's no small thing, considering that one must use all one's energy just to keep going, get from one place to another without dying, which means that thinking, on top of this, and trying to come to grips with life, must be the stuff of epic. They plough their way onwards through snow and wind, two men in search of themselves; will they find the gold or just dull stones? At first they walk somewhat above the seashore, but then are forced to move lower, closer to the sea, and in some places all the way down to the beach, which can be dangerous, not because of the waves that rush cold-blue onto land, but because of the snowdrifts that have accumulated along the high banks; the tide eats its way into the drifts and leaves empty spaces, caves, to some extent, meaning many tons of snow can hang for weeks almost in thin air and collapse at the slightest disturbance. It's easy for the locals to avoid "the traps", as they call these drifts, in broad daylight and preceded by their sheep, but Jens and the boy naturally see nothing now and aren't aware of this perilous hazard. Yet Jens realises the danger when the sound of the storm fades, leaving only a peculiar silence. He stops, looks around, listens, grabs the boy's shoulder and quietly explains the danger to him: they have several tons of snow hanging over their heads; don't say a word, one word could do us in.

They're relieved to make it off the beach and stand for several moments side-by-side, as if to contemplate the bizarre fact that they're still alive, and then they keep going, pass by farms without noticing them, turf farms buried in snow, invisible in the light, let alone in a dark storm, people and animals are breathing beneath the snow, like the grass waiting for birdsong and sunshine. They walk and think. But it isn't easy for an ordinary person to control his thoughts; they can be unrulier than any sheep and run off as soon as you slacken your grip, run off and vanish in the distance or dissipate like smoke. In fact, the boy's mind is mainly filled with utter nonsense. A little image or two from his memory, events from the fishing station, Andrea laughing between him and Bárður, Pétur silent, Pétur reciting obscene verses to fight the cold as they wait over their fishing lines, Árni's friendly face, the dance steps that Guðrún took for the boy and Bárður, perhaps particularly Bárður, while in the evenings the boy felt as if he would never get to sleep due to what he thought, at the time, was love. He thinks about Bárður and it's so good that he forgets himself for a long time, the trek becomes easier, as if Bárður were right next to him, he *is* next to him, not cold and dead or sternly reproachful, but rather warm with life, and streaming from him is an energy that seems to make existence easier and removes all difficulties. The boy thinks about Bárður and misses him. He who dies never returns, we've lost him, no power in the universe is able to bring us the warmth of a vanished life, the sound of a voice, the hand movements, the touch of humour. All the details that comprise life and give it validity have vanished into eternity, vanished only to leave an open wound in the heart that time gradually transforms into a swollen scar. Yet he who dies never leaves us completely, which is a paradox that comforts and torments at once; he who dies is both near and far. You're dead, yet you're here, mutters the boy, and Bárður smiles and it's easier to walk, the cold wind jostles him, causing him partly to stumble, yet that's alright; I'm to deliver a message from them, says Bárður, they're watching you, they hope and they believe – thus you know what you should do. No, says the boy sincerely, that's precisely what I don't know and it hurts, tell me what I should do? But then there's no Bárður, the boy is just talking to the falling snow and the glacier is somewhere behind the storm, as massive as the end of all things. The snow swirls up from the ground and is whipped into their faces, if they intend to live longer than this night, they must find shelter, but where is it? Jens doesn't like the idea of digging a snow-cave, creating shelter within the enemy itself; a refuge so risky that it's little more than a death trap. They plod along, two men, two living beings, two lives in weather much too foul. The boy is tempted to rest his weight on Jens' arm; you look after him, Helga had said, and Jens replied, yes. Of what worth are words if one doesn't stand by them, of what worth is a man himself then? And who decides whether we live or die, whether we die of exposure in the snow, freeze out on the sea, perish from loneliness; for some reason Jens presses on against the storm. He's half blind from the icy shell lying over his face, yet they find a farm; it's almost completely buried in snow and has long since fallen to ruin. But it is shelter, even good shelter; they find a place to rest, have a bite to eat, the boy mutters something, recites a poem, thinks about the people who lived here, and then they shiver themselves to sleep. Sleep in the dilapidated farm. Or doze. What happened to the lives that burned here, why do all of man's hours evaporate, to be lost entirely, is there no-one who writes it

VIII

The men blink and look around. It's early morning of a spring day, but the spring light, sometimes harsh, sometimes soft with sunshine, is barely visible; it drifts down in fragments between snowflakes that the sky pours out over them. And once again they set out. They don't see the glacier but sense it; it's on their right, extending outward behind the falling snow. A glacier is of course just a gigantic mass of old snow, snowflakes many hundreds of years old, yet it changes its entire environment. Everything grows greater when the summer sun shines on it, a bit as if the countryside were blessed, and then its people would rather die than move away.

You're certain of the way? asks the boy in the first shelter, far too many hours from when they set out. They'd recovered from their stiffness, sometimes were even able to walk off the cold. Still the same precipitation, still the same wind, still the same blowing snow. Are you certain? he asks, but only to say something, really; people who talk to each other aren't quite as much at the mercy of the world. Jens stares straight ahead, silently, knocks ice from his beard, yes yes, he finally says.

The boy: It's good to know the way.

Jens: We head north-east, then north-west.

The boy: When do we turn?

Jens: In good time.

It's good to know the way, says the boy again, because it's also good to express oneself in a few direct words; no nonsense, no giddiness, just facts. He sits there next to Jens and grows from this. To be a man is to know where one is heading and not waste too many words on it. Women are attracted to such men. It's just the way it is. And then of course he starts thinking of Ragnheiður, there's nothing he can do about it, yet she's the daughter of Friðrik and that can't be good, not at all. Good that she's going to sail to Copenhagen and lose herself amidst the towers and people, with her cold eyes. With her body that's a taut string, with her firm breasts. But he had never been kissed. And then she kissed him. With moist, soft lips.

How is it possible to forget that?

If he could only touch her breasts; something must happen when a man touches what must never be seen.

He stares into nothing, silently. It's good to feel one's member rise in bitter cold, in a dark storm. It warms a person up a bit. One forgets oneself. And then it isn't good any longer; in fact it's just shameful. Nor is it good to say nothing; the world isn't as interesting, and in the silence there's a risk that one will start to think of what is best not to think of. Do you know any poems? he asks. No, says Jens, without looking up. Should we sing, then? No. But you must know some poems, maybe by Bjarni, a man like you . . . No, says Jens. Jónas?[8] No. Then shouldn't we talk a bit? No. Why not? Why, then? Well, we're two men out in a storm far from human habitation, having hiked under difficult conditions for twenty-six or twenty-eight hours, and still with a long way to go. Jens says nothing. And one feels less lonely. Jens says nothing. Are you thinking? I'm resting. Have you thought a lot? Thought, for what? You said you needed to think, remember, and I . . . Think, yes, not talk. They go together sometimes. Hardly. Reinforce each other. No. What's her name? Who? The woman. What woman? The one you're thinking of. Who says it's a woman? So it's a man? You're tiring. I mean, you want to walk for days and days in storms and snow in order to think; it must be some woman! Jens is silent. Well then, says the boy, I'll just recite a few poems to myself, forgive me if I recite them out loud, I just find it better, I feel the words better that way. What's the point of that? asks Jens grumpily, but the boy says nothing and starts reciting, there within the storm and snow, next to a man who doesn't like words, two poems by Jónas, two by Steingrímur Thorsteinsson, two by Kristján Fjallaskáld,[9] he recites them well and Jens doesn't protest, he simply steps back and looks away, as if to escape. And then, after numerous words about blossoms, love, regret, clarity and

8. Bjarni is the poet Bjarni Thorarensen (1786–1841); Jónas is the poet Jónas Hall-grímsson (1807–1845); both were chief proponents of Romanticism in Iceland.

9. Steingrímur Thorsteinsson (1831–1913), was rector of the Learned School in Reyk-javík and a great translator, having translated, among other works, *One Thousand and One Nights* and fairy tales by Hans Christian Andersen. Kristján Jónsson Fjallaskáld ("poet of the mountains"; 1842–1869) is a typical representative of a late-Romantic poet in Iceland.

darkness, the boy recites a poem by Ólöf from Hlaðir. Old books say that it's a bad omen to recite poems by women during storms. Never for love in return I ask, says the boy, laying his icy mitten over his weather-beaten heart, and:

> Never for love in return I ask,
> – with questions and hope young minds are rife –
> the daily struggle, the laborious tasks
> Have made me a crone; have wrung out my life.
>
> Desire a profound abyss does conceal,
> In silence and sound you are told.
> Not once have I opened my hand to reveal
> Withered flowers; never proffered you lips pale and cold.
>
> For you my love shall never take end,
> Without it my life would be death.
> Nor God nor man my heart could mend,
> Deprived of its wealth, its breath.[10]

10. Originally from Ólöf's second volume of poetry, also entitled *Several Ditties* (*Nokkur Smákvæði*; Bókaverzlun Odds Björnssonar: Akureyri, 1913).

he has to bring to his knees, in a fight to the death. He attacks the storm, which surrounds him with howling, mocking laughter. It laughs mockingly at him, Jens Guðjónsson, the man, his life, his weaknesses and betrayals. Nor God nor man my heart could mend, deprived of its wealth, its breath. Stop here on your way back, Salvör had said to him before he set out for the heath a week ago, they stood outside the farm, both lacking sleep; the bags under her eyes could be seen well in the hard light, the knives of time, the knives of life. Yes, he had said, of course. Are you going to think of me? Yes. When? Always. Always, that's a beautiful word, and what will you do when you return? I'll kiss you, he said, and set out for the heath. Never for love in return I ask. I loved my husband, she said once as they lay together, that beast. You were young, said Jens. Yes, but isn't it strange that I could love such a man; he beat me but I still loved him, until I started to hate him. I recall him once being handsome and kind, he just wasn't strong enough for life, it made him a beast and a wretch. I thought that I would never love again, she said in the darkness of the family room, and they were likely both grateful for the darkness, it's easier to speak such words in darkness, to hear them, and to receive them. Of course Jens said nothing, but wrapped his arms around her, let his arms do the talking. You know that I love you, she said, but shut his mouth with a kiss, before he could say anything. But let it be known to all that I still love you, that without this love my life would be death; what will you do when you return, I'll kiss you. Did she wish to hear a different reply? Because one kiss, what is that? Wasn't she asking for one life, wasn't she

234

asking for everything that he can give, all his days, all his strength, all his weakness – and he asked for one kiss! Jens struggles onwards and the storm is howling, mocking laughter, because despite his wanting to think only of Salvör and nothing but her, of her voice, of the kisses, of the hollow of her neck, of her long legs, of her warmth, he also thinks of the housemaid in Vík, Jakobína; he can't help it. He wasn't sleeping when she rubbed his cold legs, he was well awake yet didn't stop her, even though her hand crept up and touched what she absolutely must not touch; he couldn't stop her, didn't want to stop her.

Those who betray their country and king in war are shot, but what are we to do with those who betray themselves, betray life itself?

Why has he never asked Salvör to come with him, seriously, determinedly, instead of settling for saying it almost nonchalantly, in the summer light, and accepting half an answer? What is he afraid of, his weakness? That he isn't a whit better than the beast, her husband? And does she fear the same, that he's weak and will therefore end up like her husband? Beat her, disgrace her. Perhaps I'm as damaged as that devil, thinks Jens, tramping frenziedly through the drifts; he opens his mouth and screams.

Screams loudly, no doubt; it resounds within him, he trembles beneath this scream, but the boy doesn't hear it, he only hears the wind, has long since lost Jens, that devil vanished into the storm, left him alone once more, damned crazy bastard, this postman, there must be something wrong with my head to want to keep chasing him instead of turning back, as he proposed. The boy presses on, tumbles over twice, lets himself be tempted just as often to shout out for the crazed postman but only the wind replies; he sinks, once slides down a slope, a long distance, has no idea where he is when he finally stops, hasn't the slightest idea which direction is most sensible and for that reason heads nowhere, really, just rambles on, tilts his head, tries to protect his eyes as he glances in every direction, peers between snowflakes yet naturally sees nothing but snow. Damned bastard, he thinks; he curses Jens but soon gives up doing so, doesn't have the energy for it, simply goes on. Well, he doesn't exactly go on, it's not as good as that; he wanders, rather, alone in the world, as the wind shakes him, jostles him. They were heading uphill when he lost Jens, had been doing so for quite some time and therefore it's likely safest to keep doing so. But the higher that he goes, the more difficult the going becomes. Sometimes he's stuck, sunk in snow up to his arms, even; takes a long time to free himself and loses precious, dwindling energy. Then he slides downwards, a long distance, and doesn't dare go back up, in fact descends even further yet tries to keep heading north-west, what he thinks is north-west. Then he gives up on this as well and thinks only about staying alive, which is also a splendid goal. He's driven off course by the wind, seeks out the easiest paths, avoids snowdrifts, retreats when he starts sinking in snow, tries elsewhere, but then can do no more, stumbles, sinks to his knees and is unable to stand up again. Yet he crawls on for a bit, tries to find cover and finds it, maybe not cover, not exactly, yet someplace not completely exposed; and there he lies down. It's splendid.

The wind rages above him, but the boy no longer cares.

Yet it's extremely lonely here, as if he were alone in the world and everyone has died a second time, everything good is dead, all hope is withered. He also feels something extending from the middle of his heart up his neck, it's a column of tears, it reaches that high now and wants to go higher, wants out, it lifts itself and fills his chest cavity, fills his neck. To comfort himself, he starts humming a lullaby from the depths of his childhood, an old folk song, an extremely simple and fragile tune with four verses that contain the dreams and solace of a thousand years. His parents often hummed these verses to him, half under their breath, and the melancholy melodies followed him into sleep and down into his dreams. He hums to himself, he hums and sends the fragile melody out into the storm, hums until it is carried to his mother, who takes it in her hands, follows it all the way to him, so this is where you are, my dear, she says, lifts him lightly and takes him with her; whither he doesn't know, hopefully just out of this storm. And away from this loneliness called life.

X

One might think you had someone looking after you, says Jens, who emerged suddenly from the storm and put the boy on his feet, woke him, shook him; don't sleep. Yes; it's so good. That's right, but you won't wake up again. And why should I do that? asks the boy, but Jens says nothing, doesn't need to, the boy was awake and could feel the storm again, the cold, and his mother was gone.

Jens is standing over him, his face so icy that he looks much more like a messenger from Hell than a man. I thought it was hot there, says Jens. No, Hell is cold, it's a maze of ice. Where did you get that? I don't know; where did you get the idea that Hell is hot? Isn't it in the Bible? Anyhow, the Bible wasn't written here in Iceland, says the boy, no, that's right, replies Jens, before adding, there's someone looking after you. What do you mean? asks the boy, slightly cross at having to return to the cold and life, the tranquillity was so sweet and his mother was with him.

Yes, Jens had left the boy behind, had simply trudged on without caring a whit for anything, but came to his senses high up the mountainside, where he found himself alone. You went so fast; I tried shouting. I failed, says Jens, directly. You did? I should have taken care of you, I promised, and even though I promised nothing, no-one leaves someone behind in such weather. You just went too fast for me; that's not failing. I left you behind, once again, that's how it was. Well, why then? Jens doesn't reply, his anger had left him when he was on the mountainside, the boy gone. It wasn't good to discover this; it prompted self-contempt. Hardly possible to find a person in such weather; hopeless, rather. But it's also hopeless to live in this country, yet here we've lingered for a thousand years. Jens took out the postal horn and blew, started back and blew several times. Reckoned that the boy had soon given in to the wind and steepness, searched with that in mind, yet was on the verge of giving up, it was so meaningless, he started to tire, lose his sense of direction, his energy dwindled fast, but then he spied a shape ahead. Thought it was the boy, shouted, headed towards it, cursed when the shape seemed to retreat, and quickly at that, he could barely keep up but then nearly fell over the boy, sleeping in the snow.

Was I sleeping?

Like a baby.

Damn.

Yes.

A shape? the boy asks, taking the frozen blood pudding that Jens hands him, what did it look like?

Jens: Didn't see.

The boy: What's it doing here?

Jens: It was a mirage; it was just the weather.

The boy: Was it a person, do you think?

239

Jens: A mirage, I said.

The boy: That led you to me?

Jens: I shouldn't have mentioned it.

The boy: Must have been a person; I wonder if it was, you know, living?

Jens: Aren't you done with your blood pudding?

The boy: Jens, isn't there damned little likelihood that it was living?

Jens: Dead people don't meander about. No likelihood of that at all.

The boy: I don't know where we are, except that we're far from everything living, somewhere far up in the mountains, in this god-awful weather, it's been dark and stormy for days, meaning no-one's out and about, yet someone appears before you and leads you, shows you to me, and vanishes. Which is strange, whether it was a living person or a dead one. And the dead seldom want to save lives, rather the opposite; they call the living to themselves. So what is this shape doing, and it just disappeared, do you see it now, how does it look? The boy glances around, gnaws at the blood pudding, Jens sits on his haunches, hardly anything else is possible in this little shelter that's almost no shelter, the wind rocks him like a pebble on the beach, he shakes his head.

The boy: Does that mean no?

Jens: If you wish.

The boy: And no to what, precisely?

Jens: Do you need to talk about everything?

The boy: No.

Jens: That's not what I hear.

The boy: I don't talk so much. But sometimes one needs to ponder things, isn't that so?

Jens: Why?

The boy: Oh, to come to a conclusion, I suppose. You know, two people together, utterly lost in a dark storm, appearing to them is a ghost that seems to want to save lives; isn't that enough reason to talk to each other?

Jens: It's time to keep going, and you don't do that in words.

Words are fine, says the boy, insulted; they help us to live.

Jens: I've missed that; finish your blood pudding, we're leaving.

The boy: Some words bring us happiness.

Jens: Of all people, I had to end up with you.

The boy: And some bring us unhappiness. Truth to tell, I think that words are the seventh wonder of the world.

Jens: You must have been beaten at some point.

The boy: He who beats another person usually does it to cover over his own paltriness and lack of talent.

Jens: Now we're leaving. Unless you're determined to chat us to death.

No, the boy didn't want to do that. But he needs to unburden himself of a few things before they continue, out into the unknown, the tempest. What do you mean? That I need to defecate. Defecate? You need to shit, shit is shit and fancy words don't change that. But they change you, says the boy, and starts doing what they call by so many different names, but no matter what words are used it isn't at all cosy in this damned cold, blowing snow and wind. The boy tries to bare as little as possible of his flesh, it goes badly, his clothes are stiff with frost, his fingers are benumbed with cold, they curl up with numbness as soon as he takes off his mittens, gasps for breath when he bares his bottom and feels the cold wind. A sudden gust of wind knocks him down, he lies there with his pants around his ankles and Jens laughs. The boy scrambles to his feet, props himself up better, leans into the wind, tries to hurry to finish, if the wind were to die suddenly, as is its wont, the boy would fall backwards, even with shit sticking halfway out and then Jens would laugh himself all the way to Hell, but hopefully not back, thinks the boy sullenly and finally manages to squeeze it all out, big, hard as rock, then hikes up his pants as quickly as he can.

The wind is transparent, it's just air in motion, air that's in a hurry, without having any place to go. It blows without visible reason. It thus makes it damned hard to hold one's course and yet be forced in the end to give in to this transparent phenomenon, to have a purpose yet be forced to yield to purposelessness. The wind, now blowing slightly to the west, drives them slowly but surely to the north, far into the mountains. The boy thinks once, we're heading north, not north-west, but prefers not to pursue it, doesn't have the strength for it, he couldn't care less where they go, is too tired to have an opinion on it, just follows Jens, places his trust in this man who doesn't like words. And Jens tries to keep walking with the wind, find easier ways for them, though nothing's easy here and they have only two choices, difficult or unconquerable. He chooses the former, hasn't enough confidence in the boy for anything else, he himself has grown apathetic, doesn't care which way, it's so ridiculous to race to deliver the post at a determined time, ridiculous to take punctuality and a grudge against one man over life itself. What matters is just to keep going, but precisely where is irrelevant, just make it out of this alive, find shelter and wait out the storm's fury and then deliver the post without endangering one's life, and the boy's. Make it home, where Halla has begun to expect him and asks their father thirty times a day, isn't Jens going to come? But first he has to stop at Salvör's and take the step, say what needs to be said, at some point one likely has to say something, open oneself, open one's heart, otherwise one might lose one's life, forfeit happiness and condemn oneself to loneliness. But what should he say; and is he able? Why must everything be so complicated between people? he thinks, tramping onwards; the cold assaults them, they're completely lost, no doubt, but it doesn't matter. Several times he thinks he sees a shape appear and he follows it, even though it means changing direction slightly; he does this almost automatically, what does it matter if it's a dead person, the living haven't proven to be particularly good to him, existence is too dingy and why not place his trust in the dead, what do they gain by betraying life? And the shape leads them to shelter. Good shelter. The best shelter of the journey and it's so good to get out of the wind and the chilling, blowing snow that they feel emotional, awkwardly; they look at each other, white and weather-beaten, Jens is no longer able to move his head, his beard is frozen fast to his clothing, frozen over his mouth, they look at each other and think, what a first-rate fellow!

What a bunch of bollocks, thinks Jens to himself, before endeavouring to free himself from his armour of frost.

They sit close together, feeling each other's presence quite well, so well that it should be uncomfortable, and completely intolerable for Jens, to be so close to another man. Yet he doesn't move and the boy finds that just fine, he wrapped his arms around this big man in a bed on Vetrarströnd, and life seeks out life, it's natural and for that reason he presses closer to Jens, like a puppy. Jens looks at him; are you cold? he asks, not overly harshly, but just a little bit, and the boy moves away. It was wrong of me to leave you behind, says Jens, when the boy has moved far enough away from him. You came back. Little excuse if you'd died. Again they fall silent, the boy dares not speak for fear of ruining the good that they unexpectedly share, and then Jens says, I've never told anyone. What? says the boy, almost frightened by this unexpected closeness and not certain that he wants to hear more.

Jens: I've seen and heard things, and it's caused me particular concern. I've been on heaths and seen things. And heard things. I've seen mountains in July nights and they've been like sleeping birds. And then I've heard them sing. But mountains don't sing; it's ridiculous.

The boy dares not look at Jens, says nothing until he's certain that nothing more is to come from the postman for the moment, then says hesitantly, I've also heard them sing, the mountains. I was afraid of that, says Jens. Again, silence. Finally: Why were you afraid of that? It isn't healthy to hear mountains sing; they aren't birds, birds are small, they fly, mountains are huge and don't fly.

in this blinding, bone-chilling storm, cold, thirsty, hungry, and preferably never lose sight of this big man who seems inexhaustible, has heard the mountains sing like birds, allowed the boy to sit close to him and uttered these beautiful things, so strange coming from his mouth, but shortly afterwards turned a bit savage and now never looks back to see whether the boy is still there, just presses on, looks neither right nor left, perhaps knows where they're heading, perhaps not, but while they move they're alive, which is really something in this Hell. But what hour is it?

Will evening come, night and possibly morning again?

Or does time press on in such heavy weather, does it get any further than the men, isn't time roaming around lost as well, and where will they end up then? Behind the world, no doubt, thinks the boy, where storms never subside, where it never warms up and never stops snowing. Twice he tries eating snow to quench his thirst but becomes even thirstier, is even tempted into talking to himself and reciting lines of poetry, because there come moments in a man's life when he's unable to orient himself except through particular lines of poetry, in some incomprehensible manner some of them have the essential in their depths, understanding itself, the way itself, contentment itself, even though the poet himself may have been lost and in the hands of trolls all his miserable life. But the lines crumble into pieces on his frostbitten lips, crumble into pieces in his mind, as well, he can't keep his thoughts straight, he thinks about Andrea and she transforms into lines from *Paradise Lost* that transform into Kolbeinn's munching mouth at the breakfast table and the skipper transforms into a raven waddling around the farm where the boy lived more or less like an outsider after his father drowned and the raven transformed into Geirþrúður's hair that transformed into a wet dream about Ragnheiður who transformed into dying mice.

And Jens is gone once more.

Swallowed up by the weather and the boy is alone. Once again he forgets himself, loses himself in a poem and in the meantime Jens disappears.

He stops, ceases to struggle onwards and stands still, forces himself to stand, though the temptation simply to sink is so alluring; he stands still and shuts his eyes. Now I shut my eyes, and if I'm meant to live, he thinks optimistically, then Jens will be standing before me when I reopen them. He stands with his legs spread wide so as not to be blown over and it's incredibly good to have his eyes shut, as if he's made it to unexpected shelter. The wind is certainly still blowing coldly against him yet it's no longer of any concern to him. It has grown distant, it's no longer threatening. It would be too easy, perilously easy to sleep like this; open your eyes, he commands himself, and that's what he does. Opens his eyes to see a woman standing before him, just an arm's length between them. Rather tall, erect, her head bare and her long, dark hair blowing over and from her stern face, her dead eyes penetrate his skull and drill themselves into the centre of his mind. Then she turns and walks away, against the wind, and he follows. Follows her without thinking. He cannot resist, dares nothing else. Follows a dead woman with ice-cold eyes, doesn't take his living eyes off her as she moves effortlessly through the storm. Dares not blink for fear that she'll disappear or what's worse, turn back and look at him like that, dig herself into his skull with her ice-cold eyes, he's still cold from the first time. But it simply isn't possible to keep his eyes open without blinking, it's impossible to stare into this storm without occasionally looking away, and he does so, once. Blinks, looks quickly away, then looks back and the woman has merged with Jens, who presses on ahead of him.

A long time has passed since they last huddled under cover, finished their food and could breathe decently, untroubled by the storm; how long it was in hours the boy doesn't know, but in his body, every cell, he feels that it's been far too long. This is why he's so enormously relieved and thankful when Jens finally stops in a sheltered spot that he can imagine hugging the postman, which of course he doesn't do; one doesn't hug a man like Jens, just not at all, never. But the space is so narrow that they have to turn towards each other, face each other standing close together, like close friends, are forced to do so if they want to avoid having snow blow into their faces. If the Devil created anything in this world, apart from money, it's blowing snow in the mountains. You're alive, declares Jens, or rather, mumbles something along those lines, his beard so frozen that he finds it difficult to speak. I suppose, replies the boy, just as unclearly due to his cold-benumbed facial muscles, trembling from the cold and awkward affection, before asking, do you think she's leading us to Hell and the end of the world?, asking in some sense to settle himself down, prevent himself from suffering the shame of hugging Jens. What,

248

who? asks Jens after struggling with the ice in his beard for some time.

The boy: The woman we've been following.

Jens: What exactly are you talking about? The boy watches the postman scrape icicles from his beard; Jens' expression is so blank that it's off-putting, his grey eyes are stern and ice-cold; I would rather cut off my arms than hug this bastard, thinks the boy, suddenly feeling disgust well up within him, absolutely unbridled, violent, but also bracing, and downright liberating, you damned dickhead, he says. Jens continues scraping with the dull knife he'd taken out.

The boy: Did you hear what I said?!

Jens, scraping: What?

The boy, trying to raise his voice, though it's difficult, numb as it is, and besides, everything sounds feeble in this wind: You're a damned dickhead, I said! A damned prick, a bleeding dickhead!

Yes, yes, is all the postman says, as if the boy were asserting something so obvious that reacting to it wouldn't be worth the bother. For several moments disgust and hatred seethe in the boy, his arms twitch as if in preparation to strike, but then it all fades away, it's so useless to hate in such weather, in this place. I meant the woman, he then says, almost calmly. What woman? asks the postman, without putting away the knife.

The boy: Oh, the one we're following, naturally; have you seen anyone else, there aren't exactly a lot of people here.

A woman, says Jens, letting the knife sink; a woman, he repeats, as if trying to remember something.

249

The boy: Are you going to insist that you haven't seen her, I mean it, the shape, which is in fact a woman?

Jens starts scraping again: The shape, yes. Hard to say under these conditions what one sees and what one thinks one sees.

The boy: One sees what one sees.

Jens: You don't know much.

The boy: No, but I have good eyes, and a poorly dressed, bare-headed woman here in this hell-hole can't easily be ignored.

Jens: Tired men, cold, hungry, and jaded, see a lot of things. I've got lost with others and have had to hold them down by force so they don't rush out into the storm after some person they think they see.

The boy: Yes, dead people, ghosts, I mean, try sometimes to lure the living. I've read stories and anecdotes about it.

Jens: The only ghosts that I've seen are living people.

The boy: So you didn't see her?

Jens: I'm not always sure of what I see.

The boy: But we've been following her for a long time.

Jens: I know nothing about that. I saw a shape before; that's right, twice, thrice, maybe it was a boulder, I find that quite likely. Do you see anything now?

The boy, peering out into the storm: No, not now.

Jens: There you have it.

The boy: But always now and then! Unclearly, of course; it's impossible to see in this weather.

Jens: What did I say?

The boy: But I saw her very well when I lost you.

Jens: Did you lose me again?

The boy: I shut my eyes, opened them, and she was just standing right in front of me, not quite as close as you now, yet not much more than an arm-length away.

Jens: Did you lose me?

The boy: What, yes, for a while. And then all of a sudden she was standing before me, signalling me, or I think she did, and then walked off. I followed and that's how I found you. You didn't see her?

Jens: You can't trust anything in this weather. It mixes you up.

The boy: I saw her; that wasn't just bollocks.

Jens: If you say so.

The boy: And she must be dead.

Jens: If you say so.

The boy: What's a dead woman doing up here in the mountains, and what does she want with us? I mean, when have the dead wanted to help the living, help them live, I mean? I saw her, just as clearly as I see you now. She has the coldest eyes that I've ever seen, and I've seen a lot of different eyes; I've looked in dead eyes and hers were much colder. Maybe she's death itself!

Jens: Lord, how you can talk.

They lean into the shelter, an ice-covered boulder. Try automatically to move far apart, but then the snow hits their faces like cold, groping hands. If they're going to stand here, under cover of this damned rock, they need to move closer to each other than they can bear. Feel each other's breath; the boy sees every single vein above the postman's beard, little red veins, tiny, like red brooks beneath a veil of frost. It's painful to stand so close to another man. Very painful. Physically painful. As if they need to sacrifice something to do so, and it stings and irritates. Two men whom malicious fate bound together and cast into a nonsensical journey. You cross two difficult heaths, Helga had said, otherwise it's just boat trips and they're your responsibility; on the other hand, trust to Jens on land. Right. Trust this man who tried to leave him behind and now stares at him like an enraged bull. The boy knows such men far too well; they're rigid, inflexible, so rigid that they shut out all softness, all play, all carelessness, so rigid and inflexible that they try instinctively to subjugate their environment. So rigid that they spoil life. So rigid that they kill.

The boy: I don't give a shit about your manliness. Geirþrúður was right.

Jens: Do you think we're at the end of the world?

The boy: Whoever's in your company has come to the end of the world.

Jens: What do you mean?

The boy: Where the Hell are we?

Jens: Listen.

The boy: Listen, to what, the weather and your panting?

Jens: Listen. And what do you hear?

The boy: The damned storm, what else?!

No, says Jens, listen in this direction, and he points to what the boy imagines is north. Hell and the end of the world, he mutters to himself; he pushes his cap off his ear and listens, tilts his head better and listens. At first hears only the moaning, haunted wind, the whistling of the snow, but just as he starts to pull his cap down over his cooling ear, he discerns something distant, behind all this. At first vaguely, like a suspicion, but it grows as he catches it – a low, heavy booming. He hurries to pull his cap over his ear.

Jens: It's the Polar Sea.

The boy: The Polar Sea?

Jens: But you can call it the end of the world and death. Words have no influence on the sea.

The boy: We're off course; how bleeding far we've veered off course!

They tilt their heads away from each other; somewhere out there the sea echoes off sheer cliff walls. Shouldn't we turn around? blurts out the boy, a growing knot of fear in his gut. Of course, if you're so tired of life, says Jens.

The boy: Damn it.

Jens: Are you scared?

The boy: Damn it all to Hell!

Jens: It's just the sea. You've been on the sea.

The boy, shaking his fist at the postman: I don't give a shit about your manliness! Whoever doesn't fear this sound is downright stupid. Whoever isn't afraid of walking off a precipice in such weather is a stupid numbskull. A man with less imagination than an earthworm. I shit at your manliness, shit at it. Now I know what the priest's wife meant when she said that men were irresponsible, when she said that it was the women and children who constantly had to bear the consequences. She meant that manliness wasn't just ridiculous, but also dangerous, because it thinks only of itself, about looking good; that's what matters to you: appearing strong, courageous, fearless, making a show; to look good in the end matters more to you than life itself!

Jens has straightened up, and he towers over the boy: Manliness means daring. Never giving up. And never bending!

The boy: Sometimes men like you are just cowardly, they don't dare stop. My father drowned in horrendous weather; they went to sea despite the bad outlook, while most others stayed at home. Pétur knew the foreman. A great man, he said, feared nothing, ever. You should have seen Pétur's eyes when he talked about that foreman, should have seen how they lit up when he described the courage of the man who dared not yield to a storm, dared not yield to danger. All six of them perished. And do you know how many children lost their fathers? How many families were broken up because of the foreman's manliness? How many needed to be raised on farms here and there and never again saw anyone who mattered because they all died? To think that you're left alone in this bloody world because the foreman was so bloody manly. This goddamned manliness of yours suffocates everything that's good and sensitive and beautiful, it kills life itself and I shit on your damned manliness, shit an entire dung heap on it. Now I'm turning back; I'm going no further!

The boy shouts these last words. Spittle flies from his mouth onto Jens, lands on his nose and freezes instantaneously. Jens can't be budged; he just absorbs all these words, this sputtering, before saying calmly, you're absolutely not turning back. I certainly am, says the boy loudly, so angry that he desperately wants to hit the postman. There, he says, pointing out into the storm, in the direction of the low sound, is nothing but death, and I'm planning on living a bit longer, I have some unfinished business, goodbye and let go of me and may the Devil take you and gobble you up!

Jens has grabbed the boy by the arm: He'll take me sooner or later, but you'll be killed if you turn back.

The boy: Life or death, what does it matter to you?

Jens: You do nothing but ask questions. Are you always like this, forever asking; do you think there are any answers?

The boy: Let go of me, or I'll hit you.

You can't, says Jens, and we're going north, towards the end of the world, if you want to call it that. I'm not planning on dying. Just so you know. Though it's none of your business. My father is old and can't live without me. No more than Halla. They need me and would both be dependent on the parish if I weren't to return. They would be placed with strangers, and not in the same location. You don't know how Halla is. Haven't the slightest idea. Everything becomes better in her presence, though she's just a poor wretch who pisses and shits herself when she isn't looked after. In some places people like her are tied up like dogs out in front of the farmhouse or shut into cubbyholes and tossed food, just some scraps. She would be filthy and no-one would brush her hair. Father brushes her hair every morning and she closes her eyes, you've never seen that. When is Jens coming? she would ask the first few months, many times a day, so often that people would get tired of it and kick her. And you can't even bristle at her before she starts crying. Then she'd stop asking for me, and only because she would have forgotten me, forgotten our father, forgotten everything, and then she'd believe that her life was supposed to be so, and had always been so, tied up out front, shut into a cubbyhole, filthy and beaten. You can do what you want and what you feel is right. I'm heading into the wind, to the north. If you want to live, follow me; I'd highly recommend it. The only thing that I know how to do properly is to survive storms far from humankind. Which path do you choose?

XI

Life is so varied it's absurd, incongruous, beyond most words; it's much more sensible to whistle a few random, amusing notes than to try to describe it in words.

First, Jens lets it all out, telling of things dear to his heart, telling of his fears, of what drives him, and all the anger is sucked out of the boy. Then Jens says, maybe we're nearing a bay, where we'll find a cottage. A house to shelter us? asks the boy doubtfully, and they step out from the cover of the boulder, head into the storm, the malicious wind, the bitterly cold, blowing snow, the boy is blown two or three metres before he regains his balance, nearly losing Jens again.

They head north. Stumble onwards and see nothing, particularly not the woman who is perhaps no woman but rather a hallucination conjured by fatigue, hunger, and thirst. Jens is right; a man's mind is mysterious, more mysterious than the deep sea, and it's impossible to say what it can invent. Of course the boy saw no dead woman! Dead people don't ramble around the mountains, neither in summer sunshine nor in merciless winter, though of course it should be spring now, except that here in Iceland there's never any spring, strictly speaking; we don't know that pleasure, it's winter and then comes reluctant summer; there's nothing in between. Dead people don't go anywhere, they just lie still in the ground, their flesh rots, their bones turn to dust and soil, and over time become fertiliser for vegetation that drinks in sunshine and rain and enlivens existence. Thus everything has its purpose, or we try at times to convince ourselves of this. The land starts to decline; it slopes downward. The thundering of the Polar Sea turns into a nearby scream; damn it, shouts the boy, but Jens continues marching towards the sound, which amplifies; condemned souls must make such a sound, thinks the boy, and who knows, maybe most of the dead vanish into the sea and scream there over a thousand years for solace or oblivion. They feel the dampness of the cold sea and a chill comes over Jens, as if the cold and fear have momentarily spread through his bones. He stops, so abruptly that the boy runs into him and for a moment they stand on the slope, seized with uncertainty about what comes next, fearful of the thundering, but then Jens goes on, and shortly afterwards they spy the outline of a house.

A farm! cries the boy, grabbing the icy postman; a farm, damn it, he croaks, bursting out laughing and spreading his hands. A farm that is of course buried in snow, yet not like the farm where the farmer is afraid of words, a woman covets books and a little girl coughs so forcefully that her life hangs by a thin thread; how must she be feeling now, and I wonder if they've covered the sheet of paper with drawings, verses, words, and taken it out many times a day to look it all over; will the sheet even go with one of them and be examined over a long period of time, decades, when nearly everyone is dead, examined by decrepit eyes, wept over, laughed at, missed and remembered?

This farm, rising from the snow, half blind and weather-beaten, is seldom entirely buried; the wind blows so strongly here that even the greatest snowdrifts of winter don't manage to submerge the house completely. But where's the dratted door?! shouts the boy after they search fruitlessly for something resembling a door, making it very difficult to enter the farm. I don't know! shouts Jens in return, but then they hear the insistent barking of a dog, followed by the sound of a high-pitched human voice calling out hellooo, who goes there? Jens bellows something in return as they struggle towards the voice and the barking; the voice within calls out again, a bit louder, or closer, less noticeably thin, have you come alive or dead – shut up, Nellemann! The barking stops and Jens shouts back, half stuck in a drift, the snow unbearably soft and very difficult to walk through closest to the house; damn it, we're dead if we don't find the bloody door!

A man awaits them in the doorway, bearded, with dishevelled hair that has started to thin. He retreats into the passageway when they come, when they more or less fall in; *shut up*! he snaps curtly at the dog, which had started barking again; it stops but then growls softly, a large animal with a dark coat. Who are you? asks the man, regarding the two, who try to stand upright in the narrow, murky passageway, giddy after escaping the storm so suddenly, so white with snow and frost that they hardly appear human. Jens shakes himself and words trickle from him as he catches his breath, Jens . . . postman, I am . . . the postman. The boy slumps against the earthen wall, so exhausted that he sees stars. I could have expected anything but a visit from the postman, says the man; Bjarni, he adds, farmer here at Nes, and then grabs the dog's snout gently yet firmly, and it stops growling and retreats into the passageway.

Bjarni shows them into the family room, where the household is waiting for them, many curious eyes. A little stove in the middle of the room; you need to get out of these clothes, says Bjarni, and the boy starts pulling off his frozen clothing, weakly. Jens hesitates, perhaps hoping for assistance; pulling off one's clothing is women's work, because it's always been that way; men come home jaded, wet, cold from the sea or the fields, plunk down onto their bunks and the women pull their clothes off and take care of them as the men rest, dry the clothing as they sleep, they go to bed late but wake before everyone else, prepare and serve while the men sleep, while they read, learn to write, while they educate themselves and gain the upper hand, power invariably engenders injustice and although life might be beautiful, humans are imperfect. You'll fall ill if you don't take off your clothes, says Bjarni, his voice deep, not thin, as it sounded from out in the storm that howls over the house. They stand there shivering in their homespun clothing next to the stove and for the first time have a proper look around. The dog watches them from a shadowy corner, its fierceness having faded; its tail moves slightly when the boy looks towards it. Four children stare at the visitors; two boys, two girls, the youngest hardly more than two years old, the oldest an eleven- or twelve-year-old girl who quickly goes out and into the kitchen. A big, bullish man sits with the youngest child on his knees; he has thick lips, a broad face and small eyes. He puts down the child and stands up straight, nearly reaching the ceiling, steps over to the visitors, two steps and he's there, extends his big hand, Hjalti, farmhand here. He and Jens shake hands, so large and hefty that the family room is too small for them. The stove doesn't provide much heat, yet some, and at times *some* is downright magnificent, making the difference between the bearable and the unbearable. The visitors rub their hands, keep themselves near the warmth, try to expel the deepest chills from their bodies before pulling out extra clothing from their bags, cold and damp yet better than nothing. The youngest child crawls along the earthen floor, keeping itself far away from the strangers, crawls quickly over to the dog and cuddles up next to it. The animal stands to position itself better, licks the child's face and then curls up around it. Soon you'll be having seabirds and coffee, says Bjarni, needing to raise his voice slightly to be heard above the moaning of the wind, and then a pile of rags on one of the bunks moves and an old woman sits up on her elbow, her head shrivelled by age, her face so covered with white hair that it appears mouldy. Coffee, she says shrilly. Yes, you'll have coffee, mother, Bjarni shouts at her before she lies back down, changes back into a raggedy pile.

They're served salted seabird and gobble it down, gulp their thin coffee along with it, try as much as they can to restrain themselves, maintain some semblance of manners, the girl makes trip after trip outside for snow to turn to water. They sit side by side, half hunched over their food and trembling with cold, relieved that the sound of the storm fills the silence, the household doesn't take their eyes off them, follows along with every bite, every sip, except for the old woman, who lay back down after Bjarni helped the girl pour a few mouthfuls of coffee into her, a few mouthfuls that ran as much down her chin as into her, before she lay back half whimpering with bliss and sank into the silence and fog of old age. We haven't had visitors here for fifteen weeks, says Bjarni finally, after they've come a long way with the bird, so salty that its rancidness can hardly be tasted; sixteen, grunts Hjalti. Yes, says Bjarni, fifteen or sixteen, what does one week matter? But the postman has *never* come here, he adds, after a long silence. And to tell the truth I don't understand how you two managed to come here, and even less, why. The Devil has kicked them here, says Hjalti, and then he laughs, opening his mouth wide, revealing his bare gums and brown teeth. The old woman chirps; Bjarni looks alternately at his mother and Hjalti with an impenetrable expression. We got caught in a storm, says Jens, and lost each other. I got lost, says the boy, and went far off course; he found me in time, just in time. There weren't many options under the circumstances, says Jens, it's tiring to travel long distances against a storm, uncertain of the route. Yes, says the boy, and then . . . but he shuts up when he sees Jens' expression.

Bjarni: Yes?

The children and farmhand all stare at them, except for the youngest child, who sleeps cuddled up to the dog. The boy and Jens exchange a brief glance, and then look aside – it's as if they notice for the first time now, and both at once, the obvious absence of the housemother.

Bjarni: And then what?

Jens straightens up, suddenly becoming twice as big as the boy. This lad here thinks that a woman came to us deep in the mountains and led us here.

The boy, obstinately: I don't think it; she saved me. It isn't any more complicated than that. And led us here.

Bjarni clears his throat; a woman, says he, that's peculiar, how did she look? Well, says the boy; tall, I would say, yes, surely tall and with bright, dark eyes and dark hair, long, slender, yes . . . and . . . he scratches his head through his dirty, greasy hair, too preoccupied with remembering the woman's face to sense the odd, if not unbearable atmosphere in the sitting room. Jens' shoulders slump, as if he's growing smaller.

Hjalti: Bloody hell.

The older boy, seven or eight years old, red-haired, lies down in bed, slowly, as if tired; he lies motionless for several moments before his thin, emaciated body starts trembling slightly. Bjarni takes a long look at the boy, reaches out to him with both hands, stops, withdraws his hands and places them in his empty lap.

The farm shakes beneath a powerful gust of wind, making it impossible to talk. Then it subsides, everything eventually subsides, happiness and unhappiness, pain and pleasure, and then comes the sound of suppressed weeping, but so soft that it could be missed. The older girl stands up furtively, goes to her brother and lays her arm over his trembling body. She says nothing, and it's as if she lay her hand there by chance; we must rest our tired limbs somewhere. She even directs her gaze elsewhere, towards the youngest child who sleeps in the warm comfort of the dog, but her arm lies over the trembling body and says, you're not alone, brother, I'm here too, I'm not leaving you. In other places in the world it would likely add, I love you, but things like that aren't said at the end of the world, even arms can't say these precious words. A few train-oil lamps burn, giving off decent light but leaving behind shadows here and there, as if the world were torn apart in some places by the darkness. There are dark rings under Bjarni's eyes, as well as under the eyes of the girl who provides comfort with her silent arm, her warm palm; she's so gaunt that her eyes seem to overwhelm her face. The others in the family room hang their heads, as one does when one wants to avoid words, when there's something threatening or painful in the air and whoever speaks first cannot help but evoke it in his words.

Bjarni closes his hands, transforms them into fists, opens his mouth to say something but first has to clear his throat, and does this so forcefully that everyone but the old woman starts. The dog looks up briskly, perks its ears, the child starts to murmur, whimper, but the dog's tongue licks its hair until it goes back to sleep. A woman, you say, in this weather, up there, I find that doubtful. And what business would anyone have up there? This storm has lasted for ten days and no-one is out and about; those who venture too far from home are as good as dead . . . She was tall, you say? These last words, the question, Bjarni nearly spits out, as if it pains him to ask, as if he fears the reply, and the entire household, apart from the youngest and oldest, stare at the visitors. The boy regards the dog, and the child, they keep each other company and warm, have their happy moments, irrespective of the world.

Bjarni, calmly: I mean, for a woman?

The boy, shivering slightly from deep-rooted cold: Yes, she was tall.

Bjarni: Dark hair, thick?

The boy: Yes.

Bjarni: And did you catch a glimpse of her face? No, hardly . . .

Jens: One never knows in such weather, up in the wilderness. People often see things that don't exist, that are just imagination, mirages.

The boy, quickly: I saw her clearly. And her face. When she saved me.

Bjarni: Saved you?

Hjalti: How so?

The boy: I'd lost Jens, was overwhelmed by fatigue, and she just stood next to me.

Bjarni: Did you see her eyes? And her nose, was it just a bit bent, humped?

The boy: I saw her clearly but didn't think much about her appearance; it was also so, well, unreal. But her nose had a hump, that's right.

Bjarni, almost indifferently: And her eyes?

Hjalti, curtly: As if they entered you?

For a moment the boy envisions the woman's eyes, ice-cold with death. Yes, he says, as if they went right through me.

Hjalti: Bleeding devil.

Bjarni, pale: That's absolutely not the right word.

Daddy, says the younger girl, staring at her father. Daddy, she says once more, plaintively, pleadingly. Then no more. Bjarni stands up, sits back down, tries to smile at her, then looks at the two children now lying curled up together in the bed, son and daughter, you'll wet the sheets with your tears, my poor things, he says finally, his voice almost as thin as when it was carried out into the storm, and then asks the girl to put Sakarías in the bed with Steinólfur; and you lie down with Beta, it's best to sleep now. There's nothing we can do, he adds, perhaps in explanation, or solace, useless solace, and the girl stands up and her twelve-year-old hands rub her aged eyes. Her name is Þóra and she takes little Sakarías from the dog, which whines softly and woefully when the boy is taken. This is Nellemann, says Bjarni, meaning the dog. Like the Minister for Icelandic Affairs? asks Jens,[11] and Hjalti laughs as Bjarni smiles dully, it's not bad to be able to cultivate such elegant and powerful men. The four men look at the dog, amused at its having this name. But a child's mind isn't as agile at turning away from pain, and Beta rises as Þóra lies down next to her, looks with red eyes at her father, it was mother who brought these men, wasn't it? Bjarni gives his daughter an almost terrified look and the good humour over the name of the dog

11. Johannes Magnus Valdemar Nellemann (1831–1906), a Danish jurist and politician, occupied the position of Minister for Icelandic Affairs from 1875 to 1896.

turns to nothing. Go to sleep, my dear, says Hjalti calmly, gently, it's best. Beta lies down obediently next to her sister, but rises again immediately; do you think she's still out there, shouldn't we open the door for her, she must be cold. She's dead, says Þóra, tugging Beta back down; so she's not cold, she's just dead. But why doesn't she come in and join us if she was outside with these men? Þóra turns; Daddy, she says, Daddy, she asks. There's nothing we can do about it, says Bjarni. But maybe she's not dead! shouts Beta suddenly, having risen again; she shouts so loudly that the youngest boy wakes up, starts to cry, the dog whines softly but Steinólfur puts his arms around the little one and he falls asleep. I'm scared, Daddy, says Þóra. It's alright, I'm here. I know, she replies.

I'm sure they'd like more coffee, says Hjalti, following a long silence, as the wind shakes the house. Bjarni has no problem at all letting Hjalti brew yet another pot of coffee in this house over such a short period of time, even twice the usual amount; he's completely fine with it though the coffee is running out, only a ten-day supply left when the men showed up. Of course he's on the verge of shouting to Hjalti, make it weak; but is too proud to do so. The boy yawns, can't help it, longs for sleep but has to hold it just a bit further at bay. Bjarni clears his throat, spits, gets up to check on the children; crying children fall asleep faster, there's always solace to be found in this world. Hjalti brings the coffee; his gait is unsteady. They drink it, drink the weak coffee, they say well well, Bjarni rocks slightly in his seat, asks Jens about his postal journeys yet seems not to listen properly, even though everything that Jens says is considered major news in this place; he interrupts the postman in mid-sentence and Jens stops, as if he'd expected it. She died ten days ago, says Bjarni. The same day as the storm hit. That's why we haven't been able to go anywhere. It takes a lot of arms to transport a coffin over the heath here. How? asks Jens calmly. She'd been in bad shape all winter, replies Bjarni, his eyes on the coffeepot.

Hjalti: And then she started putting the nappies under her shirt.

Bjarni, glancing up: That's enough of your twaddle.

Hjalti: It isn't twaddle.

Bjarni: That wasn't the reason. She'd been in bad shape all winter, I said.

What nappies? asks the boy. From the little one, replies Hjalti; they were so damp, he was cold, the poor thing, and Ásta put his diapers under her shirt to dry them properly. After that she got worse.

Bjarni: I already forbade you to mention this.

Hjalti: They're asleep. And besides, I'm just telling these men how she was. The purest pearl, he says, looking at Jens and the boy.

The pile of rags moves, the old woman rises on her elbow, oh oh oh, oh oh oh, she whines. Bjarni curses softly, stands up ponderously, goes over to the bed, takes the blanket off his mother and an odour of urine fills the room. Oh oh oh, she whines.

It's bloody awful being old, says Hjalti; may the Lord protect me from it!

Fatigue pours over the boy as Bjarni tends to his whining

mother, the world darkens before his eyes, now I can sleep, says Jens at his side, yet somehow from a great distance. They share a bed, it's narrow; damn you're big, mutters the boy, trying to settle himself, can't you cut something off, do you really need all of this? Shut up, mutters Jens, and Hjalti extinguishes the stove. Why did she come looking for you? asks Bjarni from the middle of the room, a vague silhouette in the gloom, holding their wet, stinking clothes, the boy smells the stench as he lies there on his side, has no other choice due to the lack of space, and looks down at the floor. Maybe to save us, says Jens behind the boy, it's odd how someone's voice changes if you can't see the person but can still perceive his or her presence. I wouldn't put it past her, mutters Hjalti, sitting on the side of the bed; he pulls off his clothing, his big white body glimmers through the darkness; he sits naked and motionless despite the cold that presses in on them now, after the stove has been extinguished.

Bjarni: Dead people don't climb mountains, and never have done.

Hjalti: I've experienced this and that over the years, and know people who've both seen and lived certain things. And what about all of those stories; are none of them worth anything?

Bjarni: Stories aren't reality.

Hjalti: Oh, what the Hell are they then?

Bjarni: I don't know.

Hjalti: But you witnessed a thing or two when you lived in Berg. And you weren't exactly a picture of calm when we heard these men outside here.

Bjarni: It isn't the same. And who expects visitors in such weather? Did you really see something? Weren't you just tired and tattered?

Jens: It was probably something.

The boy: I saw a woman. Clearly.

Bjarni: I don't understand this.

Hjalti: Damn it all. It's only God who understands.

Then comes the night.

Hjalti lies down ponderously, with all his hundred and something kilograms, and immediately starts snoring; those who have little on their consciences and don't let existence confuse them sleep immediately, as if they're blessed. Jens has also fallen asleep; Bjarni as well, after having tossed and turned, muttered a bit, sighed, but now he sleeps and the snores of the three men cut through the chill air of the family room. The old woman moans weakly in a dream, the boy lies crammed against the bedframe, feels how Jens pushes against him every time he inhales; so I'll never get to sleep, he thinks; he lies there on the verge of despair, longs for sleep, rest, longs to get away. I'll never get to sleep, he mutters, yet falls asleep. Then wakes to a sound, the room is still engulfed in shadows and everyone is sleeping; just the weather, he thinks sluggishly, but then he hears the sound again. It seems to come from the passageway. The dog? He opens his eyes but shuts them again immediately when he discerns Nellemann in his place. Damn, he thinks, frightened, convinced that it's her coming down the corridor, with her dead eyes. Listens but hears nothing more, opens his eyes a crack and catches a sidelong glimpse of little Sakarías, the child has sat up and looks around guardedly, as if to determine whether the world is bad or good. The dog whines softly and Sakarías clambers down, crawls as fast as he can to the dog, which stands up to curl itself around the child, licks its hair and then they both sleep, a little boy, a big dog, so perhaps mercy does exist in the world. And isn't the storm subsiding? It isn't gusting so violently against the house. The boy smiles, smashed up against the bedframe; he'd started to think that the weather would never calm down again, that he and Jens would be driven like this from farm to farm in black storms as long as the world turned. Maybe spring has come, he thinks, feeling sleep drawing closer once more, with its bag full of dreams. He hears a vague, half-suppressed noise from Bjarni, opens his eyes a crack, sees the farmer wriggling, he's having a nightmare, thinks the boy, and shuts his eyes hurriedly again so as not to frighten off sleep.

He and Jens are alone in the family room, apart from the old woman. The boy wakes up abruptly, sits up immediately, still addled with sleep; Jens is standing next to the stove, his chest bare, trying to warm himself. The storm has subsided, says the giant, and it's true, there's no wind on the roof, the snow has even been cleared from the membrane windows, daylight trickles in and the heavy booming of the Polar Sea is heard clearly through the calm, nearly overwhelming the sounds of children's voices from outside. Well then, says the boy, and starts looking for his clothes. Jens does the same. Two semi-naked men in search of clothing,

enough of it, he adds quickly, before going into the kitchen to fetch the black drink. Should we drink up all their coffee? asks the boy softly. No other choice, replies Jens. And there can hardly be much food left, either, says the boy, and adds, when Jens says nothing, did you see the bags under their eyes, you know what that means! Jens sighs. Exactly, says the boy, they're starving. I've heard of how it is here in the northern regions, little left but salted seabirds by the time spring comes; people lie bedridden with scurvy, folk in their best years, some even need to be moved to other farms, to other districts, to get them back on their feet. Are given proper food for a few days, so that they can make it back home on their own. This must be the end of the world, declares the boy, and then Bjarni comes with the coffee.

They avoid speaking for some time in order to enjoy the drink better. Bjarni sighs softly. It's been a long time, many weeks, since he allowed himself to brew such strong coffee, and it's incomparable; the taste and the pleasure come immediately, he doesn't need to smack his lips over the drink in order to coax them out.

You feel that we live at the end of the world, says Bjarni, not looking in any particular direction, although it's no secret to whom he's directing his words. The boy feels his face grow warm. I heard you, says Bjarni directly, when the boy says nothing. The old woman laughs softly, very softly, from a great distance, sunk in the land of childhood, down in the green homefield of life, where everyone is alive and because of this there's no reason to cry. Even the most miserable have their dreams.

The boy: Yes, this is undeniably . . . a bit distant from everything. Behind the mountains, a little bay behind the mountains and then the *Polar Sea*.

Bjarni: Nothing wrong with the Polar Sea.

The boy: But when you stand up on a mountain and hear the din of the sea, you start thinking about the end of the world, the place where everything ends and the wilderness begins. All roads lead away from here.

Bjarni: And no roads lead here?

The boy, smiling apologetically, ashamedly: That's probably not true.

Bjarni: It's alright. But it's good to be here, there are plenty of fish in the sea, birds on the cliffs, we have fifty sheep, it's quiet here, no-one to push you around. He who lives here is free. That must be something. The end of the world, what's that? What to you is the end of the world is home to me.

The boy: Do just the two of you go to sea?

Bjarni: A third would just get in the way. Hjalti equals more than two; he's even a full three. But before it was always just me. You don't have to go out very far.

Jens: No cows?

Bjarni: No, we had one for a long time but she was bored here and stopped giving milk. Cows are social creatures. Sometimes she stood the whole day and mooed at the mountains. I was going to slaughter the creature but spared her because of the children. Brought her over to Stóruvík and sold her. She had company there.

The boy: Nice of you to spare the cow, because of your children, I mean.

Bjarni, shrugging his shoulders: I would probably have gotten more for her dead than alive.

The boy: You didn't want to get another, and have two?

Bjarni: Who can afford two cows? And where would I get the hay for such stock? The sheeps' milk will have to do. Naturally we won't have much to eat if spring comes late, but no-one is going to starve, and little variety in one's diet for two, three weeks kills no-one.

But, says the boy, unable to restrain himself, you hardly have many visitors here!

Bjarni: Yes, yes, last time in October, and now you two.

Jens: Little run of visitors, that's excellent.

Outside the dog barks, a child laughs, Bjarni turns around and for several seconds appears not to know properly what he should do with his arms, and then the moment passes. Didn't expect, he says, to see anyone before May, when the ships anchor here; they buy eggs and water from us, there are foreigners as well, you get various useful things in return, the children get chocolate and Ásta . . . yes. He stops, stares into the air, and then offers Jens chewing tobacco. Brilliant, says Jens. Yes, brilliant, says Bjarni. But, says the boy and Jens curses softly, it must be difficult sometimes, damn it, not to have any news for ten months. Not to be able to know what's going on!

Bjarni: Why should we know what's going on? And with whom? How does distant news help anyone?

The dog barks again. Nellemann's a bitch, says Bjarni; though it doesn't matter, he adds when they give him curious looks. You look to be the equal of two men, says Bjarni to Jens; just like Hjalti. Jens shrugs.

Bjarni: I'm always counted as something. The three of us can easily be reckoned as six, and that should suffice.

Jens: Suffice? For what?

Bjarni: For bringing Ásta down to Sléttueyri.

So she's here? asks the boy, looking around instinctively, as if he expects her to appear.

Bjarni: I'd thought about waiting until a bit later in the spring and then transporting her by boat. Need calm weather to do so; it's quite a distance by sea to Sléttueyri. But now I can't wait any longer.

Why not? asks the boy, who simply can't control himself; he tried to hold back from asking, but the question was out before he knew it. Bjarni, however, seemed almost to welcome it. I dreamt badly last night, he says, speaking hurriedly, as if to express something uncomfortable quickly enough; I dreamt of Ásta, she came to me. Certain dreams are unwise to scorn. It isn't good to dream of dead people, even if it's Ásta . . . she was a good woman and it'll be difficult to keep living here without her. A man is only half himself without his wife, and what can half a man do? She wasn't particularly happy about moving here back in the day, but she accepted it. Over time. We had these children, and one that died. The children miss her. She always kept herself busy.

Hjalti can be heard outside; his heavy voice cuts through the children's giggles and the dog's barking. It sounds as if he's playing with the children, that they're having a great deal of fun. What is the end of the world? thinks the boy.

She came to you in the night, says Jens calmly, knowing precisely when to speak, when to remain silent, what to say and what to keep silent about. Yes, says Bjarni. She wants to be put in consecrated ground. That's why she came looking for you.

Jens: Do you have a sled?

A sled frame, says Bjarni, from when I brought my father over several years ago. He takes a long look at the boy; his eyes are light blue and have a resolute gleam, his hair is dark and his beard is starting to grey. I'd like to ask you to stay here in the meantime, look after the sheep and mother, the children can look after themselves, or Þóra will see to them. Not more than three, four days, depending on the weather; I'll pay you. The boy avoided his gaze; pay with what? he thinks. I could put something on my account for you in the shop in Sléttueyri, says Bjarni, as if he'd read the mind of the boy, whose eyes are fixed on the floor.

It would certainly be nice to take a rest here.

Have done with the heavy going. The weather. The damned mountains. He feels nearly exhausted just at the thought of setting out again, let alone of dragging a corpse along. No problem minding fifty sheep, and the girl, who's named Þóra, will look after the siblings; the boy needs only to entertain them, help them to forget themselves sometimes, but what about the old woman? Of course he could manage changing her bedclothes and clothing, even though she smells as she does; he's smelled smells before and a smell has never killed anyone. Yet there's something he's afraid of: her fingers are bent, like claws.

It's easy dealing with old mother, says Bjarni, and somewhere I have some reading material for you.

The boy, surprised: Reading material?

A few journals, says Bjarni apologetically, *Skírnir* and *Iðunn*. I suppose I might even have something there in the postbag. Then there's the *New Bulletin of the Icelandic Society in Copenhagen*, which belonged to father. I reckon that you enjoy reading, and the journals should keep you occupied the days that you're here. We also have hymn books, but I guess you young folk wouldn't have an interest in such things. Oh, a few volumes of poetry. And *Njál's Saga*, *Grettir's Saga* as well, they're from father, he wanted to have himself buried with the latter, but of course I didn't fulfil his wish. I don't really believe that folk read in the grave, and books are for reading, otherwise they're useless, and it's bad if something is useless. Did he read a lot? asks the boy. Never grew out of it, even in his ripe old age. At one time he had around thirty books and a considerable number of manuscripts that he'd copied; he spent a lot of time doing so instead of resting, and wasted the oil, mother would usually add. It all came to nothing when the cottage burned. Then they moved here. The books burned? asks the boy. Yes, along with farm implements, a dog, and clothing. Father went into the fire, but not after the poor dog, who was good enough, but rather the books, although he only managed to save *Njál's Saga* and *Grettir's Saga*. It would almost have been appropriate if *Njál's Saga* had burned, says the boy.[12]

Bjarni: He didn't recover well from the smoke, and died a few years later. The damned books killed him, mother always said.

The boy: Do you read?

Bjarni: It's a bad habit.

The boy: But you read anyway.

Bjarni: We need to get going. This calm spell isn't going to last long; the next assault is on its way.

But it's spring, damn it, says the boy, almost accusingly.

Jens: Where is she?

Bjarni: Out in the smokehouse.

Out in the smokehouse? exclaims the boy, and Jens glances at him with an expression ordering him to shut up.

Bjarni: I didn't like the idea of keeping her outside. Besides, she could have gotten lost beneath the snow. It was the only way.

Jens: So, let's go. We need to get up the mountain before the storm. I'll take Hjalti and the boy.

Bjarni, shaking his head: He'll hardly do. It's a job for men.

Jens: He isn't quite as pitiful as he looks. He's a tough little thing when put to the test; he just talks too much. But your place is here; the children are motherless.

Bjarni had sat down, and continues sitting when they stand up. Sits and appears to have aged around ten years, but the boy's

12. The medieval Icelandic *Njál's Saga* is sometimes referred to as the *Saga of Burnt Njál*, due to the fact that its eponymous hero is burned alive in his house, along with his family. Hence the boy's comment.

languor is gone in a flash; he's prepared to fight mountains. Despite their being ten, and surly.

The air is almost white with light; there's a vestige of sky where the April sun burns behind the clouds. The Polar Sea extends outward like eternity itself, it breathes deeply and waves crash against the cliff somewhere below. Jens avoids looking down, but the boy spies a winch near the edge of the cliff, meaning the people here have to lower the boat and then haul it up when it's in danger from the crashing surf below; damned drudgery that must be, he thinks, looking around for the boat but seeing only snow. Jens adjusts the postbags, perhaps ten kilos each, fifteen; there were journals for Bjarni: *Skírnir, Iðunn.* Nellemann comes running, stops next to Bjarni, looks up at him enthusiastically, tongue dangling, yes yes, he says amicably and the dog sits down in the snow, looking as if it's been awarded a medal. The children and Hjalti are a good distance from them; they've made snow-men, an entire family, every member alive. Hjalti rolls a large, growing snowball ahead of him, holding the youngest boy like a sack beneath his other arm.

The children don't dare come near the visitors, keep themselves at a distance but stare at them. Steinólfur gnaws at his woollen mitten, Hjalti holds Sakarías, then hands him to Þóra and says, we're leaving. You all go in, says Bjarni to the girl. But Daddy, says Steinólfur, it's so nice and bright outside! Is it? says Bjarni, look-ing around, as if first realising it now. I want to be outside with

Hjalti, says Beta, without taking her eyes off Jens and the boy; visitors stop only a short time and seldom return, she'll hardly get another chance to see these men. They're going to take your mother, says Bjarni sharply, almost scoldingly. Beta looks from the visitors to her father; take her where? To a churchyard, of course, says her sister. She shouldn't be going anywhere, she mustn't; otherwise she'll never come back! She's gone, says Bjarni, before adding, hesitantly, my girl. I want to see mummy, says Steinólfur, removing his mitten from his mouth, and then the youngest starts to cry, perhaps because of the cold, perhaps not. Go inside, says Bjarni sternly, and the girl walks off with the crying boy and the others following reluctantly behind. Watch what you drink, says Bjarni to Hjalti as they walk towards the smokehouse. You'll keep your eye on me, I suppose, replies Hjalti; they walk side by side, the farmer looks old and fragile next to the big farmhand.

Bjarni: I'm staying behind.

Hjalti: What?

Bjarni: That's how it's going to be. I'm staying behind with the children. They have it hard enough.

Hjalti: Damn.

The cottage is nearly buried beneath the snow but it's clear that they've shovelled snow off it regularly, last time that morning. The smell of smoke meets them as Bjarni opens the door, goes in and comes out pulling a simple sled, the coffin on top of it, made of rough driftwood, not a beautiful piece of work but neither is

281

death. I'll accompany you up the mountain, says Bjarni; you'll need the help. The boy looks up. The mountains stand in a semicircle around the bay; in some places sheer crags and pitch-black cliffs stare obstinately out at the sea. They set off with the sled, which glides easily through the snow. Don't you want to tell the kids? says Hjalti. I already have. I mean, that you're not going all the way. Bjarni stops, looks down at the farm, the children haven't gone in but stand just outside the door, along with the dog, watching them. You go, says Bjarni; then you can say goodbye to them. I actually did so before you came out; said I needed to make a short trip with the visitors, but it can be done again. The big man runs off, remarkably light-stepped; onwards, orders the farmer and he and Jens pull, the boy brings up the rear, pushing, looks twice over his shoulder, sees Hjalti lift Beta up high and rub his big head on her belly.

He's quick to catch up with them and it's hard-going inching the coffin up the slope; it takes at least four living men to drag death away. The boy works up a great sweat; sometimes has to go down on his knees to push when the slope is steep. They crawl their way up, unbearably slowly, cut across the slope where it's easiest, though it's never easy, and when the boy goes down on his knees he puffs and pants on the coffin; his warm breath slips in through the chinks. But it's no more than three hundred metres, says Bjarni when they stop to rest; we've done just over half. The farm is a little speck down below and the children are gone, as if they'd never existed; I'll never see them again, thinks the boy sadly. It isn't always good to go up high and gain a view.

They see the sea; they see that it's endless. The higher you go, the smaller you become and the greater grows the sea.

Bjarni bids them farewell at the crest of the slope; ahead of them is an undulating, high heath. Just over a day and a night if the weather stays calm, says Bjarni, avoiding looking in the direction of the horizon, where the world is darkening. I'll watch what I drink, says Hjalti. Bjarni looks at the coffin and the others turn away, suddenly preoccupied with looking around. Hjalti, pay for your lodging with the sled, says Bjarni, looking west, over heaths and mountains; he clears his throat and adds: God be with you. Then shakes all their hands and begins his descent. They head in the opposite direction, westward, which seems in some mysterious way to be due north. As if it's the only direction here. The boy pushes, the others pull, it goes well; splendidly, in fact. Two hours later it starts to snow. At first gently, and then of course everything grows dark. Hjalti curses just as the winds awaken.

XII

Four individuals on the move, three living, one dead.

At times the boy is in front of the coffin, along with the demi-giants, a thin stick between two tree trunks, but is unfortunately more often behind, pushing, laying his hands over the rough wood, applying force, using all his might, and several centimetres below his palms is her face, blue with death, white with cold. It's harder to pull; one sinks often, needs constantly to cut a path, yet it's better to be there, there he seems closer to life than here behind the coffin. Of course it provides a bit of protection from the storm, especially when he bends down, but then he feels the icy breath of death on his skin. He tries to keep his arms ahead of him, so that his head is behind the coffin, not on top of it, but he can't avoid it when they ascend slopes, hills, struggle up out of depressions; Jens and Hjalti pull and he has to spread himself over the coffin to gain leverage, his face directly over her, her dead eyes penetrate the coffin lid and meet his living eyes; if he shuts his eyes he hears her voice in his head. It isn't good to be dead, she says, it's cold and the cold makes me cruel; don't fail me.

He tears his eyes open and doesn't give a damn though the blowing snow hurts his pupils, because the voice immediately falls silent. Just keep them open! But then the slope becomes so steep that the boy has the coffin in his arms once more; he keeps kicking his way upward, shuts his eyes reflexively during the struggle and simultaneously hears the voice; are you trying to hug me, dead as I am?

Do you know the way? asks Jens as they pause to gather their breath, much later. The mountains that had towered over them at the start of the journey are gone; they grew hazy in the snowfall and then disappeared entirely, and with them the directions, the horizon, and everything that one generally needs to journey in the mountains, in cold weather, a biting north wind. Do you know the way? asks Jens, perhaps a bit worriedly, but also relieved, since they put more distance between themselves and the Polar Sea with every step; it had reached into his dreams the previous night and touched his breast; he woke with an icy heart. There's knowing and there's knowing, replies Hjalti; what does a man know, I've made this trip before. They kneel on the lee side of the coffin, under cover of death, the boy like a puppy between the two men, who knock icicles from their beards. It's demanding work, travelling with a dead person. Of course the sled is good and sometimes there's a decent crust of snow, sometimes difficult going, soft snow, drifts, snow-filled hollows and depressions; the two giants pull, the boy pushes, they sink in snow, alternately sweat and feel chilled. Somewhere behind them, far away, is a cottage with children and a farmer and a dog and the old woman; it's half forlorn now that Hjalti is gone. His absence also calls to mind the death of Ásta; it's almost as if she's died again. Bjarni sits numbly, staring into space; Sakarías gains safety and solace from the dog, which has such eyes, such a broad and soft tongue; but the other three must look after themselves, they are vulnerable.

The three men have made good progress, stopping only briefly to gather their breath after ascending the most difficult slopes; the boy and Hjalti have exchanged words, conversed, while Jens was silent, said nothing. But now they rest. A few more hands wouldn't have hurt, says Hjalti, not to complain; he just tells it like it is. How is it to be almost on top of her? he then asks the boy. Cold, says the boy. I believe that, but does she speak to you? When I shut my eyes, the boy blurts out. It's impossible to speak anything but the truth up here in the mountains; lies and half-truths go nowhere, since there's no-one to cultivate them. The dead don't speak, says Jens.

Hjalti: Oh yes they do, and more than you, in all likelihood.

The boy: She speaks with me . . . or to me.

You lack resolve, says Jens bluntly, as if in explanation; their backs are turned to the coffin, it seems easier to rest that way, and to talk. That may very well be, says Hjalti contemplatively, his blue eyes looking at the boy from beneath his ice-covered eyebrows, but it doesn't change the fact that the dead speak; I know it, and there's little in me but resolve. It takes life to speak, says Jens, shaking himself; the icy chill is intensifying, this atrocious chill that comes from within.

Hjalti: There's death and then there's death; two very different men in front of the coffin, but it becomes ever more difficult to distinguish them from the falling snow; people have vanished in these parts, turned to snowfall, never to be seen again, in the summers melted into the earth along with the whiteness, a more beautiful death might not exist, though it's never pretty to die, it's just life that is beautiful, and the men pull the coffin along.

Jens curses his right arm, which falls numb now and then. Damn, he thinks, damn; glances back over his shoulder, the coffin, the sled and the boy are white with snow, but he's still there. Jens sinks in snow up to his knees and thinks about Salvör. Take me, isn't that what you men want, difficult to forget these words, they always smell him out, assault him, accuse him; can you live without betraying me? she'd whispered once, it was a summer evening barely a year ago, they lay among tussocks, sheltered from the world, the redshank complaining incessantly above them, otherwise silent; the clouds blue-grey, taking on shapes, the wind slept in the grass, the blades barely moved, a butterfly or two flew about and drank in the few moments given to it. Fluttered its soft wings, mysterious as silk. Salvör held out her bare arm, cautiously, held out a finger and a butterfly alighted on it, as if by magic, and its wings trembled. She brought her finger near to his face, extremely slowly so as not to frighten this living being with its dreamlike wings. Is it beautiful? she asked. Yes, he said, holding his breath so it wouldn't fly away. Why do you say that? Because it's beautiful, I suppose. How so? Its wings, he said, moving nearer; the butterfly had settled down and no longer trembled. Isn't it a bit like life? mused Salvör; beautiful

288

from a distance, but when you come closer you see that it's just a winged worm? She blew the butterfly gently off her finger and asked, whispered, as if she hardly dared ask, perhaps because she feared the answer, can you live without betraying me? He'd taken her hands in his, he'd brushed the hair from her face, this face that meant more to him than the sky itself, brushed the hair back and said, I'd rather die than betray you, and then she wept, from happiness or because it's so much easier to speak than to live. She beheld the treachery in me, thinks Jens, wrenching himself up from the snow, more than knee-deep; she wept because I'm a wretch, as her husband was, betrayal at the first drop, and not even needing liquor for it. He pulls hard, so hard that the sled jerks forward and the boy falls face-first into the snow. Hjalti snorts when Jens speeds up, but he keeps up with him, doesn't want to be less of a man; males are primitive, predictable. It's all the boy can do to keep up with them, but he's barely a man, trudges along behind them, for a long time without pushing. But why, thinks Jens, do I go to Sodom? Is it just because I like the hotelkeepers? Is it because I find Marta amusing, her comments and thoughts? Is it because of the liquor? I can drink it at Geirþrúður's, even at The World's End. Isn't it first and last to look at Marta, so I can feel the excitement, the damned desire, so that I can think about how she moves when I'm here in the mountains, so that I can think about her when I'm on heaths? You look at me so much, she once said, one summer night when the sun hung silently and sleeplessly just over the surface of the Deep. Jens said nothing, simply drank more, and she smiled; so look, she to build a wall to break the strongest gusts, builds in haste and it works; it's almost as if they've retreated further, come further away, the roar of the wind grows distant, the gusts weaken, they see their own breath and a sense of tranquillity comes over them, they almost feel well, stare out nearly contentedly and the boy allows himself to doze, allows dreams to flood reality. Hjalti and Jens fade into the distance, move into another world; sleep slowly and gingerly knits a protective cloak around him. The boy makes muttering sounds, his mouth half open, he slobbers a tiny bit and it freezes on his chin. Jens is first to come to his senses, due to his experience, character. There's something wrong if one feels well on such a journey; that's when one is in danger. He shakes off the numbness of tranquillity, spreads out his cold fingers in his frozen mittens, moves his numb toes and sees the boy slipping into a deep sleep and dreams. At first you sink into dreams that are blue, but that turn very slowly and cosily into black death. It can be everything at once, beautiful, sad, and terrible to watch a person fall asleep, to witness the slackening of the facial lines, catch a glimpse of the subconscious, a person's inner landscape that he tries all his life either to hide, lose, or discover. Jens hesitates, as if he doesn't dare nudge the boy; Hjalti just stares into space, hardly conscious. Finally Jens sighs quietly and drives his elbow hard into Hjalti, who straightens abruptly and shouts, damn it all to Hell!, nearly screams it and the dreams are peeled away from the boy. Thanks for that, mate, says Hjalti to Jens; I've never welcomed violence, but I thank you for your elbow, I'd actually fallen asleep and thought I saw Ásta standing here outside the opening, she motioned me to come, I felt as if I'd set out, yet sat tight. People are killed too easily here in the mountains; it's enough just to shut your eyes. But bloody hell, it would be good to eat something now. Something decent, I mean. I could kill for some good smoked lamb, a big slice. Aren't you hungry? I could eat an entire sheep.

If not two, says the boy. Stop talking about food, says Jens; he crawls towards the opening, sticks his head out to assess the situation but the wind tries to cut it off; it's worsened, he says, spitting out snow.

It's difficult to stay awake. Fatigue trembles in their muscles, boils in their blood, they shake themselves now and then like animals and say little, hardly anything at all, their thoughts are like obtuse fish in stagnant water, barely stirring, barely a vestige of them. If they think, they think about food, and without realising it the boy has started to croon to himself, a homespun folk song, *Children should be given bread, to nibble on at Christmas*, stares out dully but wakes when Hjalti joins in with the catchy melody, softly at first, but is soon belting it out; his voice fills the snow-cave, strong, pure, softly shadowed. The boy also raises his voice, they sing other Christmas songs, sing loudly, almost scream them far up in the mountains, inside a snow-hole, far from human habitation, in winds bent on beheading, with their backs up against a coffin, and it's the end of April. Their singing becomes so hearty, so ridiculous, so deranged that Jens inadvertently joins in at one point, hums along, the enchanting tune catches him, but he soon stops, just listens and doesn't object. They sing, and in the meantime forget their hunger. Sing all the Christmas songs they can remember. Then Hjalti has to pee. The boy inhales deeply, sucks in the air and smells the aroma of smoke. At first he thinks that his memories of smoked lamb at Christmas are so strong that he perceives its smell, but then he starts sniffing the air like a dog. Moves his head in a semi-circle and sniffs. Do you smell smoke? he asks, I mean, does it smell like smoke in here? Like smoke, up here? What nonsense! says Hjalti, having just peed, but he starts sniffing, as does Jens. Damn, mutters Jens, getting up quickly, having even paled slightly, while Hjalti presses his nose against the coffin. The Devil with it, he says, his eyes closed, it's the smell of smoked lamb! He flares his nostrils, his mouth half open, his stomach grumbles and he moves as far away from the coffin as he can, which isn't very far in the constricted space. Jens and the boy try to push themselves to the side, the postman drives his shoulder into the snow wall and it collapses on him and a bit on Hjalti, who utters a string of curse words; it's healthy for a man to curse, almost as healthy as praying, and sometimes much better. The boy shuts his eyes and simultaneously hears soft, cold, and mocking laughter in his head; are you hungry? asks the voice. It's no good being here, says Jens. But it's better than leaving, says Hjalti. Damned storm, curses the boy.

It's night outside the snow-cave.

The boy rocks regularly in his seat, recalling snippets of poems and stories; Jens widens the opening when the smoky smell intensifies, allowing the wind to come in, which it's quick to do; they immediately turn white with snow. Jens narrows the opening; it's better to endure the smell than the snow. I haven't been with a woman in three years, says Hjalti. Tomorrow, no, we're already at today; it's been precisely eleven hundred days.

Jens: Eleven hundred days.

Hjalti: It's an awful thing for an able-bodied man. I'm on the verge of looking at the sheep.

Where did it happen last? asks Jens. Now he speaks; now, when the boy doesn't know what's appropriate to say.

Hjalti: At Sléttueyri; where we're going. Blessed Bóthildur, a housemaid for the physician and his wife, damn it; we went at it like beasts. Like we wanted to devour each other. Such an angel, that woman. Strong as a bull, beautiful as a summer bird.

Have you seen her since? asks the boy.

Hjalti: Yes, last year. But just briefly, and in company.

The boy: And then?

Hjalti: Nothing, and that's the way it should be; can't be any more.

Why not? asks the boy in surprise.

You're so young, says Hjalti. I have nothing, except for these hands, and I mustn't drink, because then I turn into a bloody bastard; I would destroy us both. Better to have good memories than ruin them through further acquaintance.

Jens crawls up to deal with the opening; takes a long time. They're cold, the ice has long since melted off them and transformed into a chill; they move to keep warm as best they can in the narrow space and breathe in the strong smoky smell emanating from the coffin. The boy and Hjalti forget where they are and

295

start humming Christmas songs; one of them starts and the other joins in immediately, and sometimes they sing a song all the way to the end, even raise their voices and the notes are carried out into the storm, which tears them into pieces. Jens doesn't object; merely stares sullenly. Christmas cakes with raisins, says Hjalti after they finish singing *Children should be given bread* for the fifth or sixth time.

The boy: Fried flatbread.

Hjalti: Porridge with sweetened milk. And candles.

Jens: Smoked lamb.

Hjalti: Now you've got it! Smoked lamb and candles, my lads, that's bliss. One shouldn't complain, just live, but I've had a piss-poor life. As a child I was kicked here and there, welcome nowhere, didn't have it good anywhere expect with blessed Ásta, though not because of the wealth and comforts; it's tough living there, you should see the waves raging and roaring against the cliffs, the earth shudders beneath the house and your courage clatters inside you. And then come summers that are nothing but drizzles and fog, for two years the sun shone for two days in the summer and those days there were storm-force winds, otherwise it was never-ending drizzles and all the hay more or less ruined; the following winter was heavy and there was nothing left to eat by spring, you'd be gnawing your fingers yet giving the children their portions, awful to hear a child cry from hunger, it's like being cut open alive. Finally Bjarni didn't dare say the Lord's Prayer, because little Beta would start crying when he came to "give us this day our daily bread". All the same, it's been good have been my bloody pigheadedness. The only thing that I longed for was to grow big so that I could pound those who kicked me, and I got my wish. Don't know whether to thank God or the Devil for that. The farmer at Gil is named Jósef and his wife is María, just like Jesus' parents; existence can be comical like that, lads. They're still alive as far as I know; I sometimes ask about them, it's actually easier to hate living people than dead ones. Jósef's a real jokester and often made fun of my fear of the dark; as a child I saw ghosts and all sorts of horrors in every corner. He liked to sneak up on me in the dark and breathed heavily behind me. He told me horrible stories in the evenings before I was sent into the passageway to sleep. Into the passageway? asks Jens. It was crowded at Gil, says Hjalti, crowded in the family room, crowded in their hearts; I was made to sleep out in the passageway, in a nook by the main door, with some old rags of clothing over me for a blanket. At first I was as scared of the damned dog as the ghosts; it was a big creature and black with ferocity, but we came to accept each other after several nights, and that probably saved my wretched life; I would simply have died of hunger and cold and fear if it hadn't been for the dog. He was my best friend, companion, and saviour. That's why I knew what had to be done when Ásta died and poor little Sakarías came to experience the harshness of the world. The dog was named Blackie, but I called him Trusty, and that's the name he preferred to answer to. But you know how it goes; someone has to go out around four or five in the morning in the summers to fetch the sheep; that someone was always me, my feet wet in the morning cold, nothing to eat before I finished my chores and then I was given little, you're not going to eat us out of house and home, said María, always giving me meagre portions; I was hungry all my youth and have been hungry ever since then, can never get enough. Well, those were still the best moments, Trusty and I out alone in the early morning and sometimes in beautiful weather. At those times we were happy, just us, the grass, brooks, and birdsong, and sometimes I lost track of time and was given a few whacks for my tardiness. Hardly from pure malice; more like stupidity, nothing else crossed their minds. Yet worst was fetching water in the winters, for the household and livestock, seven to eight trips every morning; in my memory there's an eternal north wind and two wooden buckets, heavy and covered with frost. It usually splashed over me with every step. Once I fell terribly ill from this, when I was nine or ten years old, and was as good as dead. The boy is going to die, I in my delirium heard someone say, and I was rather content with that; I expected easy access to Heaven, still innocent of evil; the only thing that bothered me was not getting to take Trusty with me; we two would have been perfect for herding the sheep in Heaven. But one day, in a brief moment of clearheadedness, I saw a coffin standing upright, just within my reach; that blessed light of tranquillity, Jósef, had had business in town; he used the opportunity and brought back a coffin for me. Then, unfortunately, I felt rather spiteful and remember that I thought, before the delirium swallowed me again, you're going to be stuck with your damned coffin! And it was right then that I lost my innocence, I suppose; my damned spitefulness saved my woman who smells like smoked lamb and the spirit of Christmas, this would be alright, it would be possible to sing and think something beautiful. But for some reason the coffin becomes ever heavier, death becomes heavier with man's every step, it says somewhere, and these three living men would wholeheartedly agree to that. Just as well that the two of them are worth five, thinks the boy, pushing on the coffin, he catches a whiff of smoke now and then, but it's dull here beneath the wide sky.

They didn't dare wait longer in the snow-cave, the odour was driving them mad, sleep was defeating them, but bloody hell it was cold abandoning it, dragging out the coffin, even Jens gasped for breath in the freezing wind. The first hour was completely dark; they stumbled onwards without getting anywhere, nor were they heading anywhere either, were just focusing on not being blown away, staying on their feet, not losing the coffin and each other, but then the fury abated slightly, the skies cleared for a moment, and Hjalti could say those blessed words, yes, we're here. And they kept going, four individuals, three living, one dead, isn't that a rather favourable outcome? Was noon approaching, midday, or was just another night descending, perhaps? They proceed step by step and their happiness at Hjalti's words fades away; they pull, push, sink, gasp for breath, Hjalti and Jens' moustaches and beards freeze around their lips and the boy can't feel anything but his eyes. The mountain slopes vanish once more; the blowing snow turns the world dark again, the wind picks up, it blows almost directly at them, evening approaches and the boy shuts his eyes, his vision darkens from fatigue. Happiness can't last, says the woman in his head, but bitterness can last a long time and is more faithful to you, doesn't abandon you; love falters, hatred abides. It isn't true, objects the boy. What isn't true? Love is ... what do you know about love? she asks, interrupting him; what have you loved and where are the days, where are the years that have passed in this love of yours, whom do you love? Mother, he wants to say, father, Lilja, Bárður, but then doesn't, because they're all dead. Forgets that Ásta is inside his head, nothing is hidden from her and her laughter is cold; of course you only love dead people; why do you think you can speak to me? All the best is on this side. Don't resist; or can life offer you what death holds? Does the truth burn you? she asks as he opens his eyes wide, tears them open to get rid of her, and the storm, which seemed to have grown distant, crashes down on him again with all its weight. Now I can always speak to you, she says, and it's likely true; his eyes are open but he still hears her. He catches vague glimpses of Hjalti and Jens in front of the coffin. They'll be relieved to be rid of you, she says; you're a burden to them, you're weak, they're strong and this Jens has long since grown weary of you. The boy tries to think of Ragnheiður, instinctively seeks the warmth of the blood, the opposite of death, lust, enamourment. Thinks of the sweet that she stuck in his mouth, glistening with her saliva, thinks of the warmth when she pressed herself against him momentarily at the hotel, her shoulders white as the moon, her lips soft with moisture, her lips ... do you call that love? asks the voice in his head. Yes, it's love, it's surely love, what do you know, you're dead. But why are you also thinking of this woman

XIV

I don't know why I looked back, says Hjalti to the boy as they kneel in the shelter of the coffin, the two demi-giants having just pulled him up out of the snow. The boy had done what Ásta said and lay down; he was on his way into a downy-soft and beautiful world when they yanked him up, shouted something, screamed, tore him from softness and beauty into this damned life and this cursed weather, and he struck out as hard as he could, but his blows missed their mark and these big men held him down with embarrassing effortlessness as he came to his senses. No, I don't know why I looked back, says Hjalti, it was difficult enough to look ahead, let alone turn my head, this damned chunk of ice is frozen solid to my clothing and I have to turn my whole body to see what's behind, but maybe you have a guardian angel because when I looked around you were gone, we were pulling only the coffin and you were nowhere to be seen. Just a few steps more and we would have gone too far to find you; here whatever falls to the ground vanishes and is lost, vanishes and dies.

Jens pulls out a snuff-horn, reaches beneath his parka and produces this heavenly glory, as Hjalti words it; have you had that this whole time, you bastard?! For emergencies, yes, replies

Jens; he takes a pinch, as does Hjalti, in both nostrils, they sigh blissfully and order the boy to do the same, order him in such a way that he can't avoid it. Haven't you ever tried snuff? asks Hjalti, shocked when he sees how clumsily the boy handles the snuff-horn, and then sneezes repeatedly for two or three minutes. Nothing better for waking you up than this, declares Jens, before replacing the horn. God has truly created you, says Hjalti, cheerful from the snuff, slapping the postman's back. They have to speak loudly, the shelter is meagre, the wind rages all around them but the coffin provides just enough cover for them to crouch there and rest a bit from the wind, that transparent monster.

Jens: How much further do you think it is?

Hjalti: The Devil if I know; two hours, twenty, what matters most is to live, and with tobacco in our veins everything is possible; how much do you have left?

Jens: Enough for one pinch per person.

The boy: I'd rather die than take another pinch of that damned stuff.

Hjalti: That's what I like, men should talk like that – then we know they're alive! But we'll sit here for a while and take advantage of Ásta's cover.

The boy: Damned unreliable cover.

Hjalti: Never any unreliability as far as Ásta's concerned. I'm coming to realise little by little that it's impossible to live on this godforsaken earth without a wife, and then someone like Ásta; otherwise you're just lonely, and lonely people wither.

Jens: Wither?

Hjalti: Just like that, and blow away like dust. What sort of existence is that, anyway?

Jens: Wretched, I reckon.

The boy looks at the two men, these demi-giants who have saved him, pulled him from the downy-soft embrace of death, just before it hardened and turned cold. They're completely unrecognisable, white with frost and ice; the only thing human about them is their eyes, which don't freeze as long as one is alive. They crouch, all three, try to make themselves smaller to utilise the cover better, move closer to each other, sit almost in a semi-circle and look down between their legs, down at the snow. It's so good to crouch and feel the presence of another person, feel the presence of life under cover of death. Jens, says the boy. Just this name and its owner replies reluctantly, yes; yet he does reply; that's how much closer they've come to each other on this trip. You're not alone. No. I mean, you have a woman. What's her name? asks Hjalti when Jens says nothing. They rock beneath the gusts, they half doze, and Hjalti and the boy have almost forgotten the question when Jens says, Salvör; he says it towards the snow, where he's looking, as are they all, and they don't look up. Salvör, repeats Hjalti when he realises whence this reply came; it's . . . so you don't live together? No, it's not as good as that. So you live alone? Yes, no, with my sister and father. Halla, says the boy, tries saying it, uncertain, but Jens nods.

Hjalti: So why don't you live with her?

She reads me like an open book, says Jens.

Hjalti: Yes, that can be difficult.

Jens: She was married.

Hjalti: Was, that's a good word in this context; promising.

Jens: She killed her husband.

Hjalti: Damn.

Jens: Burned him inside his house.

Hjalti: That, of course, is . . . worse.

Jens: Yes.

Hjalti: But he probably had it coming; wasn't he a rough fellow?

Jens: A damned brute at home, beat her and disgraced her and even the children were afraid of him, especially when he was drunk.

Hjalti: Liquor is an invention of the Devil.

Jens: And he was often drunk. When he was home. Was hardly ever sober his final years.

Hjalti: Where was he, by the way; at sea?

Jens: No, it was odd, he went around entertaining people with stories and the like. A popular man, charming, I understand, but he changed into a monster when he came home. One night, after beating her and disgracing her in the worst imaginable way, Salvör set their home on fire and burned him in. Fled with the children to the nearest farm, and has been there since. This was fifteen years ago. In the winter, in cold weather. A three-hour walk between the farms and the younger child didn't endure it; she hasn't yet forgiven herself for it.

Hjalti: She did it to save her life, and the lives of her children; that's a sacred thing. He was marked by the Devil, it's no more complicated than that.

Jens: But she failed, the youngest didn't survive the trip, the cold. And then the older child, the girl, was immediately settled on another farm, not very far away, yet far enough. Salvör's patron prevented her from being prosecuted, but some still call her a murderer. She hasn't seen her daughter for three years, I understand; she was sent away, a second time. To another community, another district, even.

Hjalti: You don't know where?

Jens: No idea. I don't even know her name.

Hjalti: But what's standing in your way?

Jens: She doesn't want to tell me.

Hjalti: Damn it all, man; I mean of you living together?

Jens: She says she doesn't want to betray her employers by leaving, after all they've done for her.

Hjalti: It's one thing to be grateful, another to sacrifice yourself.

Jens: I also think it's just an excuse. But I understand her well. I'm not reliable. It's a fact. People like me are bitten by the Devil; they can't control themselves.

The boy, who is nearly blown over but manages to grab Jens: Bitten by the Devil? You haven't abandoned Halla, or your father; that's something, it must be something!

Jens: Her husband drank like a beast. The wine transformed him. Made him a monster.

Hjalti: Sometimes I think that the Devil has spit into every single beer bottle in the world.

Jens: Maybe. I let people down when I drink.

Hjalti: Has she seen you drunk?

Jens: Doesn't need to, she reads me like a book. And that's why she doesn't trust me. Not any more than I trust myself. There's nothing as loathsome as beating one's wife; both hands should be cut off any man who does so. Yet what would I do after five years, after ten years? Can I trust my hands?

He looks at his hands as if in search of an answer, but they're hidden in his mittens and give away nothing.

Hjalti: We're stuck in god-awful weather, sheer devilry, and it's uncertain whether we'll all make it back alive, three living people and one dead; isn't that too good a ratio to be true? But you, brother, you need to make it down alive and then defeat the dark storm inside you; that's your fight, it's where you're to engage in your life-and-death struggle. I reckon the chances for victory or defeat are even. If you do nothing, there's no chance of victory. If you do nothing, you betray all those who matter to you, and probably life itself, though I know nothing about that. You're fortunate, maybe not blessed, no, not at all, but fortunate; fate is giving you a chance! That's why you have to make it back to civilisation, go to her whom you call Salvör and say, and swear to Heaven, that you'll engage in a fight-to-the-death with yourself to be good and reliable. Then say: Do you want my heart?

Jens: Do you want my heart?

Hjalti: Yes.

The boy: That's rather good.

Jens: No-one speaks like that.

Hjalti: Yes, yes, when everything depends on it, we speak like

310

idiots, believe me! And she'll say yes. I know it. She's just waiting for you to open your damned trap, open it so wide that she can finally see how your heart looks, actually, and then she'll say yes. Then she'll know that you dare to challenge yourself.

Jens looks up from the snow, smiles, albeit dully, rocks in the wind. Maybe you're right. You're a funny sort. But what about that Bóthildur, isn't she waiting in Sléttueyri?

Hjalti: It isn't always easy to chase dreams.

The boy: Why don't you help yourself, like you're helping Jens?

Hjalti: One only helps those who deserve it.

XV

Does it seem as if it's subsided a bit? Isn't it as if someone, the world, God, the supreme power, has taken pity on these three men, maybe simply because the three of them sat down, three lives that were distant from each other, but had moved considerably closer by the time they stood up? Because something more beautiful or better than words had bound them? Has the wind subsided, has the storm's murderous desire slackened, or is it just simpler to survive as one whole rather than as three separate pieces? Now they set off again, no skulking, hesitation, half-hearted struggle; they simply continue and face it all, the sky and the night, because it is night, another night in the mountains.

But then it too has passed.

I'm starting to get my bearings, shouts Hjalti; it's daytime, noon, we're approaching that damned Eyri, maybe an hour more, two hours and we'll be looking down at the fjord, if there's any glimmer in this damned world!

But perhaps there is no glimmer; the wind whips up again and a frenzied storm hits. They've certainly got to know the wind on this journey, but it's never been as fierce as now; it's a scream from Hell. They walk and they crawl along, inch by inch, dragging glimpse of sleep like mild sunshine and silence behind the madness, but starts in alarm at an elbow from Jens, tears his eyes open hastily and the booming of the storm hits him again. Hjalti is warning them of the ravine that will be lying to their right, so deep that it scratches the roof of Hell and has swallowed eleven men in the last hundred and fifty or two hundred years, although two of the last were Norwegians, and are therefore rarely included. The story goes, yells Hjalti in order to overpower the wind, which doesn't like anyone but itself having a say; it's the wind that tells the stories here, but Hjalti has a strong voice and he moves nearer the others so that they can hear him. The story goes that back in the day a young mother cast herself into the ravine where it's deepest, with her dead child in her arms, in desperation; it was in the autumn. She was a housemaid and her master was said to have treated her badly, disgraced her, beaten her and threatened to take her child from her if she resisted him. What's a mother without a child? She endured all of his abuse. The folk on the neighbouring farms, and of course on the farm itself, knew this, or suspected it, but the man was a bigwig in the parish, respected, popular, and stern. People feared him for his severity, but also admired him and respected him for the same, and looked the other direction to avoid witnessing his misdeeds. A person can forget most things or deny them just by looking the other direction, and it's nearly always easier to look away rather than watch, because he who watches has to acknowledge what he sees, and then work against it. The child died of the croup, said most, but they knew it was a lie; this monstrous master struck it too hard when the child tried to defend its mother; think about it, lads, just a five-, six-year-old kid. She crept with it out into the autumn night, there was a pelting rain and she came to a little abode where a female acquaintance of hers lived. You can just imagine, the blackest night and a rain squall; her acquaintance heard a knock on the windowpane and her name whispered, or however it was the mother got her out, and not everyone would have gone alone to the door on such a night, but she went, half asleep, wrapped herself in something and outside waited the misfortunate mother. What do you have in your arms? asked her friend. My child, said the mother. In this weather?! exclaimed the other. It won't feel any more pain, said the mother, pushing the rags from the baby's face to reveal the congealed blood, and saying, at the same time, he did this. She was bareheaded in the storm, was even barefoot, her feet already bruised and bloody; come in, said her friend, God knows that that fiend shall be punished, even if I have to do it myself! God has no interest in poor women, said the mother, and you know as well as I that we can't touch him, and if we tried I would be sent to Bremerholm[13] for the murder of my own child. But I'll call for ten men; that will be my revenge. What do you mean? asked her friend; come in, you'll die out here in the night, dressed like that. But then the mother supposedly laughed and shouted, do you really think I'm planning to go on living, after this, and leave my child behind alone in death – tell them to look in the ravine! And at that she

13. Bremerholm was a prison in Copenhagen (from the sixteenth to the mid-nineteenth century) to which many Icelandic criminals were sent.

disappeared, ran out into the night and vanished. So quickly that her friend lost sight of her immediately. She wasn't found until many days later; or rather, her remains; she'd leapt into the ravine where it's deepest, a hundred metres down, crashed to the bottom without letting go of the child, it must have boomed in Hell when she slammed onto its roof.

The boy: Hopefully someone has dealt with the householder.

Hjalti: Are you such a child? He was a nob, a drinking mate of the parish administrator and the priest. The mother was said to have lost her mind; they all lived long and died happy. The only people punished in this country are those who have nothing, haven't you realised that? The others are never punished except in stories. But now nine others have joined her there; the Norwegians were drunk and lost their way, had gone up into the mountains to shoot ptarmigan. Nine gone, one to go. Of course I should go to her down there, and in doing so defeat the demon in the liquor and provide her some comfort. But remember this: when it suddenly starts sloping steeply, we're safe; then we've made it off the mountains, but the ravine is dangerous in such damned weather. The path lies close to it and huge cornices tend to slip out from under heavy people; that's how some have gone down; with the snow. How far is it until we're there? asks the boy, so tired that it takes him a great effort to ask; hopefully not more than half an hour, he thinks, I can't take more than that. Half an hour, says Hjalti, in decently calm weather, three hours now, no less, if we come across the path; it's easy to get lost, end up in the Devil's arms and freeze there.

*

They stand, no, half lie, in a semi-circle. Do you hear that? whispers Hjalti; they've huddled together instinctively, as if trying to take cover, and to feel a life besides their own. It's her, it's her calling for the tenth! Stop with your rubbish! Jens more or less shouts back. Hjalti moves even closer to them, comes right up next to their faces; they feel his breaths, see deep into his eyes, and it's as if his pupils have been scratched by disappointment, pain, weakness: Damn it, lads, does a man come into this life just to die?

And what can the answer to that be; nothing, of course, yet for several moments it's as if they all try to find the answer, or the answers, perhaps they're just hanging their heads blankly and are simply exhausted, nothing left, unconscious, aware of nothing, yielding to fatigue. And the sled slips away. Slowly, as if it's sneaking off. Jens feels something brush against him, looks up, sees the sled crawl slowly away; there goes the coffin, he thinks, bends down again. Yet hardly more than for two, three seconds before he springs up, so abruptly that he's almost blown over, shouts: The coffin! and runs off. The boy and Hjalti simultaneously realise what's going on, scramble to their feet and go after it. The sled has gone over a little knoll and is increasing its speed. The hill is very steep and the wind is blowing and the three men run after it. If it's possible to call such a movement running. These men are exhausted, and besides, Hjalti and Jens are stiff, entirely unused to running, most resembling confused seals; both are immediately panting, open-mouthed, yet they press on clumsily. On the other hand, this is the boy's moment. Because if there's anything he knows how to do, if there's anything he can do, it's run. The fatigue that had paralysed him just before is gone, wiped away by the thrill of the chase, which surges through his veins; he easily passes the demi-giants, dashes between them and hears them gasping for air. He runs after the sled and the coffin, runs terribly fast on the dizzying slope, with the furious wind at his back; it's as if he's flying, yet he's able to go even faster and laughter bubbles up within him. He runs, he flies, he draws closer to the sled, he reaches out with one arm, grabs hold of the coffin and immediately makes a leap, is lifted up and the wind tosses him onto the coffin, so harshly that he's nearly hurled off, but he manages to hold on, gets up and straddles the coffin, holds on to the ice-hard cord, manages somehow to thrust his mittens beneath it and hold on that way, no matter how the sled races on, no matter how the coffin tosses, the sled even flies once off a high overhang but he manages to hold on; the slope becomes steeper, it's a plunging incline and there's a living boy and there's a dead woman and it's likely impossible to go any faster, the wind screaming behind them, on the verge of losing them, the snowfall cuts the boy's icy cold skin, his nostrils flare and he smells the smoky smell, the powerful smell of smoked lamb and he's stopped laughing, long since stopped laughing and he shuts his eyes to protect them from the snow and the frost and listens to her cold, flat, and malicious laughter, which fills his head little by little, fills it with cold, and frost settles on all his memories, his dreams; eternal winter has hit. Is this how a man dies? he thinks, opening his mouth. First in the hope that the cold will be alleviated and the woman silenced, but then he starts to shout. Perhaps it's his life's reaction. And the reaction to everything behind him. The it's just a different fog for him, an even worse one, the final bottle is empty; he can't sleep any longer, sits at his desk among all the words, among the munificent, useless words, because what are words without another person, what are words without touch, Kjartan listens to the storm pound the house, what good are words if you can no longer bear to touch your wife, what good are words if you've stopped believing in life?; the boy screams, he shouts and he weeps because a teenage boy died of exposure fifty years ago, froze to death though the farmer held him in his arms and whispered, I'm sorry I'm sorry I'm sorry, until his lips were too cold for words and then the farmer died as well and now no-one remembers their lives, just their deaths. Whither went all the good moments that they lived; do they become nothing in death? The mountainside is endless, they rush on and down and down and down, perhaps heading straight to Hell, and the coffin is breaking apart, a dead woman and a living boy who in despair and rage holds on to a frozen cord, his eyes shut and screaming and shouting because so many people have drowned here, the sea is full of drowned lives yet people only catch fish, never dead lives, the boy screams because we can't row out onto the sea of death and fetch the ones we miss, tossing and turning in the night in silent agony, what can we do to fetch those who left too soon?; is life completely powerless and are there no words that can break the laws, are there not any sentences powerful enough to overcome the impossible, why in Hell do we live and die except to surmount the impossible? The mountainside is by now vertical, the sled is tossed from side to side, takes a sudden dip, rights itself just as quickly and the boy's

XVI

You're incredible, the boy says to Jens; he is unbroken, landed in a soft drift; how the Hell did you manage to find me? But Jens says nothing to this; he simply says, bloody Hell you can run, before setting eyes on Ásta in among the wreckage of the coffin; her eyes are shut but her mouth is open in a sneer, her teeth yellow-brown. Jens goes all the way up to her; so that's how you are, he says. He has to kneel slightly to get a good look at her face; her legs are partly buried in the snow. Jens appears to take it as natural that the woman, who a short time ago was inside a coffin, is now sticking up from the snow, sneering, leaning slightly and her left hand pointing stiffly into the storm; go there, she's saying. But of course it's slightly remarkable that Jens has managed to find the boy so quickly, and effortlessly. The sled had raced on and to the side on its wild trip down, turning well off course; Jens had run ponderously after it, tumbled, slid uncontrollably for several dozens of metres on the postbags, waving his arms, resembling a huge and ridiculous insect in his powerless attempts to turn to the left, turn away from the deep ravine, heard its whine excessively near, managed to stop, dragged himself lost and confused to his feet, turned in circles, calling out for Hjalti, calling out for the boy, blew several times on his postal trumpet but it was only the wind that answered, so he trudged on, the ground no longer sloped beneath his feet and then by some incomprehensible luck he stumbled upon the boy. Who asks about Hjalti. He'll manage here, says Jens, and easily, if he has only himself to take care of, but we've got to keep going. I can't stand up; I'm finished, I'm just going to rest here, the wind will subside at some point and the snow will stop falling. At some point will doubtless be too late; are you cold? asks Jens, no, replies the boy, that's the problem, I feel just fine, so why should I stand up, I'll just be cold again if I do. The most dangerous thing of all in such weather, says Jens, is that when you no longer feel the cold, you fall asleep within half an hour.

The boy: And never wake again?

Jens: Not any more than Ásta here. They both look at the woman, who leans, sneering, but is no longer cold.

The boy: Is this her?

Jens: What do you mean?

The boy: Isn't this the one that you saw, you know, that appeared to you?

Jens: I don't know what I saw, or whether I saw anything.

The boy: I saw her. I looked at her. It's her.

Jens: Well then.

The boy: I thought it only happened in stories that a dead person travelled a long distance to visit living people.

Jens: Don't close your eyes, boy! Then you'll be just as dead as she, and what use is that?

The boy: I was just listening, but I can't hear her anymore.

flow in his veins singing him into soft sleep, but he opens his eyes and looks in surprise at Jens. You, tired? he says. Jens looks away, his beard a solid chunk of ice, and then looks back at the boy. You were bleeding, he says. I thought so too, but it's hardly serious? No, says Jens, looking at the woman again; I can't keep going, any more than you, have never been as tired and never been as cold, but now it's not a case of what you can do, but what you do. He bends down stiffly, extends his half-numb right arm and pulls the boy to his feet; they stand there side by side, the storm rages all around them and a dead woman sneers at them. I'm cold, says the boy. Good, says Jens, but now we need to know what direction we take. The boy regards Ásta, steps up to her; it's as if she looks through his eyes and deep, deep into his mind and consciousness, but gently now. She's pointing in the right direction. Jens shakes his head, but then says, no worse a direction than any other. They stretch a bit, they look around, peer into the storm, upwards, what they think is up, but of course see nothing but the snow. Jens shouts, he reaches for the postal trumpet and blows, thrice, with a brief pause in between, the sound slinks up the mountain and they wait as long as they can, but nothing is heard and there's no sign of Hjalti. They set off, before the cold, the hunger, the fatigue, and the thirst bow them for good; they set off following the indication given by Ásta, who has turned entirely white with snow and will soon vanish, no doubt; Jens fumbles for the wooden remains of the coffin, sticks them into the snow around the woman in the hope that this will help to locate her, if the two of them make it to the village, which is somehow so far-fetched;

326

doesn't it seem as if they've walked out of time? Walked out of the world and are condemned to wander in a storm alongside life for the next thousand years or so; some of those who live will catch sight of them, like a vague suspicion, in the moments between sleep and waking, like a distant despair that nothing can ease, least of all time.

Nor is it possible to say that they're walking now. They totter, they fall, they crawl, and sometimes one of them starts giggling and then the other laughs, and then they sit and laugh or scream, impossible to distinguish between the two, then scramble silently to their feet without looking at each other. Jens falls and it takes the boy a long time to help his heavy body up. The boy falls and Jens has to use all his dwindling strength to heave him up and then the boy hangs for some time on the postman's shoulder, like a peculiar postbag; Jens has to plant his feet firmly to support the weight that he could have, under normal conditions, borne long distances without even noticing. I don't love her, mutters the boy in the vicinity of his ear. Whom? Ragnheiður. What Ragnheiður?

The boy: You know, Friðrik's daughter.

Jens: Have you had something to do with her?

The boy: I don't know, no, I haven't had anything to do with anyone, I just know that she has shoulders made of moonlight.

Jens: Damn it, keep away from those people, boy.

The boy: I'm powerless when I see her; is that love?

Jens: Why are you asking me?

The boy: You love.

Jens: Stop spouting such words.

The boy: It's just my heart beating, Jens.

Jens: I have no interest in saving you from frost and mountains if you're going to go crawling to Friðrik.

The boy: It's she who has shoulders of moonlight, not he.

It's all the same, says Jens.

Perhaps I don't love at all, says the boy; but she could possibly order me to die. Damn, to hear you talk, says Jens. They haven't moved; they sway to the fury of the wind, lean their heads together as if seeking cover, are too tired to tear themselves from each other, too powerless to think, they just talk, the words come up to the surface and they gather them there. Are you going to go to her? asks the boy. Yes, replies Jens. Then you've got to survive this. Can't avoid it, says Jens, and they tear themselves apart, keep going, downwards, since it starts to slope, and then it slopes steeply, and the wind tries to blow them over. Better not lose your footing, shouts Jens, who inches his way downwards, trying at the same time to resist the wind and the inclination, it's hard to know what lies below. No! shouts the boy, maybe a great promontory, then just a precipice and the sea below, we'll plunge off into the dark blue sea! Damn it, yells Jens, his anger flaring up at how this boy can never shut up, oh Hell! he shouts, and loses his focus for a moment, steps incautiously and that's all it takes. He falls, simultaneously sweeping the boy's legs out from under him. And instantaneously they're flying, helpless. Two men dashing madly on their backs down a slope, a mountainside, perhaps with the deep sea below. Perhaps they'll soon plunge off the verge of a great cliff, hover like snowflakes for several seconds, like angel's wings, like the sorrow of angels, then drop like stones to their wet deaths. They tear downhill and Jens is first to scream. Then the boy. Two screaming men on a rapid descent down a mountain, down a slope, through night and through storm. Two screaming men who finally slam forcefully into something hard. First Jens. Then a second later the boy, half a metre from the postman. And then the world goes out.

A GUIDE TO THE PRONUNCIATION OF ICELANDIC CONSONANTS, VOWELS AND VOWEL COMBINATIONS

ð, like the voiced *th* in *mother*

þ, like the unvoiced *th* in *thin*

æ, like the *i* in *time*

á, like the *ow* in *town*

é, like the *ye* in *yes*

í, like the *ee* in *green*

ó, like the *o* in *tote*

ö, like the *u* in *but*

ú, like the *oo* in *loon*

y, like the *ee* in *green*

ei and *ey*, like the *ay* in *fray*

au, no English equivalent; but a little like the *oay* sound in *sway*. Closer is the *œ* sound in the French *œil*

JÓN KALMAN STEFÁNSSON was born in Reykjavík in 1963. He is the most recent winner of the P. O. Enquist Award and his novels have been nominated three times for the Nordic Council Prize for Literature. His novel *Summer Light, and then Comes the Night* received the Icelandic Prize for Literature. Spellbound Productions are making a film of his trilogy of novels – of which *Heaven and Hell* (2010) is the first and *The Sorrow of Angels* the second – for release in 2014.

PHILIP ROUGHTON is the translator of works by Halldór Laxness and *The Islander*, a biography of Laxness by Halldór Gudmundsson (MacLehose Press, 2008). He lives and works in Reykjavík.

Jón Kalman Stefánsson

HEAVEN AND HELL

Translated from the Icelandic by Philip Roughton

In a remote part of Iceland, a young man joins a boat to fish for cod, but when a tragedy occurs at sea he is appalled by his fellow fishermen's cruel indifference. Lost and broken, he leaves the settlement in secret, his only purpose to return a book to a blind old sea captain beyond the mountains. Once in the town he finds that he is not alone in his solitude: welcomed into a warm circle of outcasts, he begins to see the world with new eyes.

Heaven and Hell navigates the depths of despair to celebrate the redemptive power of friendship. Set at the turn of the twentieth century, it is a reading experience as intense as the forces of the Icelandic landscape themselves.

MACLEHOSE PRESS

www.maclehosepress.com

Subscribe to our quarterly newsletter

Jón Kalman Stefánsson

THE HEART OF MAN

Translated from the Icelandic by Philip Roughton

After coming through the blizzard that almost cost them everything, Jens and the boy are far from home, in a fishing community at the edge of the world.

Taken in by the village doctor, the boy once again has the sense of being brought back from the grave. But this is a strange place, with otherworldly inhabitants, including flame-haired Álfheiður, who makes him wonder whether it is possible to love two women at once; he had believed his heart was lost to Ragnheiður, the daughter of the wealthy merchant in the village to which he must now return.

In this conclusion to an audacious trilogy, Stefánsson brings a poet's eye and a philosopher's insight to a tale worthy of the sagasmiths of old.

MACLEHOSE PRESS

www.maclehosepress.com

Subscribe to our quarterly newsletter